Rory Gleeson

Rory Gleeson was born in Dublin in 1989. He
graduated with a BA in psychology from Trinity
College Dublin, and went on to earn degrees from
Oxford, the University of Manchester, and UEA.

Praise for *Rockadoon Shore*

'Savage comedy and inevitable tragedy are unflinchingly
and dauntlessly intermingled in this impressive debut,
which has a flawless sense of place' *Sunday Times*

'Fresh in its unpredictability . . . gutsy and ambitious' *Guardian*

'Gleeson has energy and enthusiasm; he is a
talent to watch' *Sunday Business Post*

'Crackling with wit and fine writing . . . An
exuberant dispatch from the front line of youthful
narcissism and despair' *Mail on Sunday*

'Gleeson is particularly good at skewering the unspoken
tensions between his characters as the weekend falls apart
spectacularly . . . This is an uncomfortable read that's like
being in a slow, but mesmerising, train crash' *Daily Mail*

Rockadoon Shore

Rory Gleeson

JOHN MURRAY

First published in Great Britain in 2017 by John Murray (Publishers)
An Hachette UK Company

First published in paperback in 2018

1

© Rory Gleeson 2017

The right of Rory Gleeson to be identified as the Author
of the Work has been asserted by him in accordance with
the Copyright, Designs and Patents Act 1988.

A CIP catalogue record for this title is available from the British Library

ISBN 978-1-47363-410-7
Ebook ISBN 978-1-47363-409-1

Typeset in Sabon by Hewer Text UK Ltd, Edinburgh
Printed and bound by Clays Ltd, St Ives plc

John Murray policy is to use papers that are natural, renewable and
recyclable products and made from wood grown in sustainable forests.
The logging and manufacturing processes are expected to conform
to the environmental regulations of the country of origin.

John Murray (Publishers)
Carmelite House
50 Victoria Embankment
London EC4Y 0DZ

www.johnmurray.co.uk

To Ma and Da

Day 1

Malachy

They had that look about them, that self-important snarl of youth that said, 'We're going to give you no peace, and you'd better get used to it.' He was finishing the building of a rock wall on the edge of his field when he spotted their car arriving. He stared from up on the hill as it crunched across the gravel car park, past the little church and the graveyard with the slanted headstones, and pulled in to the large white house opposite, the Rockadoon Lodge. A nervous-looking girl with thick, curly brown hair slid out of the back seat. She walked to the long gate blocking the driveway and opened the latch. One fella, big and tall and hardy-looking, though with a droop in his shoulders, followed her and helped swing the gate open for the car to drive in.

Though it was still early enough in the afternoon, the sky was grey and the day dark. A thick mist had formed in the valley that morning, and now the air was wet, the ground soggy. Malachy watched as the car advanced into the drive and jolted to a stop. Once the engine was cut, a skinny, fidgety lad wearing a small vest stepped out from the passenger seat. He beat his chest and gave a wild howl that echoed across the car park and into the fields around.

—YEEEEEOOOOOOWWWWWWW!!!

His shout faded away, then he started to shadow-box in the misty air. Behind him, the driver's door swung open and a blonde girl emerged. She brushed herself down and slipped a big pair of sunglasses from her head onto her nose. Though the sunglasses covered most of her face, Malachy could tell she was gorgeous. She seemed to snap at the skinny fella and immediately he stopped

3

boxing and let his hands fall. An athletic lad in trackies jumped from the back and started doing leg stretches on the gravel. A shorter, pudgy girl followed him clumsily, catching her jeans on the car door and tugging them free. She seemed to hide inside her hoodie. After a few moments to themselves, the six of them drifted towards the front door of the house as the brunette started to point out features of the property. There was an air of excitement about them as they looked over everything, kicking at the gravel drive and slapping the white walls of the Lodge like the side of a horse.

Malachy felt himself sinking in the mud, his wellies planted. He still had one large rock left in his barrow, so he squeezed his knuckles in under and felt the weight of it slippery and muddy in his hands. He hefted it up and placed it into the wall, wedging it firmly in beside the other rocks. He made sure it was steady then started trudging back to the gate. His front field and house overlooked the church, the graveyard and the Lodge. The Lodge's back garden sloped down to a rock wall, then opened out to gnarled, twisted trees and overgrown hedges, ferns and bog land. Both houses had a view of the lake, half a mile or so down the way.

When he reached his front gate, Malachy leaned forward on it and watched the new arrivals unload their car. The skinny fella put a crate of beer on his shoulder then stood waiting as the brunette searched under some flowerpots outside the front door for the key. Fifth on the right, Malachy knew, in a little plastic Ziploc bag to stop the rust. He understood how things worked in the Lodge. After several moments looking under different pots, the brunette found the key and let them in.

As used as he was to watching the house, to seeing all kinds of people coming and going, there was something about these ones that bothered Malachy. Whatever that fucking look was, they had it.

Cath

She started off searching under the flowerpot she remembered from the last time she'd been round, five years before, but that didn't work out, so then she went down systematically looking under every pot that lined the front wall of the Lodge. It was her suggestion to come out to the house in the first place. That meant the responsibility was on her to make the weekend work, but now she couldn't even find the key to let them into the frigging thing. Not the greatest start in the history of mankind.

They'd enough money pooled for two nights in the house and the drive home. The last few months had been rough with all the exams and DanDan's trouble, so Cath just wanted to clear her head of all of it. She wanted plenty of things, but DanDan wasn't one of them, no matter what anyone said – he was her mate and she was his and it wasn't that way.

That morning they'd travelled three and a half hours west from Dublin out to Carrig, and she'd kept catching him looking at his own reflection in the car window, his eyes slicked over like he might weep at any moment. She'd no idea how to deal with him. Which did you address first, the part of him that was grieving or the part that was dumped? She wondered if she could get him to cry. Cath enjoyed a good cry. You got this amazing, fresh feeling into your body afterwards, like the tears had washed every bad thing away. If she could make him cry then maybe it'd cleanse him, give him a rebirth. Make him less frigging mopey at the very least. It wouldn't take all that much, no more than a gentle nudge, to push him over the edge.

As she checked under the first pot to the left of the door, she looked around and found him staring off into the distance. He

5

was tall and big-shouldered standing behind her in his grey T-shirt. Though he was still slim, Cath could tell he'd put on weight since Jess had died. His height and build carried the weight well, concealed it, though his face, the edges and angles of it, had softened, and made him appear only sadder still.

Maybe if she got him high, maybe that would loosen him up. Get his tongue going, his tear ducts swelling. JJ had brought a bag of weed and some pills he'd gotten off a lad on Camden Street. She'd never tried pills. They'd been given drugs awareness meetings a few years before in secondary school. A sweaty counsellor told them that if they took pills their brains would shrink. They'd dehydrate, try to pull their veins out of their arms then jump out a window thinking they could fly. This was followed by a cautionary tale about a teenager who'd gone down to the tracks to smoke weed and a train knocked his arm off. They'd heard that same story in Sex Ed but with blow jobs subbed in.

She began to feel a dry heat in her chest as she came up from the left pot empty-handed. Behind her, Merc tut-tutted and checked his phone. She ran one last time to the pot she remembered and tugged the whole thing out from the earth, rolling it to one side. She found the front door key lodged in the dirt underneath. The pressure in her chest flooded out. She unearthed the key and turned to the five people waiting behind her, brandishing it, turning it like a display model.

—Now. Hardly a wait at all.

She wiggled the key into the lock and let them in.

The house hadn't been used in a while. It belonged to her mam, who'd always said it made her feel sick whenever she came back. Bad memories. They normally just let the house out as a holiday home to tourists or allowed relatives use it as a getaway for dirty weekends and post break-up retreats.

She stepped through the hallway until it opened out to the main living room. It was better than Cath had hoped for, actually. Dusty and damp but liveable, and still very much like how she remembered it from years before. A big mouldy sofa and some creaky chairs were circled around the stone fireplace. A massive oak dining table stood in the middle of the room, with a vinyl record player placed in the corner. The walls were decorated with oil paintings and bits of things other houses didn't want: an old 1950s framed ad for HP sauce, a yellow deer-crossing sign. A broken sewing machine. There was an old bookcase filled with big piles of yellowed childhood books from earlier, more manic times when it was a holiday home for all the young cousins aged five to fifteen. Cath wouldn't be surprised if some of her baby pictures were down here; her mam habitually gave them away to relatives. There was a supply of briquettes already there, and fire-lighters for the fire. Less prep than she'd thought.

There were three bedrooms upstairs. Two of them had double beds, while the third was a games room with a bunch of mattresses heaped up and a table tennis table in the corner. Cath and Lucy would share the main bedroom; they didn't mind spooning. Steph liked her own space so she got the other bedroom to herself, and the guys would share the mattresses in the games room.

They were used to sharing accommodation. They'd all met for the first time when they were housed together on a freshers' surfing trip. In the shabby front room of a seaside cottage, three hundred metres away from the main cluster of the other surf houses, they'd managed to make some connection through an experience going wrong, when the heating broke and they'd had to keep the fire going all night to keep warm. Their shared reluctance to brave the windy path to the rest of the houses had also helped bond them. They were comfortable being in close proximity from the very start, and that physical closeness had led to a kind of shamelessness among them, a lack of embarrassment about acting out or being a bit grotty. Their group friendship had lasted them even after they left the surf house, cold, tired and grinning. On their return to Dublin, they went for a drink that turned into a night of drinking, and then that was it, they were together.

In the kitchen, grimy plates were propped beside greasy cutlery and burnt pots. The fridge had been switched off, the door left wide open, but there was still a smell of gone-off milk coming out of it. Old five-litre bottles of water were stacked beside the back door. Good job they'd brought their own. Couldn't have people getting typhoid on her watch.

The LPs by the record player were mostly trad music, bluegrass, old show tunes and musicals. The soundtrack from *Chicago*, The Carter Family. Every now and again there was some classic stuff – The Beatles, The Rolling Stones, The Clash – hidden among multiple copies of The Dubliners, The Clancy Brothers and records of obscure Donegal fiddlers. The sleeves were all covered with a film of dirt.

She ran around trying to check that the place was okay, that everyone was happy. The heating worked fine, but Steph kept sneezing because of the dust. Every time someone sat down on the couch a big puff would burst up and float over the room and Steph would start sneezing again. The dust would go away, Cath hoped, once it'd been knocked about a bit. She tried to find sheets and covers for the beds, and get all the lights and appliances going.

Once she had the most important things covered, she paused a moment. A faint rain was falling outside. By the time they'd unpacked the car and gotten everything set up, the mist had set in proper and outside was a mix of grey, black and navy.

The front door had been left open, so she went to close it. As she did she saw a dark shape outside resting in the grass. It was DanDan. Jesus, that woman had done a number on him. He'd always been so energetic, never one to sulk or get moody. Now he was out by himself, lying alone in the garden, getting wet in the rain.

She went out to check on him. As she left she could hear JJ, Merc and Steph shouting at each other from various rooms, and the clatter of Lucy banging pots in the kitchen. The sound was low for the moment, but she knew they'd get louder and start roaring soon enough. It would get completely out of hand before long. She just hoped it would be the good sort of chaos, not the bad, and that it'd knock DanDan out of his fug. Something would happen to him before the weekend was over, she knew that much. It'd either be really good or very fucking bad.

DanDan

The cold closed around him in the garden. He needed the air. Whenever he went inside to the damp, earthy smells of the dusty house, the mould smells and turf smells and fun smells, he longed to be out of it. The lights from the house lit halfway down the garden, shining the grass a bleak yellow. When he looked up into the light escaping from the upstairs bedrooms he could see a soft rain falling down.

Rock walls circled the garden. The rocks were stacked up on top of each other without cement, the tops covered in moss. He sat on the nearest wall, felt how firm and steady it was, and pushed on a piece of moss. His finger came back with moisture on the end. His hair was wet and he could feel the rain coming down his back. His beer had gone flat and a bit milky.

He could hear a river somewhere nearby. The rush of it was so constant that he'd not really acknowledged it when he first came out, but the more he listened to it, the more he noticed little bubbles and trickles that didn't repeat or varied from the usual sounds, and he felt like he needed to swim. He finished his can and threw it out into the garden.

The grass was long, about a foot high, and completely soaking. What would it be like to lie down in that wet grass? It looked inviting enough. He dived down into it. Straight away the moisture started gathering up through his clothes, chilling him. Now it was cold. He turned onto his back and tried to look up through the rain, to the skies above hidden by clouds. DanDan just wanted to shut everything down. Shut himself down.

He'd promised himself he wouldn't cry on this trip. He'd never been a crier, not so much as a child and not at all as a teenager.

He'd kept himself completely free of tears all through his first year of college. Then Jess had dumped him in an arcade. Took him in behind a row of air hockey tables and told him it wasn't going to work out, and he'd felt it rising up in him, a gulping wetness that caught in his throat. He'd cried all over her as she said sorry, that she'd made up her mind. She still loved him, she'd said, but not in the same way any more. He'd sniffled and snotted and moaned all the way home, into his bed, and all through the week. Then she'd gone and died ten days later.

His ma had delivered the news to him while he lay in bed, her standing by the door with the mobile in her hand, distraught-looking, and him shocked and useless under his blankets, unable to move or do anything to stop what had happened. She'd had a heart condition all her life, had been already living beyond her life expectancy, though she'd told no one. He'd had to show at her funeral, and everyone there crying and mourning, looking at him like he was nothing, like he hadn't deserved her, and had wasted months of her life, time she could have spent with them, her friends and family, instead of arguing with him. He'd had to leave the ceremony with his eyes closed, so he wouldn't see anyone, and they wouldn't see his tears and his weak fucking face.

He lay back in the grass and squeezed his face tight. The darkness felt so natural when it came over him, so inescapable. When it did he couldn't feel that happiness had ever been in him, he had no sense memory left of it, and though he knew he'd been happy at one time, remembering it just felt like watching a film unfold of another him in a different time and place, watching another person who looked like him smiling and laughing, but not connecting with it in any way. The misty rain washed his eyelids. Every bit of energy was sucked out of him and he felt he could lie down like this forever, his eyes shut against everything. Like Jess's eyes. Shut forever. Gone and in the ground. He wished he could sink farther into the ground. Past the grass and into the earth. Sink down and greet her below.

Then he heard a voice. Cath's voice. It was always Cath.

—DanDan, you okay?

Why was she always asking him was he okay? She'd asked him a hundred times on the drive out. Okay? Okay? Okay? It was like she was trying to get him upset. He felt the lump in his throat turn hot and liquid, rising up through his face and into his eyes. He was going to cry. He tried to breathe.

—DanDan?

—Yah?

He looked up at her from the ground. The house lights shone behind her through the light rain and he could see individual strands of hair floating away from her head. She was good-looking in her own way. Her face had occasional gawky bits, the snaggle tooth and the bump in the bridge of her nose, but overall she looked well, with her thick hair, the tight jeans and stripey top. They were too close as friends for any nonsense, though. She was waiting for him to answer.

—What're you doing in the grass?

—Having a think.

—Think about what?

She just wouldn't leave him fucking alone. He would never have time to himself. She'd be poking at him for the next two days. Poke poke fucking poke. He wanted to scream at her, to use a proper raging, mean voice that belittled her, to turn to her and say 'What the FUCK do you want? What the FUCK, do YOU want?' But he managed to keep his silence. She'd stood by him all this time, being there for him, talking late into the night, consoling him when everyone else had just wished him the best and moved on. He owed her for that.

She stepped closer. As she got near to him, he propped himself up on one elbow. He wiped the rain from his eyes, and sighed loud like she'd disturbed him.

—Nothing important, Cath.

He raised his arm and pointed behind her, down the back garden.

—What's down there?

—Just more fields. A river runs down by the side.

—Where's it go?

—Down to Lough Gorm. That's where the pier is.

Her breath clouded around her head, steam rising from her shoulders as she stood in the gloom. She moved forward and rubbed her arms, wrapping them around her body so that she hugged herself as she spoke.

—You can't go swimming in the river, though. It's too shallow . . . You okay?

He looked beyond her.

—Go on inside, I'll be in.

—Okay. I'll put a drink out for you.

She went inside, back into the warmth. What had she said about the river? Too small or too dangerous? She probably thought he was thinking about drowning himself in it. He liked that at least she was worried. The rest of the lot inside weren't worried. He could hear them, howling, shouting at each other, laughing. Morons. The lot of them. Not a modicum of respect in any of them. Not a brain cell between the fucking lot of them, just running around laughing like goons, drinking themselves silly, killing themselves stupid with alcohol. He took a breath.

Just ignore it and sink down, down into the grass.

Malachy

He'd spent almost seventy years watching over the Lodge. When he was coming up it had belonged to Billy and Mona Rourke. When they died it went to Billy's teenage daughter Tara. She had the place painted over, rented it to the Neville family, then moved to Dublin. The Nevilles kept to themselves. Whenever they passed they'd nod at Malachy and his father, but in the twenty years they'd stayed there he couldn't remember talking to them much. Their children grew, they repainted the Lodge, and moved on. A French couple rented it for a few years as a summer house, letting the garden go to shit in the off-season. Eventually they gave it up and the Lodge went back to Tara Rourke, where it lay silent and small against the valley, and he'd continued to watch it.

Developers had bought his own farmland for a housing estate ten years before. He hadn't wanted to sell any of it at first. What would be the point at all? All his life he'd been a farmer. What would he do, he asked them, if he couldn't farm?

But they pursued him and pursued him. They offered him more and more, and every time they did people in the village said, 'Go on, Malachy. It won't last forever. Do it now, while you can, Malachy.' The developers had kept at him, about his age, about what he would do when he grew too old to work, even as they upped their offer. Eventually the money got so ridiculous, so out of kilter with the established order of what he'd always known – that land was worth so much, then sheep and cattle worth so much again – that he'd lost sense of it. He'd never been poor, or down on his luck, but he had the farm and his tractor and the sheds and all the right gear without ever being rich. Any profit

13

went back into the farm, or doing up the house, and anything left over just sat in the bank.

What would happen, they asked, if he hurt himself, did his back in? He'd no family, no one to look after him, no sons to work the land. The farm would go to pot. He'd bankrupt and have to sell the land and the house anyway, only for a much lower price than the one they were offering. Though he knew they were only a cluster of swindlers, saying whatever the fuck they had to to get what they wanted, in a way they were right. He'd no one, and the farm had always been too big for just one to manage. Eventually, he'd signed.

He'd somehow believed that that would be it. He'd sign, they'd go away, and nothing really would change. Then one morning he woke up and his acres were gone. And what was the reason for getting out of bed then? There were millions in his bank account, but he just left it sitting there. So much money he'd no idea what to do with. People in the village told him that it was his time, 'Time for a wife, Malachy, with that fortune.'

'Too fucking late,' he said.

He wondered for a short moment what to do with himself, but his da had taught him, time and again, whether it was work or pain or fatigue, 'Get on with it, just keep fucking going.' So he did.

The next ten years he kept himself busy. He got up at the same hour and went out to work as usual, only instead of going to the farm he started to repair all the stacked stone walls around his remaining land. When they were fixed, he did all the other walls in the area. He repaired three miles of ruined walls on the road to the Doon Shore. Then, when they were done, he built up new stone walls on the land he had left using the rocks he pulled from the earth. And from the hill he watched the builders as they put up new houses on the land he'd sold. Modern ones heaped on top of each other, all straight lines and equally sized square gardens, front and back, a road in and a road out, and a one-way system in place. During that time of building it was like the valley had stirred into life. Cars and vans came and went, bringing workers and letting agents and prospective buyers and light and noise, and for a few moments Malachy had felt almost good about the whole thing.

But then the crash, and no one moved in. The valley was quiet again, and the houses around quiet, and up over the hills all the other houses in winter were quiet and it was like nothing had changed at all. And he felt dirty almost, like the downfall of the estate was his fault, that he'd conned someone, somehow, or cheated him. So he stayed guard in his little house looking down on the lake, and the estate, and on the Rockadoon Lodge that had been there before any of them.

When he'd had his tea Malachy brought the chopping stump out to the front garden so he could keep an eye on the house down the way, the lights now on in every downstairs room, and through the mist came drifts of sound he'd not heard in ages, yowls like wild animals, the sounds of shouting and laughter and music mingling into short waves that came upon his ears then receded.

He chopped wood out the front until he worked up a sweat. A dull ache began to take hold in his shoulder but he kept going. The aches were nothing new, and he took a satisfaction from working through them, a kind of cheeriness that he could still do it, still take it, even if it hurt him. Fuck the pain of it.

He felt the soft rain moisten his lips and cling to his eyebrows as he watched one of the house guests, the tall broad one, leave the house and sit outside drinking a can. The young lad's shoulders were slumped and he drank his can slowly, rolling it in his hand. Then, without warning, he threw his can away and flopped down in the long grass out the front of the Lodge.

Malachy leaned on his axe on the stump. Mona Rourke used to sit in that very spot in the garden. Billy Rourke would drink inside while his poor, sad wife sat out in the long grass every night. The young lad was now in the exact same spot where she used to sit. The grass was a violent green, heavy and dripping with moisture.

A strange, floating feeling came over Malachy, something that felt like numbness in his stomach. It was probably just the cold.

15

He stayed watching the lad in the grass and wondered what he got from it, what the attraction was in lying down in it.

He dropped his axe into the stump then went down slowly on his left knee. He waited a moment before bringing his right knee down under him. It took a second or two but he managed it, and only mild pains. Malachy paused on his knees, watching the house, the young lad in the grass, before he flopped down in it as well. His large, strong hands broke his slow fall. He felt the grass tickle his face, his front getting cold and soggy as he sank into the ground. He left himself there a few moments, then turned over and went onto his back, letting it get soaked.

He closed his eyes and tried to imagine how the young fella felt, but he had no access to it. What the fuck was he doing? Too old for this, now. People were fucking useless, and none more so than Malachy, who was soaked through from copying a youngster. He got up and brushed himself down. He took one last look at the young lad in the grass, then went back inside.

The strange feeling he thought was just the cold stayed with him the whole way. As he began to warm up inside, it didn't fade as he thought it would. It stayed in him, in his stomach, knotted up. He went into his living room and sat in front of the fireplace. He gazed into the grate, letting his clothes dry, the fire flickering softly burning down.

Steph

She sat deep in the couch, put her head back and closed her eyes. Her nose was trembling constantly with the dust but fuck it, she'd survive. She tried to just relax into the cushions, let all the stiffness from driving seep out of her. It'd been a long drive and JJ'd been annoying her constantly the whole way out, trying to get her to play games of Would You Rather and Never Have I Ever, competing with Merc at inventing the most bizarre and disgusting scenarios involving bodily fluids. Some quiet time now, just for herself, would be nice. She exhaled and settled in.

Then JJ vaulted over the back of the couch and squashed right in beside her, pushing her into the armrest. He started a drumbeat on his legs, using her knee as a cymbal.

Bum TSH BumBum Bum TSH.

She put her head resting in her palm, her elbow on the armrest of the couch, and tried to block him out. Only a year and a half before, when they'd all first met, they'd started talking from the minute they got in, the drink already in them from the bus ride. They'd pushed for information on each other, what course they did, who they knew, whether they were single or not, where they wanted to go, did they want a drink, do you want a drink? There'd been an electric buzz off the night as they glued far faster than any of them expected. But now it was comfortable, and that potential of new love and sly possibilities, it wasn't quite as potent as it was then. It had dulled. Now, all she wanted to do was sit down for a while before dealing with the shopping. That worried her.

She decided to let JJ away his drumming, she could tune him out, but then Merc nudged her over, trying to wiggle himself in beside her. He shoved her elbow aside with his arse until he was sitting next to her on the arm of the couch. They had her sandwiched in, the pair of them. Merc started to join in with the drums, and the two lads, without saying a fucking word, started using her whole body as a drum kit.

Bum TSH BumBum Bum TSH.

She held her elbows in by her side, and closed her eyes. This must be what it was like having kids. She allowed it to continue, until Merc tried to use the top of her head as a snare. She jumped up from the couch.

—Fuck, Merc.

—Sorry.

He shrugged and she crossed the room to search through the shopping bags they'd left on the big wooden table after unpacking the car. Her nose trembled and Jesus . . . Jesus . . . Jesus . . . CHRIST she sneezed hard into her shoulder. She gasped and went back to the bags.

It was turning into an expensive trip. Merc had bought a slab of cans and a gigantic bottle of sambuca. JJ, on the other hand, had bought two bottles of vodka and twenty-four cans, a twelve-pack of Red Bull, skins, two packs of rolling tobacco and forty Marlboro Gold. He also had weed on him and some MDMA. JJ was going to die young.

They'd bought enough food to make some kind of a curry and a bolognese maybe, then loads of nibbly crap, crisps and things. Lucy was supposed to be sorting out the kitchen but Steph hadn't seen her. No one fucking helping. She was worried about the next two days, what she would do if it turned nasty, or just plain aul boring. Or she hit one of those phases when she felt as if her eyes opened, and she looked around her and couldn't see why she was in the place she was. The only thing she'd ever been able to do when that mood came over her before was to get up and walk out the door and never come back. She'd done it before with old friends, jobs, boyfriends. Walking out on Fergus, her first long-term boyfriend, had been a prime example.

Steph looked about her and tried to induce one of those moods, when she felt suddenly detached and alone. She thought of the strange things in the house and the strange people in it. Merc and JJ drumming on each other, and Lucy in the kitchen probably gearing up to get pissed. Cath was off somewhere with DanDan maybe. Did she care about any of these things? About any of these people? She found it hard to feel one way or another. She could take it or leave it. At some moments she wanted so desperately for them to like her, at others she could barely stand the sight of them. At the moment it was just a dull grey, neither up nor down.

She knew how to deal with it temporarily. All she had to do was up her energy levels, have a drink, make a joke and try and forget about it. But what would happen later was a cause for concern, if a mood came on her so dark she couldn't even see it was a mood, and then she'd just have one big long list of fucking problems with these people and a complete lack of desire to please or even acknowledge them, and that way spelled trouble. For better or worse she was trapped here. The only way forward was to keep drama to a minimum, hope no one did anything stupid, and just grind her way through the fucking thing.

Maybe this was why people found her a little cold. It'd been that way with her for the longest time. She knew people whispered that she was standoffish, up herself, that she thought she was better than them. Fucking ice queen. It wasn't that way, though. She just couldn't help it sometimes.

Still, these friends here, the ones she had now, she could still get on with. Cath listened to her. Lucy always wanted to talk to her. DanDan and JJ, and even Merc to a certain extent, they were fresh and they were new and they were open to being different. They still occasionally did and said mean, stupid things, but more often than not if she picked them up on it they'd apologise. She'd trained them to stop saying words like bitch and whore so frequently. When one eventually did slip out, they'd say they meant nothing by it, which she did believe. Overall, the group of them were pretty okay.

On that first trip together they'd found something in each other. They weren't altogether very similar in terms of energy or outlook. They were different in how they saw themselves and the world, what they expected of other people, but they'd gotten on all the same. They were comfortable together, and they'd spent almost all of their first year in college in each other's company, cementing their friendship with coffee and bitching sessions and late-night drinking.

As she unpacked packets of pasta and Dolmio sauce, and more bottles of wine from the bags, she looked over at the two fellas continuing their drumline on the couch. If they weren't going to help unpack, then Steph wasn't either. She rooted in one of the bags and took out a can of cider. JJ noticed immediately, stopped drumming and shouted over.

—The cider be mine.

She was in no mood for this.

—Ah would you fuck off. It'll all come around in the end.

He looked indignant.

—Okay, okay, moody.

JJ scooched off the couch and settled down cross-legged in front of the empty fireplace. He took a spliff from behind his ear and reshaped it, rolling it between his right palm and his left bicep. His arms were long and wiry and streaked with bulging veins that seemed to be forever shifting and throbbing, so that even when he was sitting still it felt like he was moving. He liked his veiny arms, she reckoned, always wearing a tight vest that clung to his thin body, hugging his brittle ribcage and leaving his arms uncovered from the shoulder down. Waving his spliff, he addressed the room, though Steph and Merc were the only ones in it.

—To health and good company.

Steph never really liked taking charge, but Cath was away somewhere and there was still some stuff to do. They needed to put some kind of organisation on it. While Steph had the two of them there she may as well enlist them. Just as JJ began to spark his lighter, she spoke in a casual, breezy voice.

—Here, before you get going with that, just help us with the shopping, yeah? And open a few windows to air the place out. And get the fire going as well.

JJ grimaced and gave a childlike moan.

—EUGH. Fiiiinnnne.

He put the unlit joint back behind his ear and started opening up the windows. Merc got up from the couch and saluted her.

—Yes, sir. Oh captain my captain, roger matey.

He clicked his heels and went to the fireplace. He made a big deal of positioning the firelighters in the grate, wrapping up newspapers for kindling and putting them on top, then stacking the briquettes over those. Once he had the whole thing lit, JJ walked round to him and clapped him on the shoulder.

—Man make fire. Good man. Good man, strong man make fire.

Merc lifted his T-shirt sleeve with a sooty hand and flexed his bicep.

—Strong man.

JJ grunted and flexed his own bicep.

—Me strong man too.

Merc rose to his feet and faced JJ. They grunted and circled each other, showing their muscles and snorting. Steph laughed.

—Stop it, the two of you.

Merc smacked JJ's face.

—Woman mine.

JJ smacked him back.

—No. Woman mine.

Steph watched them. They shouted MINE WOMAN MINE MINE before staggering into each other's arms, wrestling in front of the fireplace. JJ managed to hook one of Merc's legs and sprawl over him. Their shoes slipped on the tiles and Merc sent the fireguard crashing onto the floor with a wayward kick. JJ was skinny as anything, but he was wiry. He also had between three and five brothers, depending on who he wasn't talking to, so he was used to wrestling. Merc was stronger, much bigger and all toned and everything, but he'd grown up with sisters. JJ looked

21

like he was beginning to get the upper hand. They were all elbows and pretend messing until JJ managed to twist around Merc and get him in a headlock from behind. Steph should step in.

—Leave him be, JJ.

—Conor McGregor!

—Stop it!

—McGREGORRRRR.

JJ repeated 'McGregor, McGregor,' into Merc's ear as he kept him in the headlock. He appeared to still be messing but Merc began to strain at his arm so he got a better hold of him. Merc looked like he really wasn't in the mood to lose. He elbowed at JJ's ribs. JJ took the blows and laughed. He held his grip as he whispered into Merc's ear.

—Woman mine, I say. Woman mine.

JJ seemed to be waiting for a witty riposte, or a cry of 'No surrender!' maybe. Merc said nothing. His legs shot out, looking for leverage on something. He swung for a big dig into JJ's ribs with his elbow and caught him. JJ exhaled in pain and held Merc's body down with his legs. He broke character.

—Here, man. No need for that. Cool it.

Merc's hand went to JJ's arms. He caught JJ's flesh between his fingernails and started to squeeze. JJ wiggled his arms away.

—Chill, man. Chill.

What the hell were they doing?

—Ah here, man. No pinching.

Merc pinched harder. Steph clicked her fingers and raised her voice.

—Lads, hold off.

They were both involved now, and didn't pay her any attention. Still keeping up the pretend play but it had turned into something more than that. Merc wasn't going to stop, Steph could see, until he'd gotten some of his advantage back. JJ seemed like he wanted an end to it.

—Here, stop, man. Come on, here, ah.

Merc was bright red in the face. He grunted and dug his nails in on JJ's arm and dragged them down, scoring a crooked, jagged trail of broken white skin that oozed drops of red. JJ slowly let go of his headlock. Merc twisted out of his arms, scrambled to his feet and turned to face JJ again. JJ looked at him, rubbing his arm.

—The fuck, man? You don't pinch. You don't scratch.

—You don't get someone in a fucking headlock when you're just messing around.

—I was fucking messing till you started going mad. I'm fucking bleeding for Christ's sake.

—Your fault, you took it way too far.

—Took it too far? ME? You were the one who—

Right, she had her opportunity. Steph got her bottle of water with the spray cap out and squirted water at the two of them. She caught both of them in the face with the jet of it. They jumped and looked over, almost having forgotten she was there.

—The fuck?

—What are you doing?

—Stop acting the bollox and help me out here.

—JJ's being a prick.

—Merc, are you friends with JJ? Are you? Are we friends here? Or are we not?

Steph waited for him to answer. Merc was breathing heavy, trying to make it look like he was in control of himself. JJ was wearing an offended look; pinching was obviously against the rules in a house of brothers. She spoke at them again, calmly.

—Cool down and give us a hand with the shopping. Or else they get the hose again.

JJ seemed to like the reference. His shoulders slumped, the hackles going down, his T-shirt flecked with water drops. He shrugged first.

—Fine. No one get woman.

Steph needed to make sure. She tried her best mammy voice.

—The two of you both make up.

JJ approached Merc, his body open to him. Merc looked at him warily.

—We get each other?

23

—Yes. JJ love Merc.

—Merc love JJ.

They hugged insincerely then separated. Steph gave them a clap. At least they went through the motions. They smacked each other's backs then came over to the table to help. JJ looked at her.

—Right. What we do?

—Start on putting away those bags.

JJ lightened up, ready to move on. He grabbed the bags.

—Good. Man lift shopping.

Merc was brooding, though.

—I'll have a look at the fire again.

He went over and poked at the briquettes, which were beginning to smoke. He blew on them to make them spark, then he added more newspaper, picked up the fireguard and put it back into place. He stepped back and surveyed the fire, keeping quiet. Steph watched him feel his left bicep with his right hand. He flexed the muscle and tested how strong it was, how much he could poke it, almost as if he didn't even notice he was doing it. He was starting to do neck stretches when Cath's voice came calling down from upstairs.

—The fuck is going on down there?

Steph shouted up.

—Nothing, Cath, all sorted.

—Want me to come down there and put some manners on them?

Two minutes too late, the real mammy intervenes.

—No need, Cath, but thanks.

—You're welcome.

The mood had softened. Steph could feel it. Might not be so bad after all. She tried to stuff her mood down, tamp it right down and keep it low until the cider took care of the worst of it.

Lucy

She rolled the bottles of vodka into the freezer first then opened
the bottle of red she'd brought in, taking a quick swig of the wine.
Here was where it would happen. She was going to have her
Jennifer Grey moment in this house. Maybe this kitchen, even.
Maybe someone would lift her over their head all fancy-like,
though none of them were probably strong enough.

She wouldn't mind going into town over the weekend. Play
some pool and talk to a few local lads. Bored ones, farmer ones.
Maybe they'd lift her up over their heads. She liked the natural
muscles farmers had on them; that plain rugged hardness they
had, much tougher than city boys. They played football and were
used to doing things around the house. They usually had land or
something that required a bit of heft.

Normally when she went down the country she did well out of
it. There were so few young people about that they got bored with
each other. Any fresh meat got a good reception. A lot of them
were college lads as well, at the local club or whatever, home for
the holidays, and they were always really eager. If they went out,
she wouldn't have a problem getting one of them back to the
house. Back for a bit of fun.

She spotted DanDan coming round the side of the house
past the kitchen windows. He came in through the back door
to the kitchen, and didn't bat an eye when he found her standing there.

—DanDan!

—Hey, Luce.

—I need a hug.

She hugged herself into him, her head cushioned against his broad chest. She reckoned she could almost feel his heartbeat in there, *thumpthump*, *thumpthump*. She spoke up to him from his arms.

—Where were you?

—Just outside, I like it in the rain.

—Is it raining?

—Ah, misty kind of rain.

She detached herself and looked at him, and sure enough his shoulders were wet with rain and his face, well, his face was wet and everything, but his eyes seemed red. Had he been crying? No . . . He didn't seem the type.

He kept his eyes to the ground as she watched him, and almost out of awkwardness he grabbed up the guitar case he'd left by the back door. He held it in his arms, drumming the side of the cloth material. He coughed.

—Bathroom.

—Sure.

He shuffled out, the guitar case in his arms.

He was still being a sad sack, though surely he should be over it by now. They'd not even been going out that long, him and Jess. And also, she'd broken up with him two weeks before she'd collapsed, so it wasn't even that he lost a girlfriend. Technically, he lost an ex. But with over six months gone now, more than enough time to get over it, Lucy had made a ruling: DanDan should be back on the market.

She'd said that to Cath, giving her a big bloody wink. Cath was having none of it. Have some decorum, she'd told her. Decorum is for dry shites, Lucy'd said, but Cath insisted there was nothing going on. Maybe there is nothing going on, Lucy'd said to her, but would you *like* something to be going on? Cath'd said no again, but Lucy still suspected. How could you hang around with a fella like that and not have anything going on? And DanDan was a ride as well, the height on him, well over six foot, and big solid shoulders. A big solid man he was. How could she not fancy that?

They were all off down the country together. It was the ideal time for it. And they might go down the lake later. That'd be mad. She could suggest they go skinny-dipping, or play any number of silly games that'd give the opportunity for flirting or otherwise. Lucy had her goals and now had means to pursue them. She knew what she wanted from the weekend. She wanted rid of a part of herself she'd held on to for too long. Twenty years of age was a bit late for first times. Any one of the three lads would be fine.

She took another swig of wine. It hadn't really bothered her up to now, but the last few months she was really feeling it. If anything, it was just down to chance that it hadn't happened. She'd never had a proper boyfriend, and most of the one-night stands she picked up were either too drunk to do anything, or they got sick before they could, or they were just a little manky. One lad she'd gone back with after a party was actually a teetotaller, but when she tried to put the moves on him in his front garden he'd told her that she was too drunk, and put her in a taxi. That was when she knew she wanted to have it done and over with. She'd be twenty-one before too long, and then it'd be an actual problem. She hadn't told the others about it, not even Steph, who was perhaps the best one to tell, given she kept her mouth shut about most things and never seemed to care all that much what you did with your life. The rest would judge or pity her, and who were they to do that?

She might tell Cath, actually. Over the last year they'd shared many things out in Lucy's flat in Dublin. Cath would come out to hers at least a few times a week and they'd watch movies or talk over music. And whenever Steph came out they'd usually have a good night of it. Steph would have a mad story of what she'd done over the week, or something that pissed her off, or the latest upheaval in her research placement. She'd lean back and stretch out long and languid over Lucy and Cath's legs, look at the ceiling and say something like, '. . . and fuck me, did he not think I'd eventually notice he'd Photoshopped the abs on himself? Christ, there's a lack of forward planning,' and they'd laugh. In the end what began with coffee and a chat would usually turn into a few bottles of cheap wine and a Patrick Swayze film. Now there was a man with a fine set of arms.

Speaking of which . . .

She took a wine glass out of a cupboard and went into the living room. Steph was rooting through her handbag, JJ and Merc were draped over the couch, but Cath, where was Cath? She called out.

—Cath?

—Yeah?

Cath's head popped up from the other side of the couch. What was she doing down there?

— I meant to ask. Do you've a monitor here?

—I think so, why?

—I brought the hard drive with the movies . . .

Cath got up from her knees and walked around the couch. She left a few seconds before replying.

—We didn't come to watch films, though.

—I know, yeah, but like when we're hungover in the daytime we need something to watch.

—I thought we could go swimming in the daytime, or hiking or something.

Cath looked hurt. God help her, she really was fragile. She'd been frantic the night before, texting everyone, making sure they all knew the plan, until Steph called her and told her that she knew what time ten o'fucking clock was and that she wasn't coming if she got one more message from her. Cath had kept quiet since then but Lucy could see her worry was bubbling along all the same. She tried to reassure her.

—I know, and we will go out in the daytime. But like if we're hanging about or something, I brought some movies just in case.

Cath seemed to relax.

—Okay. What did you bring?

—You know well what I brought.

Cath looked at Lucy, and Lucy saw a little hop in her eyebrows, hope.

—Señor Swayze?

—Among other things, yes.

—Grazie, bella.

—Swayze always does the business.

Merc let out a load moan next to Cath.

—I'm not watching any *Dirty* fucking *Dancing*.

Steph chipped in when she heard this, cool as anything.

—Sounds like he's trying to put you in a corner, Luce.

—Really, Steph? That won't work.

—Why not?

—COS NOBODY PUTS LUCY IN THE CORNER.

Lucy's delivery seemed to please Steph, who nodded in approval and punched the air like Judd Nelson. Steph was so cool. Merc was almost at a sulk already.

—Whatever. I'm not spending all weekend quoting this shite.

JJ jumped up from the couch and looked at him.

—Come on, man. It's a classic.

—No.

—Come onnnnnnnn . . .

JJ started to do an incredibly awkward Swayze dance, waggling his hips and shoulders, and advanced on Merc, who sighed and leaned his head back. JJ did a twirl.

—Fucking classic movie. Almost made me turn.

Lucy poured a glass of red and put it into Steph's hand, then drank straight from the bottle herself. She wanted to get the night going, get on with the fun.

JJ danced up in front of Merc, gyrating his hips. Merc pushed him off.

—Fuck. Off.

—YOU LOVE IT, BABY!

—Seriously.

—YOU. LOVE. IT.

JJ left Merc and danced up to Cath. He started bumping her with his arse.

—SMACK THIS ARSE, BABY. SMACK MY ARSE.

—Eugh.

Cath gave him a tap on the arse. JJ howled in pleasure.

—OH MY!

Steph took a big gulp out of the wine and grimaced.

—JJ.

—Yeah?

—Turn on the music.

He stopped dancing, a grin on his face, and pointed at her.

—TURN ON THE MUSIC IS RIGHT, BABY!

Lucy looked at Steph. It must be. It must.

—We getting it started?

Steph nodded, almost wearily.

—Yeah, get it started.

—YEOW!

JJ

Big nights out, man. Who needed them?

This was better. Few good friends. Beers. Talking shite. The atmosphere, the air in the place. It smelled fresher than anything they had in the city.

Trees. Green. Fields. Rivers. The air, that floating daytime darkness that came in the windows and filled the place.

JJ felt a bit spacey. There was that gap between people, broken down by this. Lounging in the air. Good friends, good company. Break it down. Break it right down.

What was air when you thought about it? Carbon dioxide, oxygen, chlorine, or something.

Whatever, it didn't matter. What he meant though was, like, when you broke it down into its constituent elements, what was it? Nothing. Bits of a jigsaw that made no sense when separated. But, put the pieces back together and what did you get?

Air. You breathed it in and it filled you. Pure and unfiltered, untainted by anything else. Except with a flavour of the country. It was pure and it made you feel good. You felt yourself regenerating. You took in all the good and breathed out the bad. Nothing like it.

Actually no, fuck that. This was what happened when you spent too long with city folk. You started to believe all that mystical shite about the country. He was bored sick of the countryside. He'd grown up in it. City folk got all romantic about it. 'Oh look, a tree. How beautiful, how quaint.' To JJ it was just another fucking tree.

Country air was filled mostly with the smell of slurry and illegal bonfires.

Still, smelled good.

His arm was sore from the wrestle with Merc. Christ, that one had come from nowhere. They'd joked that it was about Steph. It probably was.

He was maybe a bit too high. Get back to earth. Where was he?

He was in a room.

JJ was in a room.

With friends. They were his friends.

Merc was his friend.

Friends who were playing music on the laptop by the table.

They had some sort of House mix on.

UNCE UNCE UNCE UNCE UNCE

He felt the music throb through him, massaging his heart. Ah man, there was nothing like this kind of music. It was genius. One hundred and twenty-eight beats a minute, ideal for an elevated heart rate, that's what made it so perfect, so in tune with the body's natural rhythm. Made it elemental, raw, visceral, animalistic.

UNCE UNCE UNCE

More textured and precise and full of feeling than any of that classical bollox they'd taught them in school. They'd spent half of their Leaving Cert music class listening to music that was hundreds of years old and what did it do? Nothing.

UNCE UNCE UNCE.

Wait for the Drop.

Wait for it.

Up up up it goes and there, yes, THERE. Yes, there it is.

UNCE UNCE UNCE.

And bring it down, cool it, bring it down.

Down further, calm it, cool it off.

All that time in the classroom going over time signatures and the horn solo in Tchaikovsky and musical themes, and what had it meant? 'The Love Overture' was used to sell perfume and cars and meant nothing to the people it was supposed to be about: young people, lovers. How misguided was that? Maybe your man didn't know when he was writing it that the only people who'd listen to it seriously would be in the over-sixties bracket. If you were going to write music about young people with energy and that mad kind of love, why do it in the dullest way possible? Why not write something they could understand, something they could relate to, instead of grand orchestral wank?

The song was finishing on the speakers, cooling, fading away. Wait for the next one, wait for the next. He could drink more Red Bull.

His leg was shaking. JJ's leg was shaking.

How many cans of Red Bull was that so far?

Three.

Four.

He needed something a bit more paced now, with a stronger beat, steadier, something he could nod his head to. The next song started blasting up, blasting off. But it sounded different. It wasn't coming from the laptop any more, but from the record player.

Merc was dancing to the vinyl.

What was on the vinyl?

Fucking, fucking *CHICAGO*.

WHY WAS *CHICAGO* ON?

He needed answers. He finished the spliff.

—HEY.

Steph had a large glass of red in her hand. She leaned against the wall, twirling her hair with her free fingers. She looked at him.

—What?

—Why is *Chicago* on?

—It's on. Relax.

—What do you mean?

She looked at him again and dropped her hair. It fell into her wine glass, dangling just a few millimetres above the surface of the red liquid.

—I mean relax.

—You relax.

She smiled at him. It was a warm smile. Her blonde hair. Long blondey hair on her.

Soft, long blondey hair you might want to put your face in.

He loved her.

No, no he didn't. That was the weed.

She looked at him for a second, but he couldn't see past the shades, the big Dior things she wore constantly either on her nose or the top of her head. It was a little confusing how good-looking she was, her face all smooth and symmetrical, her jawline clear, and the rest of her hidden behind the sunglasses.

She was mental, Steph. She had a quick mind. Quick mouth as well. JJ wouldn't want to get on the wrong side of her. He wanted to be on the right side of her. Difficult proposition. He'd been trying to do it for the last few months, trying to make her laugh. Sometimes it worked. He might get her to snort, stifling a laugh, or she'd build on a joke he'd made, advance the action of it, and he'd feel like they were getting close. Many other times it didn't work. He'd joke with her and she'd smile understandingly and tell him to calm down.

She could be cold sometimes. Always behind those sunglasses. Let's see those eyes of yours. He'd been told a bunch of facts about eye movements in that human behaviour lecture, but he'd been too busy having a laugh with Merc, throwing bits of orange peel at other students, to pay attention. He needed another Red Bull. Must get another Red Bull. Show us your eyes.

She looked at him reproachfully.

—You're staring at me.

—Sorry, drifting into a thought. Sorry.

She waved him away.

—You're grand.

—Cheers.

Their moment was broken when Merc started to shout.

—YEEEEEHAAAWWWWW.

Merc

—I'D MURDER THE LOT OF THEM!

He'd taken over the centre of the room and was dancing his
heart out, showing off his best moves. Probably wasted on this
crowd, but sure someone had to be the life of the party. Musicals
weren't exactly the sexiest music for a strip session but you made
do. He hadn't even started properly yet. They were in for a treat.
He high-kicked, feeling his hammy dealing with the stretch of it.
Lucy whooped.

They had show tunes from *Chicago* on. The song when they're
killing their husbands. A bunch of women gather round saying
that their husbands had it coming, that they murdered their part-
ners because they deserved it. Merc wouldn't mind any of these
girls trying to have a go at him. Be worth it.

In more than a year and a half of knowing them Merc had not
shifted one of the girls, much less got the ride off them. When
they'd first been lumped together in that surf cottage, Merc was
all set to change houses, ready to move his bag to the cottage
down the way with his mates in, but next thing Steph was step-
ping out in a bikini for the waves and he was inclined to hang
about. Then DanDan broke out the guitar and he was pretty
amazing at it, and before Merc knew what was happening they
were all sat round singing songs, drinking and talking about
where they'd grown up. JJ with his brothers down the country,
Steph with her mad parents. JJ had kept them energised, Lucy
had told steady stories about her good-looking friends doing mad
stuff back home, and Cath kept bringing out different kinds of
food and booze and coming up with things for them to do, and

the whole weekend had shot by. They'd never even bothered with the surfing they'd had so much fun, and by the end Merc had felt like it was actually good for him, being away from his usual mates. It felt good branching out, talking to people who thought in different ways to him, and not just thought in different ways but laughed and joked differently as well. He wasn't just on auto-pilot with them the whole time. He had to really listen to them to figure out what they meant; he'd to try harder to make them laugh, to get the jokes he was making, and when they did laugh it meant more to him, and he came back from that weekend with a feeling that he'd done something new and exciting.

It was nice, though. These girls listened to him, and he felt he was actually friends with them. He didn't have any female friends from back home. Not ones he wasn't actively trying to ride anyway. But with these ones, whenever he had a problem with anything, he could ask them, and their advice was always wildly different from the fellas on the GAA team. And they treated him differently; they didn't just assume he was one thing or one man or opinion, they didn't pressure him to fill his role so often, to be the mad yoke or the cheeky fella or the smarmy one. They gave him chances to talk and feel and express his opinion, and if he didn't feel like it, they just let him be.

Then again, what was the point in going down the country if there wasn't even the hint of a shift? And the past few months they were all acting off. A part of him said to hang in there, to trust in them, in himself, not to seek out a cheap ride at the expense of something more valuable, but he tried to silence that part down. If it was going to break, it'd break, and he might as well get something out of it.

—DON'T TELL ME ABOUT CICERO, LADS. I KNOW ALL ABOUT CICERO.

As he did his best boogie shuffle, he felt the muscles in his neck, his shoulders, his arms all cooperating seamlessly, sleekly, dynam-ically. He was making sure JJ got a good view of him, saw what a real man's body was. The skinny little bastard had gone too far with the wrestling.

36

—FUCKING LIPSCHITZ.

He peeled off his T-shirt, feeling the muscles twitching in his back. Lucy gave a howl. He was sweaty underneath the T-shirt. Perfect for polishing off the curve and pump of his six-pack. Steph watched him, her blonde hair spreading over her shoulders. Here was a chance now. The gates were wide open for a languorous flirt. He'd had the option earlier when she was back there sitting on the couch, but JJ'd swung in, swooped in before him and stole that chance. Skinny bastard. It wouldn't do.

What chance did JJ have, the size of him? Oh no. It wouldn't do at all.

He spun his T-shirt over his head then threw it at Cath. She caught it from the air with a smile. He did a spin, doing his best Michael Jackson impression. Lucy was rocking on the balls of her feet.

—MORE! TAKE MORE OFF.

Exactly what he wanted. He did a few squats in time with the music; the big brass section came in perfectly as he twirled again at JJ, letting him get a long look at his obliques. JJ didn't seem to care much, he was too busy tugging away at his spliff. Come on, skinny little fella, know your betters. He went slowly, slyly for the waistband of his O'Neills, giving them a proper show. Lucy squealed again.

—YES! OFF WITH THEM! DEPANTS!

He flexed his quads and started to push his trackies down. They slid down his thighs to his knees. A little hip wiggle in front of Steph, who was shaking her head at him, gave the last incentive for the bottoms to drop to his ankles. He stepped out of his cacks, scooped them up with his foot and sent them flying at Lucy, who caught them and cheered. Steph seemed to wink at him through her sunglasses, he couldn't tell.

—Charming.

Was she flirting with him? Wouldn't blame her. He danced up to her in his underwear and ground on her. She shook her head and rearranged her sunglasses. Then she laughed.

—Ah go on then.

She smacked him on the side of his arse. He turned on her.

—You'll pay for that.

—Oh I'm sure.

—And now, Ladies and Gentlemen, what you've all been waiting for . . .

He gave them a few more spins, a few more twirls.

—Give us the cowboy hat there.

Lucy threw it at him. He caught it and popped it on top. JJ was looking at him like he was about to die. That's right, man. See who's in charge now, ha? See who's preferred?

He hopped on the table, and with the brass section of *Chicago* and Lucy's whoops spurring him on, he put his hands on his balls inside his jocks, then dropped the boxers.

AND THE CROWD GOES WILD.

Lucy screamed and Cath clapped. He kept his hands protecting his bollocks while he spun an imaginary lasso over his head.

—YE'VE NO ANSWER FOR THIS! BANG!

It was all about the craic, boys. Getting on a table and getting your junk out. Lucy was looking up at him adoringly, the bottle of wine in her hand. Steph pretended to be bored in the doorway, though there was a bemused look on her face. They called that a wry smile.

This was what college life was supposed to be, what he had signed up for. Not that trite shite learning in grey rooms off greyer corridors. This was what it was. And every party needed someone, ANYONE to liven the fucking thing up. If getting bollock-naked was one way of doing it, then that's the way he was choosing.

DanDan stepped into the room. Cath rubbed his arm when he came in.

—POP BOLLOX!

DanDan always so morose-looking.

—BANG! FUCKING BANG, LADS!

Would he kill DanDan for Cath?

No, he wouldn't. He wasn't that kind of person. He was good.

—BANG! FUCKING FUCKING BANG!

DanDan looked up at him on the table. Checking him out, was he?

—Ah, Merc, come on. I leave the room for two minutes and you've got your balls out.

—Come on, Dan, you like what you see.

—Must be hard keeping that body under wraps all the time.

—Quit staring and join in.

But the tune was fading. Merc began to feel exposed with the music dying away. JJ started up another spliff. Trying to hog it all, the fucking stoner. He'd been way out of line earlier with that headlock. Merc had thought it was just a bit of a wrestle, then JJ started taking it all seriously and tried to strangle his head off. He should've booted him the minute he got free but Steph was watching so he let it go. Some people took things way too far.

He swayed on his feet, feeling the music die away. Cath was looking at him, her eyes all concerned. 'Get off the table,' those eyes said.

He sprang down and landed softly on the balls of his feet, like a proper little fifteen-year-old Russian gymnast.

There. He did it for her. He was a perceptive, generous human person.

Lucy threw him his bottoms and he trotted gamely into the kitchen to change and get another beer. He knew Lucy's eyes were on his arse.

Alone in the kitchen, a candle on the windowsill flickering, he put his legs into his trackies. He watched the candle in the reflection of the window, and though he felt energised and smiley after his dance, something rattled in him. With the beer in him, the sambuca, there was an anger building back up.

JJ had taken it way too far. He'd made a competition out of the whole thing, sucker-punched him. Merc was stronger, he knew that. All that work in the gym, on the pitch, was not for nothing. JJ was a scrawny fuck. He'd just caught Merc unawares. Merc should go in there and put *him* in a headlock, see how he liked it. Choke the fuck out of him. Strangle him till his eyes bled.

No. Calm it. Calm . . .

Merc had a handle on his emotions. Others lost theirs. They were weak. Merc could control himself. Whenever he got angry he gave himself an inner image. Did everyone else do that? Create something for themselves that represented them, that calmed them, arranged it in their mind and stayed there? Most people weren't like him. He was above all the rest of them. The candle spitting in the window, Merc closed his eyes and retreated into his mind. He made a story of himself finding peace.

He'd go there at twilight, the sky stained navy blue, like on those long summer evenings that take ages to stretch to night, when you don't notice it getting darker and darker until you can't see in front of you. He would go through a forest and down into a valley, and find himself in a clearing. A lake would be glassy still in the background, with tall trees looming all around. In the middle of the clearing, a large house would be on fire. Completely swallowed up in flames, throwing monster light onto the clearing around it, washing shadows up the trees. There would be the thundering crash and splinter of wood breaking and burning inside, the roof collapsing. Black, black smoke tumbling upwards towards the sky. The fire'd have a violence to it. It'd be beautiful; quietly, violently beautiful. Merc would imagine this in his head for the next two days if he got frustrated, or he needed inspiration for something. He would imagine himself sitting down watching the fire. Blazing, burning, billowing, the brightest light anywhere for miles, a passionate, fuming, powerful flame, with such manic power.

That was Merc's inner image. God damn it, he was deep.

His trackies on, a fresh beer in his paw, he sashayed in to join the rest of them.

Cath

Once the evening set in they gave their party pieces. She'd been planning it, looking forward to it. They sat in a semi-circle around the fireplace, some on the couch, others on the floor, and waited for someone to go first.

There was an odd atmosphere in the room. Lucy was twirling her hair and puffing her lips into little pouts as she positioned herself on the couch beside DanDan. JJ's feet were propped up but Cath could see it wasn't that relaxing, his feet at an odd angle. Merc sat bow-legged on the tiles while Steph stayed leaning against the wall looking bored. It'd never been like this before. Everyone spoke too loudly, too clearly; their movements were exaggerated, their exclamations too stagey. It was like there was a camera on them or something, like someone was recording them.

Steph was sent up to sing first, being the least willing to do so. She sang 'He's a Tramp' all jazzy and sexy. Her voice was clear and beautiful, and put them in a trance. She kept her eyes closed as she swayed gently in front of the fire, her body tracing the air in time with her voice. They gave her a big clap when she finished. Merc and JJ seemed to get into a competition over who could clap the loudest, shouting BRAVO and BELLISSIMA at her as she returned to her place by the wall. Then it was Cath's turn.

She stood up in front of the fireplace and sang 'Caledonia'. Her mother had sung it to her a few times when she was younger. She told the others that was why she sang it, because it was her mother's bedtime song. Truthfully, though, she'd heard it at other parties

41

and gatherings of older generations, and it seemed a crowd-pleaser, so she'd decided to learn it in case it ever came in handy.

'Caledonia' wasn't really what she wanted to sing. What she would have liked to sing was a strange French song she'd heard once and couldn't remember. She'd heard it on the beach, when she'd gone on holiday by herself a few months back. Her mam and dad were splitting up for the last time, and her mam took her to one side and told her she'd booked her a week in a back-packers' hostel, said she wanted her to get away for a while. Cath said it wasn't a problem, it didn't bother her, but her mam had insisted, said she never wanted her to see the kind of fighting that would happen. 'I don't want you getting cynical,' she'd said.

She'd gone on the holiday, and spent her time roving about the old town in Nice and thinking on her parents. One night she went down to the beach with a few people from the hostel. Some locals had set speakers up and played dance music mixed in with old French music and movie soundtracks. They sat in a few circles and drank cheap red wine mixed with Coke and paired off as the time drifted on. She was left with a German lad from the hostel, and this French song came on the speakers just as he leaned in and kissed her. At first she'd been thrilled about it, a beachside shift with a foreign lad, tick that off the list, but after a few moments she realised the kissing just wasn't for her. It was cold and hard and functional and the guy didn't like her, he just liked putting his tongue in her, so she broke off from him and turned away. She walked off down the beach then sat down and watched the moon. There were crabs scuttling about across the cold rocks and the black ocean before her swished smoothly. She thought of swimming out into the sea, not telling anyone, just stripping down and swimming out until her arms were too tired to turn back and she'd drown. It seemed appropriate somehow. But then she heard the music drifting on the wind from down the beach. A female voice was singing and for whatever reason she found it one of the most beautiful things she'd heard in her life, and it kept her glued in her place, kept her from going out swimming. She couldn't remember what the song was or how it went or even what it was about. She'd meant to take down the lyrics but they were in French and so she couldn't, though *mourir* was in there. If Cath had had the courage, and could have remembered, she would have sung that song for the others. But she didn't. She sang 'Caledonia'.

When she sat back down on the couch, she knew it wasn't going to be the best song of the evening. It was too popular. Too predictable. She stayed still and tried not to show it as Lucy got up to sing. DanDan was pressed in against her, and they leaned together, holding each other up on the couch.

Lucy was having a go at 'Rehab' and failing dismally. Her voice fell in and out of tune and she wobbled as she sang, her eyes closed and her words slurring.

Cath flashed a look at Steph, who looked back and shrugged. What could they do? Lucy tottered, using the fireplace for stability, and sang on.

When Lucy was drinking it was better just to leave her at it. Most nights she was grand, full of fun. Other nights, though, if she got upset, it was hard to stop. The one thing that made her worse than anything was when you asked her to slow down. She'd get really pissy and then really emotional and start crying. It might be one of those nights.

Lucy spluttered on for a few more verses before she forgot where she was and finished.

They gave her a short clap as she wrapped up. Lucy knocked over a candle then walked right by them into the kitchen, where they could hear the sound of the fridge opening. Cath's phone beeped and she wiggled it out of her jeans pocket.

How's the trip so far?

Paddy. She immediately started to key in her response.

Just settling in, baby

43

This was the game they played; once the first person texted the second would respond quick-fire to it, then they'd text and receive and text back as quick as they could until the conversation was done. Best way of doing it, according to Paddy. Get your thoughts out clean and pure.

Cool, honey

                                                            Sugar

Doe-eyes

                                                            Darling

Ride

                                                            Wetser

C.I.L.F.

                                                Cath I'd Like to Fuck?

Cat I'd Like to Fuck.
I fuck cats.

                                    Shame. I'm more of a dog person.

Doggone it.

                                                            Ha.

DanDan turned and frowned at her as she tapped into her phone. He looked down at her screen, squinted his eyes at it then moved his head away. She automatically turned the face of the phone away from him.

Would it be weird if I said
I missed you?

He'd thought it through, Paddy had. He was advancing the thing, fair fucks to him.

No.

I miss you.

I miss you too.

Come back quick.

I will. X

Cath had high hopes for him. They'd been dancing around it for weeks, flirting by text and calling each other, though any chance they'd had to meet since their first date had been scuppered. He'd had to go to a funeral, her mam had fallen ill. Still, it was almost certainly arranged now that when she got back they'd be together. This would be her last weekend as a free woman.

DanDan coughed and elbowed her as he fidgeted beside her. Ever since they'd started hanging out, DanDan had always talked about his love life with her – who he fancied, what he wanted, any problems or worries or wonders he was having. On the opposite side, though, Cath had never, ever talked about hers, and he'd never asked. When she got with fellas or had guys hanging about or she fancied someone, she told Steph or Lucy, never DanDan.

It seemed strange to her that they were so close and yet had this embargo on her talking about other men. She wondered if there was still a point to it, or if it was just too big a deal to rectify now. She waited on Paddy's response, but it was a while coming through. She sat there feeling forlorn, DanDan silent beside her, for ages, till eventually the phone vibrated in her hand.

XXXXX

DanDan coughed again and shifted in his seat away from her.

Lucy

She sat outside the front door and fumed. She'd done nothing wrong, nothing fucking wrong at all. She'd been embarrassed. They'd embarrassed her. Humiliated her. They'd tried to undermine and scorn her and for what fucking reason. To have someone to look down on. To have someone they could laugh at. Well, that was their fucking problem, not hers. She wouldn't let them make her feel like this.

She'd been looking forward to it since they'd first mentioned they might do it. When Steph had gone up for her song, they'd rearranged themselves on the couch. Cath sat in on her lap and DanDan sat down beside them. It was tight. There were legs everywhere but they fit.

Then she could feel DanDan's hand against hers. It was warm. He wasn't moving it and he wasn't looking at her. They were all packed in on each other; Cath had shifted so she was sitting mostly on DanDan's legs, but his hand was touching Lucy's, the both of them squashed somewhere between her leg and Cath's arse. Was that intentional?

It couldn't have been intentional. But there they were, touching hands. Had DanDan been trying something? Out of that nervousness, and from the horror of singing in front of them, she'd drained her drink, and started another, switching to vodka.

She'd had a little thrill when she'd gone up to sing. It was stupid, she knew that, when it was only among friends, but still. She'd turned her hips the right way, she'd tried to give DanDan a good enough look at her, let him see the curves of her, the sultry movement, and used the husky sort of voice Amy Winehouse had. She'd imagined applause, an ovation, when she finished.

She was given a polite clap that quickly died.

She was the only person who had really sung anything that meant something, really meant something. She knew, yes, that her singing of 'Rehab' wasn't the best. She might've been a semitone or two off. Steph probably thought her own performance was much better, but that was like Steph. More than any of them, Lucy'd sung something that was true to her. It had given her comfort in her life. She'd shown it to them and they'd tolerated it; maybe they grinned to themselves during it, smug that their own taste was better. She'd felt so stupid standing up there in front of them, expecting a longer clap and not getting one, and then just standing there waiting, so she'd taken another bow, and her foot slipped and she'd knocked over a candle in a wine bottle on the mantel and sent wax spraying the floor. Cath gave her another clap and said don't worry about the stain, I'll get it, and Lucy'd gone straight for the door, silence all the way. Their way of shaming her was saying fucking nothing.

She sat outside by the front door and dragged on a cigarette and sucked at the bottle of vodka. None of the rest of them could drink like her. Not even the lads. They couldn't sing like her, they couldn't drink like her. None of them. All of them in there probably laughing at her, giggling at her. Laughing devil fucking laughs with their eyes red. Her head felt full and the cigarette was making her tongue fuzzy. The vodka burned her throat, it tasted like how she imagined bin juice might taste. She should switch back to wine.

Right across the road was the church, and the graveyard. There was a little bell mounted on one side of the church door. Lucy could make that sing. She got up, and with the cigarette still in one hand, she bent down with her free one and picked up fistfuls of gravel from beside her feet. The muck went under her fingernails and it scraped her and made her feel anxious, but she picked up handful after handful of little stones and threw them at the bell. She missed the first few throws but after a few she hit the bell and it made a little ding, then she kept digging up stones and throwing them until her fingers felt swollen and her arm ached. She held her arm and breathed the cold air, trying to calm her nerves. She pulled a few strands of sweaty hair off her face.

She moved to the window and looked in at them, at JJ doing his best Christopher Walken impression. Lucy knew when they looked back on that weekend they would barely even remember her song. When they moved on and made better friends and emigrated to different places, when they'd been excited by life and humiliated and embarrassed themselves, when they looked back on that weekend, they'd still just remark, 'Lucy sang some shit pop song, didn't she?' and then pass on to some other event from the weekend, never even contemplating the generous act that had taken place. When they fucked off and got jobs and belted out children and left her behind they'd still talk about her and laugh at her. Laugh at the little posh girl who knew nothing.

She pressed the cigarette into her arm, just for a tiny second. Sparks jumped up off her and it sizzled and it burned BURNED and she dropped the cigarette. Jesus, Jesus, it stung. She rubbed at her arm, and tried to grab at it, stop the pain from coming up, but it wasn't that bad. There was just a small red mark on her; she'd not totally burned herself. Christ, why'd she done that?

She retreated from the window and made her way back through the wet grass to the door, for the warmth of inside. Rinse her arm off.

Had DanDan been watching her when she sang? She didn't know. She sang with her eyes closed.

Malachy

Malachy heard faint sounds coming from down the way.

Ping!

Ping!

He'd fallen asleep in front of the fire, the Crosaire crossword half done in his lap and the cup of green tea, doctor's orders, on the stool beside. He stood and went into the kitchen, to the window, and looked down to the house.

It'd grown dark. A thick sheet of mist had settled in the valley, but the yellow street lamps had turned on and came hazy through it, and the lights from the Lodge threw little golden oblongs out onto the lawn. He scanned the area for the source of the sound.

Ping!

The short, pudgy girl was walking around outside the Lodge. Malachy could see she was pissed. She walked slowly, unsteadily, placing foot in front of foot by the front of the house, as she bent down to take up handfuls of gravel that she threw across the road at the church, at the small hand-operated bell that hung beside the door. She missed most of her throws, but got one on target every so often.

Ping!

Malachy stood by the window and watched the girl. He was still thinking on Mona Rourke. The young lad in the field had dragged her up and now he couldn't put her down. And it was only worse with the young girl having a go at the church bell.

Ping!

The girl threw one last handful of pebbles at the bell, then lurched, stumbling slightly, to the window of the Lodge. She

49

looked in, her hands forming a screen against the sides of her head, a cigarette still wedged between her fingers. Whatever she was watching inside the house seemed to absorb her. After a few moments, she stepped away from the window and rubbed her eyes.

She dragged on the cigarette, rekindling its red glow, then she took the end of it and pushed it into the flesh of her inside forearm. Sparks flew from her arm and she dropped the butt to the ground, the sparks disappearing before they hit the grass. She rubbed her arm fiercely then held it for a few moments before turning to walk back inside.

Malachy watched her the whole time from the window. There was something wrong with these people. The way they were carrying on disturbed him. They were either lying in the grass alone or burning themselves with cigarettes. They seemed unnatural, alien and out of place in the valley. But they were also drawing him in, like he was passing a car crash and slowing to watch. Fuck it, if he was going to watch them, keep an eye on them, he'd do it properly.

He took a bottle of Jameson from the cupboard and sloshed a large measure into a teacup. He drew up a chair and placed it by the screen door so as to watch the house. With the lights on in his kitchen, they'd be able to see him just as easily as he could see them, so he switched them off and sat in the dark. He drank his whiskey in the silence, refilling the cup from the bottle whenever it ran low.

As the mist moved slowly over the house, he thought of his father. This time, though, it was different; he didn't think of the usual stuff, the memories he normally had of his father, like how hard it had been at the end, watching him struggle with his work on the farm, losing his strength. He thought instead of how, when he was younger, his father used to spit on his hands before work, a big, hocked one full of phlegm, and how he'd smile at Malachy, the left front tooth dead and blackened, as he rubbed his two palms together, drying the spit out before going to work with a spade or a pitchfork.

He continued to drink his whiskey. He wondered what his father would have made of all of this. They used to sit out and watch over the valley together, the two of them, like they were mountain watchmen, fixed and immoveable and eternal on their hill. His father had not proved to be eternal, though. He was gone years now, and Malachy could scarcely remember what he sounded like. He tried to find one solid phrase that he could remember, something definite and clear he knew his father had said. 'When I'm gone,' was one of them, but that was so frequent and said in such a dry monotone he could barely remember his father's cadence in it.

It always began, 'When I'm gone,' then it was followed by some declaration or piece of advice.

At the start it was followed by, 'This'll be your farm,' and then it turned to, 'Then you can marry,' and when that passed it was, 'When I'm gone you should go away,' until towards the end, it'd become something else, something new.

'Don't wait till I'm gone,' he'd said. 'Go now. Leave.'

Even at the end, his father, weak with pneumonia, would shiver by the fire, having refused the hospital, and croak, 'Go on now. Get going.' And Malachy, forty-five years of age, would just pat his hand and stay sitting.

'Too late, Da. Too late.'

Aside from those times, the only other sentence he fully remembered his father ever saying was about the Rourkes. Billy and Mona had lived in the Lodge then. Mona would spend the evening hours sitting on her legs in the tall grass and holding the sides of her arms in her hands. After a while, Billy would call for her or their baby girl would scream and she'd go back in slowly, seeming to count her steps. Whenever he saw her in the grass, Malachy's father would spit on the ground and retreat inside, but Malachy would stay watching her.

Only once in his life, when Malachy turned fifteen, did he ask his father about them. They sat drinking tea out the front of the house, watching the sun set over the valley, the Lodge down below them, and Malachy told his father about Mona and how she sat out in the grass, how he saw her crying sometimes, or walking as though she carried an injury, how if he met her coming down a boreen she'd drop her head and refuse to meet his eye. He asked what could be done.

His father had scratched the rim of his mug with a tough fingernail.

'There's always a tragedy somewhere,' he said. 'You just keep your own house, and get on with it. That's all you can do.'

Malachy could still feel the strength, the authority of his father's voice, and what it had meant to him at the time. But the instruction, no matter the tone of it, was one he couldn't follow. Mona sat out in the garden every night, while inside the baby screamed and Billy walked about in a rage, and Malachy was supposed to do nothing, only watch. At fifteen years old he arrived at the firm truth, that he was witnessing something wrong, something evil, and that he alone was the one to deal with it. One night he watched Billy leave the Lodge for the evening, and he followed.

The road to Carrig at the time was dark, long and muddy. No lights in those days, no street lamps. Only what light could be had from the moon. He stopped halfway between his home and the town and concealed himself behind some bushes. He breathed heavily in the undergrowth, waiting for Billy. Three hours he waited. His heart jumped at every off-noise he heard, every rustle of the branches or the leaves, and though he was young and strong and he knew that he was the one with terrible plans, he'd felt scared. Many times over he convinced himself to leave, to turn back, but he hardened himself; he was a rock, he was the fucking reckoning. Then he saw Billy's shadow spilling down the road in the moonlight, followed by Billy himself mumbling a song as he staggered home.

He waited till Billy passed, then he fell into step behind him, watching his thin grey head wilt about his shoulders. He breathed and breathed behind him, his heart pounding, then he swung his leg back and kicked Billy's legs from under him. The force of his blow, the heaviness and the realness of it, cemented Malachy in his own actions. Billy cried into the night air as he landed sideways on his arm and shoulder. Malachy was on him quickly, turning him over, kneeling over his chest. Billy screamed out again and Malachy moved to silence him. The first awkward strike of his knuckles on Billy's eye decided the outcome. Billy's head cracked back into the ground and left his chin and throat exposed. He flailed a little, gasping, trying to keep Malachy at bay with long arms and waving palms. Malachy had been skinny at that age, at fifteen, but the farm had him strong, and he used that strength on the front and sides of Billy's face. Billy retreated inside his own arms, breathing heavily and whimpering, *Jesus, Jesus*, as if already resigned to it. Malachy had expected more noise, more of a fight, or more screaming, as he beat him, but the only sounds were his own low grunts, and a short, stifled whine from Billy each time he took a blow and tried to re-cover his face. It surprised Malachy how easy it was, how gentle almost, the soft slapping of his fists on Billy's face.

He stopped when his hands started to hurt. Malachy raised himself up, checked that Billy was still breathing by putting his foot on his chest and waiting for it to move, then left, trudging away towards Carrig so he could double back around by the long way, leaving no trace of where he'd come from. And as he walked away all he heard through gargled breaths in the dark was Billy gasping, *Jesus, Jesus*.

The next morning he watched as Mona ran to the shops and came back with extra food and a bottle of antiseptic. Billy didn't leave the house for five days. When he emerged on the sixth day he had his cap down low over his face and held his ribs lightly with his left hand. He sat outside smoking a cigarette. Two days later, Mona was back crying in the wet grass.

Malachy then understood that he'd been watching something that had been going on for much longer than he'd realised. The Rourkes' lives were already winding down when Malachy's was just starting, and they'd continued to decline as Malachy had grown. He'd not really considered that they'd existed before him, that the freshness and newness he felt in everything in the valley was nothing new for them. They had the weight of two shared, painful lives on their hands, something that was strange and alien to him as a fifteen-year-old. It was not something he could change with his fists.

The Rourkes continued their routine for a few more years. Their baby Tara grew and biked around the rocky car park, never spending much time in the house, till Mona died in the back and they buried her beside the church, then Billy walked drunk off the pier on the Rockadoon Shore a few years later, whether by accident or not no one knew, or cared.

And the Lodge stood there just the same as it always had. Same walls and roof, same number of rooms, of windows. Only the tenants changed. And now it was filled with young people who were running in and out and around it like wild dogs. Acting like they owned it. But it wasn't their house, or their home. They had no right. It had been there long before them. It belonged to the valley, to the town, to the hills maybe, he didn't know, but not them. They were just occupying it, and with each passing hour he resented them more for it, for the way they were acting, for dragging things up out of him he didn't want to remember. Still, he stayed watching, drinking his whiskey down, his eyes focused on the walls of the Lodge like they might crumble at any moment.

Cath

They played charades after the party pieces. Merc made an arse
of himself trying to act out *The Shawshank Redemption* and they
laughed at him. JJ especially was giving him a bit of stick.

—Why were you knocking on your head like that?

—I was tapping my jaw for fuck sake. I said, 'Sounds like',
yeah? Second word, first syllable, sounds like: Jaw. Jaw, Shaw.

—Eh, okay, and the second thing, the stabbing motion?

—Oh come on, like in prison when you stab them, you shank
them. A shank is like a prison knife.

They'd been at each other all day, snipping and jabbing away.
Or had it been going on before that? They seemed to be getting at
each other particularly fiercely when Steph was in the room. JJ
laughed at Merc.

—How the fuck were we supposed to get that?

—If you were in any way logical you might.

—Oh fancy that, yeah.

—Fine, how would you do it?

—Like this.

JJ climbed into the centre of the room, elbowed Merc out of
the way, then mimed swimming and gasping. He wriggled on
the ground before standing up and throwing his arms to the
heavens like Tim Robbins. He kept his arms up as he looked to
Merc.

—There, that's the Shawshank.

—That was worse than mine.

—Cath, what was that?

—It was the Shawshank, JJ.

Merc glared at her. She looked back at him.

—What? It's the Shawshank.

—Whatever.

Merc sat down and took a loud gulp from his can.

They moved on playing but the heart seemed gone from it. Lucy lazily counted out syllables on her fingers and mimed opening a book, while Merc sulked and JJ rooted around for skins. Cath got up and went into the kitchen to make toast for everyone. They hadn't eaten properly so maybe they were just flagging. She brought a huge stack of toast out on a big plate. DanDan was outside again doing whatever he was doing. She should check on him.

She put the plate down in front of them and Merc looked at her; there was a nastiness in his eyes.

—Thanks, Cath.

—No problem.

—We can make our own toast, though, y'know?

—It's fine, I was making some anyway.

—You don't have to be serving us all the time.

—It's fine.

—Fucking needy, like.

Merc took a slice of toast and bit into it, chewing on it slowly. The golden butter on crispy bread passed his thin lips, and she saw it grinding up inside his mouth. A speck of butter trembled, clinging to the upper right side of his top lip. He chewed and chewed. The air in the room choked her. Why would he say something like that? He smacked his lips.

—I'm just saying.

Like fuck he was. He'd said it in such a nonchalant, off-the-cuff way, like he was trying to be kind to her, so no one had really noticed the true sentiment. Or had they? Nobody was saying anything. Lucy was bending down, trying to reach the bottle at her feet, pawing at it, her head flopping. What he'd said was getting smaller and smaller in the room and bigger and bigger in her mind. The anger was rising in her, choking up in her throat. Needy?

JJ let the silence go long enough, as he watched Merc drain his can, not a care in the world.

—Ah here.

Merc turned to him.

—What?

—Come on, now.

—I was only saying she doesn't need to wait on us. Wasn't I? Cath?

—Yeah, don't worry.

She knew she had to defend herself, to draw a line in the sand. But by the time she came to a decision to do so, she'd missed her moment. Too many seconds of silence had passed. It was too late and now JJ was just making it worse, making too big a deal of it.

—You fucking weren't.

—Fuck sake, JJ. I was only looking out for her. Wasn't I? Cath?

—Yeah, no. It's fine.

—What do you mean, Cath?

—It's fine, JJ, I said. Chill out.

She sat back down and said nothing more. JJ was looking at her, his hands open as if to say 'huh?'

Merc shook his head at her, and did a little shoulder waggle as he chomped.

—Well, what I meant was, thanks for the toast.

—You're welcome, Merc.

She'd missed it. Anything she said now would just be dragging up an old argument and being bitter, or making a big deal out of things. It was over before it began. She could feel the others knew he'd been mean. *Needy*.

DanDan came in from the front garden.

—Why are ye all so quiet?

Cath offered him the plate of toast.

—No reason. Toast?

There was a faint trill in her voice. She thought he might notice and she was sure if he looked her in the eye she'd break into tears. So she kept her eyes averted. DanDan took the toast.

—Cool, thanks.

He put it into a corner of his mouth and sat himself down. He didn't notice anything. He hadn't even tried to notice. Too locked up in his own things. He would have helped her if he had noticed, though, she knew that. At least JJ had tried.

It didn't matter. They were all a bit drunk. There were empty cans and improvised ashtrays everywhere. The place stank. Steph looked at her, her eyebrow raised ever so slightly. 'You okay?' kind of thing. She nodded her head. Steph turned to DanDan.

—Right, fella, your turn.

—What, charades? What's the clue?

—Here, I'll write it down.

DanDan started going through the motions. Two words, film. Film and book. She let herself zone out. Merc shouted at DanDan, trying to get the clue, not even looking at her, probably not even aware of what he'd said.

—Hippo! Dog! Mare!

Needy burned in her, repeated itself and echoed as she sat still. She felt it in her throat, in her stomach, coming up in waves over her, as she tried to beat it down with big deep breaths and rational thoughts.

He hadn't meant it. He'd used the wrong tone.

Forgiveness. It was the only way to go on.

Forgive, forget. How was that possible?

Forgive, why?

How long could you let someone take from you?

How much was too much?

Merc was on the point of getting the second word when Lucy heaved herself up from her seat on the couch and stumbled away. As she was passing, Cath caught her eye so that Lucy bent down to her. She mumbled through her hair at Cath.

—I'm rallying, darling. Don't worry. I'll be back in a minute.

She lumbered in the direction of the stairs and clonked up towards the bathroom. Cath watched her go but was still aware of Merc shouting charades guesses at DanDan to her left.

—Donkey! Donkey Kong! Dirty Donkey! Dingle Donkey! Fuck!

58

You forgave your friends. You let go of transient annoyances.

Needy. Needy. She heard it in her guts, in her heart, in her blood.

Neeeeedyyyyy.

—Horse! Shergar! Eh, High Ho Silver! Horse Tranquilliser! Horse!

How much of herself did she have to give, to let them take away, before she said stop? Before she cut them loose and let them drown themselves in their own petty jealousies, their vulgar competitions.

They were reaching something surely, the point of no return. They'd take everything from her.

She hoped it was just the drink speaking.

—Horse! Moon! Camel! Hump! Camel! Horse!

But then, maybe . . .

No.

—Big Horse! Small Horse! Horse! Horse!

DanDan broke and shouted at him:

—*WAR HORSE*, YOU COMPLETE FUCKING THICK.

No.

Steph

After all the songs and the party pieces and the charades – the structured fun – petered out, they settled in listening to quiet, jazzy records. JJ blew smoke up towards the ceiling. Lucy came back downstairs and tried to dance slowly to the music while DanDan strummed the cloth on his jeans. Steph needed some air. She sat outside by the back door, her back pressed against the stone wall, and lit a cigarette. The darkness of the evening had bedded in properly, making it hard to see down beyond the trees.

She was only gone a minute when she felt the back door move behind her, scratching open on the tile then swinging shut. She knew who it would be. Inside, Merc had been eyeing her. She'd felt his eyes constantly drifting down her top. Why were guys so absolutely obsessed with tits? She never really got the whole thing. But here he was now, sidling up to her. She wasn't mad about the way he'd been carrying on, but sure, didn't everyone do stupid shite when they were drunk. He sat down next to her and looked into the distance. Then he elbowed her.

—Beautiful song, before. Peggy Lee, was it?

—Yah.

—Lovely.

—Cheers.

—Seriously gorgeous. You've a talent.

She was drunk but not that drunk.

—Fuck off now, you're just ripping the piss.

He looked offended.

—Seriously, you were great. Saying I have bad taste?

—Maybe.

60

—Do you have a fag?

—Here.

She offered him her cigarette. He took it from her and said thanks. She lit another and they smoked and felt the cold and blew smoke away. Merc was quiet, subdued in a way that she'd not seen before. A quick frown formed then disappeared on his face. He tapped at her foot with his.

—Do you think . . .

—What?

He flicked the ash off his cigarette.

—I dunno. Do you think maybe Cath took that the wrong way, what I said?

So Merc could feel. Steph had been sure he hadn't noticed how he'd hurt Cath. He rubbed the end of one shoe against the other, avoiding her eye. This was a nice moment for Steph now, she hadn't been expecting it, and it was exciting to see a side of Merc she hadn't before. She wouldn't make it too hard on him, but she wasn't going to let him get away scot-free.

—What do you mean?

—Oh you know, just like, when I was saying Cath didn't have to wait on us.

—Why would she take that the wrong way?

—Well, I dunno, it looked like people reacted funny to it.

—Depends how you meant it.

—I didn't want it to be mean. Christ, I like Cath. I think she's great. I just . . .

Oh dear. Could Merc, tall, sleek, GAA legend Merc, be about to cry? Good lord. Maybe there was something about the country air that was making people vulnerable. Steph thought she'd better watch herself. She'd be the next one to go. Merc coughed. Wait for it . . . Wait for it . . . He scraped the ground with his shoe and spoke without looking at her.

—I dunno. She took it the wrong way. I mean, I was looking out for her, I was trying to tell her she's too nice to people sometimes, like I'm on her side, she just took it the wrong way, then JJ. Fucking JJ starts on about . . . Fuck sake.

Dern. People didn't change their spots that easily so. He'd been almost there. He knew what he'd done, he had the information, but had just fallen short of actually accepting it. She might as well give him a hand for trying, at least. She shifted herself slightly so she was sitting closer to him. She thought about putting her hand on him, patting his shoulder or something, but it felt weird.

Merc flicked his smoke away in anger; it sizzled out somewhere off in the wet grass.

—Do you have another one?

—Here, have mine.

She handed him the end of hers and saw his hand shake. She tried to nudge him with her shoulder. She wasn't someone who was naturally tactile, never knowing when it was appropriate to put your hand on someone's arm or not. Even with her ex, Fergus, she'd never touched him that much, which had upset him, because all he'd wanted to do was feel her and pat her and pet her and grab her and she'd have to skip out of his way all the time. Thinking about Ferg made her anxious, so she nudged Merc harder with her shoulder.

—Look, it's grand. She'll get over it. Just have a word in the morning, let her know you weren't being mean. Go in and say, 'Sorry, Cath, didn't mean it that way.' Only don't make a big deal about it. Just say sorry and she'll be grand.

—Simple as that?

—Simple as that.

—Cool. She's a good lady.

About a year before, she'd asked Cath what she should do to be more open, more physically friendly with people. Cath said she didn't know, she should be herself. She gave her a few tips: touch people when you talk to them, look them in the eye. Allow your body language to say, 'I'm listening to you.' Steph tried it for a few weeks, a few months even, and it hadn't worked. Guys always just thought she was flirting with them. She'd make a joke and touch their elbow lightly, to reinforce it like Cath said, but then next thing they'd be leaning in, trying to lob the gob. So she stopped with that one, stopped putting her hands on people. But now, with all the wine in her, she wouldn't mind touching someone. It wouldn't be all that bad now. Merc nudged her hard with his elbow.

—Good singer as well. Not as good as you, though.

—Ah would you stop. You've shite-all taste in singing.

He took a last drag on her cigarette, then he lifted his face up and looked at her, and that was when she really noticed it, how close they were and that their legs were touching, and his hand was close to her inside leg. With his outside arm he brought the end of her fag out to her, and it had burned down so low that their fingers touched a while as they exchanged it. They looked at each other for too long.

Then he leaned in slightly, and she smelled his beer breath on her cheek.

—Well, at least I've good taste in women.

—That's an awful line.

—No, it's not. It's a silly line. But it's charming in its silliness.

—You think a lot of yourself.

—I think a lot of you.

Normally, she would nip this one right in the bud. He was a mate. But she hadn't seen anyone in a while, and she was feeling the wine in her. He had good hair, and a streamlined, athletic body on him. She'd always liked the Gaelic player type of smoothness, the long torso and nice firm arms, when you could see their veins in their arms, and their lovely well-defined hands.

It was probably the wine talking.

He leaned in, and fuck it why not? She didn't belong to anyone, and neither did he, though JJ was being quiet, but who knew what he was thinking. She didn't belong to anyone. She put her lips on his.

He kissed like someone who kisses a lot of other people, and doesn't care for them; someone who puts the moves on girls late at night in clubs. His tongue went everywhere, over her teeth and down, down into her gob. She had a way of picking them.

She coughed, and made him stop for a moment.

—Slow.

—What?

—Slow down.

He slowed and she led him. After a few moments he'd gotten the idea, and she started enjoying herself, the warmth of him. His hand dropped to the inside of her thigh, and she didn't mind it there. Ground rules first, though. She pushed him away.

—This doesn't mean anything, now.

—Whatever you say.

She stood up, stubbing the cigarette out on the door frame. As she backed away from the door, scraping her arms on the coarse, rocky wall, she offered her hand to him. She felt his eyes on her, watching her move, as he followed her into the darkness.

Malachy

He drank and watched the house. After a while the blonde girl appeared outside the back door and sat down by the gravelled wall, her legs making triangles with the ground. She lit a cigarette and smoked slowly until the athletic fella, the one in trackies, came out. He knelt down carefully and put his own back up against the wall so that he was sitting shoulder to shoulder beside her. She gave him her cigarette, their fingers grazing, and lit another one for herself. They smoked a while, exchanging cigarettes a few more times, and Malachy leaned closer to the glass of his door, trying to see them. Their shoulders touched lightly as they talked, until the lad looked pointedly at her, at the side of her head. She turned to him and they kissed.

Malachy knew he should look away. He'd never seen kissing outside the house, never between Billy and Mona or with any of the Nevilles. It seemed odd and unnatural to him, but he kept watching. The couple were getting fiercer in their kissing, shoving against each other, then the blonde girl put her hand on the boy's collarbone, and pushed, parting them roughly. They stayed there, speaking to each other in what looked like whispers. Then they stood, helping each other up, and walked farther down the wall of the house, into the shadows. Though it was darker he could still make out the shapes of them.

The lad pressed her up against the side wall. His face was inches from hers, her head angled slightly to one side. She folded her arms around his shoulders, and his hands went around her hips, slipping around her back, and their fronts pressed together. They moved slowly, slowly, slowly towards each other's mouths.

The lad's hands moved down her back, and started to slide down her jeans, pushing her back against the wall. Malachy continued to watch and as he did his vision seemed to blur. He lost sight of them, he only saw their bodies moving, and in one hideous moment something jarred in him; something horrific came tumbling up out of his chest and into his head.

He was young and floating in cold water, down on the Doon Shore, bobbing up and down on his toes with Elaine Newell. She was wrapped around him, her body pressed against his, her hair wet and her breath on him. He tried to focus back on the couple pushing up against each other by the side of the house, but every time he looked at them something stabbed at him, and every time he looked away he felt a loss in him and he thought of himself in a lake, floating, floating, a warm mouth and tongue on his neck and words being whispered in his ear. He'd forgotten the heat, the burning skin against his own.

He stepped away from the door and breathed slowly in the dark. His heart pounded against his ribs. His body was still in the Doon Shore, the cold of the water compressing his chest. He looked around his kitchen. It looked different, expanded somehow, like the moon had changed its position in the sky and the light came upon the bare shelves in a different way, showing him corners of the place he'd never noticed: how grimy the brushed steel fridge was, how dirty the floors seemed, and how the moon shone on the kitchen table that was covered in the opened letters and flyers he didn't bother to read or clear away, but ate his meals on top of, though recently he'd taken to eating the whole dinner standing by the sink, washing the plate while he chewed the last mouthful of meat.

He left the kitchen and walked around to the back of his house. He could only see the start of his own fields through the mist, the first few metres of grass. It was so dark. He felt when he was growing up, years and years before, it had been brighter at night. Maybe because the place had been busy. He'd actually met people on the roads back then, and in their houses and in the village, and when he drove around there were lights all across the valley, chimneys smoking and yellow glows in the windows.

But the people had left the valley. The houses were empty now, abandoned, or owned by Germans or Americans or people in Dublin who used them as holiday homes for two weeks of the year. There were fewer lights on the hills and it felt like he was going back in time, time beyond, before people, when the hills were dark and there was nothing that could be seen but the moon reflecting in the lake. He had no idea why he was here any more, why he was where he was.

This line of thought was of little fucking use to him, he knew that. He should just go inside and put his head down and sleep, forget it all. He never slept more than five hours a night, a habit of working on the farm, though that sleep was rarely troubled or broken. His tiredness always overcame him and he slept solidly, as if nothing had happened, as if he'd simply flipped a switch. He'd sleep now, go to sleep, forget everything.

He walked back inside to his bedroom. He sat on his bed and pulled off his boots and his trousers. His heart was beating in him strong. He heard whispers in his ears, come away, come with me. It was just the whiskey talking.

His head found the pillow, and he breathed deep and hard. No one else's smells on his pillow. No one else's perfume on his sheets, no skin or hair left behind, no nails chipped and snagged on the mattress. Nothing that had not come straight from him, from his body that felt so very, very weary. He'd never had anyone in his bed before. He spat on his pillow. Just to have something on him, some foreign smell or taste that was out of the ordinary. Maybe this was what it was like to have someone sleep next to you. He crushed his cheek into the slime and closed his eyes. Go to sleep, now. Go. Forget.

JJ

He'd not *seen* anything, but Merc and Steph had been missing for ages. Way too long for just a cigarette. His thoughts were slowing down with each joint though, and it did him no good in the clear thoughts department. He drained a Red Bull, rolled a spliff, and sparked the end of it. He passed it to DanDan, who took a few sad puffs before handing it back, waving his arm to say 'no more'. JJ tugged on the spliff, burning it down in record time.

It was too cold outside, surely. How long did it take to smoke a cigarette? He tried to use his X-ray vision to see through the wall. There was a whole other scene, whole other lives going on on the other side of that wall, a life he wanted to be a part of.

He burped, and suddenly it felt like something in his face had gone two hues the wrong way and his stomach was following suit.

Ah shit. He was too far gone now. He could feel the darkness closing in.

They were just talking.

Just talking.

—I'm getting a drink.

He left the spliff to DanDan and went into the kitchen. He didn't really want any more booze. He stopped by the kitchen window, just to listen. Merc wasn't upstairs or in his bedroom, and Steph had been gone for a while; that didn't mean they were doing anything together, though. Or even, well, if they were kissing, and his lips were on her lips, and her hands on his body, no, even then, they might not be doing anything other than kissing.

But then he heard it. A thick, loud grunt.

GNUH.

It sounded like someone being punched in the stomach, like someone had come along and given Merc a kidney shot. It was low and brutal.

No more noise came after it, though he waited in the kitchen at least another minute before he turned off the light and went back to the living room. And he began to wonder if he'd actually heard it at all.

He hoped to Christ he'd imagined it.

Was that Merc's finishing noise?

GNUH.

He didn't know.

He sat at the table with DanDan and drank. He tried to forget about the other side of the wall, what was happening there. He could always look, but he was terrified of what he'd find. Steph shouldn't be with Merc. She was beautiful. And fuck it, DanDan and Cath had been very chummy-chummy lately. That was bollox as well. He wasn't being left with Lucy. Cath and Lucy were away off somewhere else, and there he was, just sitting there with DanDan, who was groaning on about something JJ didn't understand.

—I feel though, you know. Stirrings, in me. Bits of things that are feeling alive again. I'm starting to look at things fresh now, see things as they are, as if there's light in them, and I'm looking at women and thinking, yeah, you might not be so bad. Yeah, I actually fancy you a bit there. You get me, JJ? JJ?

—Yeah, I get you.

—So what I'm thinking is, if there was someone around, and you know, they were with someone else, but, they weren't *really* with them, is it all that wrong to put your two cents in, to compete for them a bit? JJ? Is it all that wrong?

—Yeah, no. No it's not, you're right.

—So I may do it then.

—Course, yeah.

—Cath's good-looking enough, isn't she?

—Yeah.

—I mean, like, she's pretty cool.

—Yeah.

On the other side of the wall, Merc was shifting Steph, at the very least. And it just wasn't fair. Merc treated people like arseholes and he cared only about himself and surely Steph could see that, but she didn't, she probably only saw Merc's body, the abs and the pecs on him, and she only saw JJ's skinny frame with no muscle on it; she just saw a waster and someone not worth her time and now she was with Merc, riding him, or doing whatever she was doing, on the other side of the wall.

JJ dragged on the spliff, and drank his beer down as hard as he could.

Cath

She stayed by herself in the bedroom as long as possible, until she could no longer be pretending to clean or pack away clothes. She felt the worst of her anger at Merc dissipating, and she began to tell herself she'd overreacted to his dig at her. She moved back down to the living room and found only DanDan and JJ, smoking a spliff at the big table. No sign of Merc or Steph. DanDan smiled at her.

—Sit down there, Cath.

—I can't get comfortable round here. Too much going on.

—Here, have a drag.

—Thanks. You alright, JJ? You look a bit white.

—Mmm, yeah, I feel a bit white. I might just, I might just lie down and not talk. For a while.

JJ stumbled up from his chair, walked to the couch and flopped down onto it. Cath giggled as DanDan went over and checked him.

—Having a catnap.

DanDan took a blanket from beside the couch and threw it lightly over JJ's body. Cath took a tug on the spliff, and coughed.

—Christ, that's strong.

DanDan laughed.

—If it's strong enough to put JJ down you'd want to watch it.

—I need some air.

—Okay, we'll go out.

They went out the front door. The air outside shook her awake and she shivered a little in her T-shirt, her bare feet wet on the sharp gravel. DanDan took his jacket off and wrapped it round her shoulders, then he stood beside her, goose-pimpled in his

T-shirt. It felt late to Cath, though it wasn't even midnight yet. It was quiet but for the noise of the river. Her phone vibrated in her jeans. Paddy. She tried to silence it before DanDan noticed, but he nodded towards her pocket.

—He's persistent, isn't he?

—Ah, it's nothing.

—How's it going with him?

—Fine. Nothing much going on, really.

They left a silence between them. DanDan kicked a few stones underfoot then motioned towards the church.

—Who's in the graves?

—Dead people.

—Ha ha.

—Ah no. People who lived nearby, I suppose. People who came. Went. It doesn't matter.

She sniffed, still waking up from the air, but the spliff in her fingers putting her down again. DanDan scratched his thumb.

—JJ told me Merc was being a spa. Don't mind him.

—I don't. It was nothing.

—Good.

They stayed out together, teeth clacking in the mist. The spliff burned down, and Cath threw it out into the long grass. DanDan looked slightly disturbed, like he'd just woken up in an unfamiliar place. Now was the time to ask him.

—Why were you lying down outside earlier?

—Just having a think.

—Jess.

—Something like that. I dunno.

—We don't have to talk about it, DanDan.

—No, it's okay . . . I'll tell you now but I'm stoned so don't be like . . . Reading too much into it or anything, y'know.

—Don't worry.

—I've been feeling strange lately. Like, I get these episodes where I get really sad and down and all I want to do is close my eyes forever. But then, they're happening less. And once they're over I forget about them, and it's as if my eyes are open and I can see clearly again. Like earlier. I was lying down and I just wanted to sink into the ground, then next thing, I'm looking at the sky through the rain, and it's beautiful. I'm coming round, I think.

—Oh yeah?

—Yeah, I mean, one minute I'm in the grass, and I feel shit. The next thing, I'm inside and I'm with you, and I feel warm. And it feels like, I dunno, like there's been a fog on me this whole time. But recently, I can start to see things through it, shapes and stuff, or places I can go, or the outlines of people. People close to me. Sorry, I'm talking nonsense.

Their bodies were close together. That was one thing she knew. He stepped closer maybe, or she leaned in. She didn't know. She nudged him.

—The shift is what you need. A big, lusty smooch off of someone. That'll do the job.

He laughed.

—Ha, maybe.

It sounded good to hear him laugh like that, even if it was only a short one, barely more than a chuckle.

She nudged him again.

—Have your eye on anyone?

—Ha.

—Oh come on. Young, handsome man like you. Plenty of courting options. They're lining up all over the nation, no doubt. Come on, who is she?

—I dunno.

He was towering over her, him in his shoes, and her without.

—Oh come on. What is she? Nepalese model? Italian princess? Spanish royalty? Living off in a French castle somewhere?

He hesitated, looking away, up to the sky.

—She's a bit closer to home than French castles.

She coughed. His arm was down by his side. He was drunk, she was drunk. They were both stoned. There was a spot of stubble on his cheek where he'd missed with the razor, a little line of it that was holding moisture in the night air. There were flecks of mustard on his jawline.

—How close to home?

—Quite close.

—Do you think she likes you?

He wouldn't look at her.

—Who knows. She's into another fella, though.

—They going out?

—Not yet.

—Oh really?

—Yeah.

—Well you've still got a chance then.

—Ah, she'd have to get rid of the fella first.

There was a long, horrible silence. She shivered. He wouldn't look at her. Was he talking about Paddy? He was talking about Paddy. He'd watched her text him earlier, he'd been jealous. He meant her, didn't he? She coughed, loudly.

—I'm heading in, I think.

—Yeah.

She went in and felt the tile warm under her feet. She couldn't trust herself around him until she thought about it. It was too much for her to do while drunk and in his presence; she needed to be alone, so she ran upstairs.

In the harsh yellow light of the bathroom, she breathed heavy and felt like she was going to get sick. She knew next to nothing, but what she did know was that she had a chance here and it might not be around again.

Now was the time. Right now. She couldn't leave it and wait, or put it off. It was now. Paddy was back home, a certainty, a horse to back, in terms of being sure to lead to something good. Or DanDan, in all his fragility and changeable moods, and the fact that they were friends and that the whole thing could be ruined. She'd never really thought about it, him and her. Or had she? She didn't know, she must have, at some point. When he'd said what he said to her, though, it had come flooding out of her. She'd tried to keep a lid on it, but it was all spilling up out of her now, coming right up out of her. It didn't seem right, letting DanDan get away. Whatever it was about him, she didn't know, but she couldn't pass up a chance with him. So she went to the phone. Poor Paddy, he'd not a hope. A text from earlier was still there.

**What's the difference between
a hippo and a Zippo?**

                                  Hey Paddy.

He texted back immediately, of course. Still playing their little game.

Hey yourself. Any news?

She thought of him back home sitting on the couch waiting for her to text, the phone held loosely in his hand, or lying nearby. She'd been doing the same the whole time with him.

                       Nothing really. Same old.

**Cool! Raining back here. Made
me miss you. Looking forward to
when you get back.**

Oh God. This was it. She had to do it. She started on a new message. Her phone vibrated a little each time she pushed a key, like it was shuddering, shaking, telling her no, not to do it.

            **Hey, listen . . . I know this sounds
shit . . . I know it's bad. But I can't
see you when I get back.**

The text remained in its little box of light in her phone. The send button was only a millimetre from her thumb. It was too harsh, surely, the text. Maybe a phone call, later? Or did she have to do it all? No. She did, she'd have to do it. Her thumb jabbed the send button. There. Done. Message sent. Her heart dropped as it went, and she waited on his reply. A light flashed when the new message came in.

Why? You drunk? Joking?

No. Neither. I just can't.

He didn't reply immediately. Would he leave it there? Just leave it there. Her phone still in her hand, as it had been all day. It beeped; her heart went thumping when she got the vibration in her hand. The text she least wanted, the worst reply possible.

Another fella?

No.

Is it? Just tell me.

This was it. There'd be no way of salvaging it now. She thought about lying, but no. If she came back with a boyfriend and he found out he'd be even more upset, and she owed it to him to be honest.

Yes.
I'm sorry.

Her phone was silent. No more lights, no beeps, no vibration.

Paddy?

Nothing.

I'm sorry.

It was done. She knew he wouldn't text back, so she put the phone down, and smoothed her hair. She thought about DanDan. She wouldn't initiate anything, but she'd be there if he wanted. They were drunk, that'd make things easier. And fuck, she wasn't going to push it, with him all bereaved, but still . . .

Malachy

He couldn't sleep. He rose from his bed and wandered from room to room, waiting for sleep to hit him. He picked up books and put them down unread. He returned the chopping stump to the back garden and tried to chop firewood but it felt far too late to be doing it so he gave up after a few strokes. He did little else but think of the people down the way and of what they would do.

He told himself not to watch them. Not to return to his seat by the screen door. No good would come from it, he knew that. But eventually, he could only wander so much. He sat once more in the dark and watched the house. He drank straight from the bottle of Jameson and decided that he'd finish the bottle, which was still three quarters full. He felt a comfort once he decided to finish it, allowing its effect come on him slow and hazy.

It was right that he should watch the Lodge. He'd been doing it his whole life, observing every tenant of the place. He watched the walls and drank from the bottle of whiskey. His ears adjusted to the quiet and soon he began to hear their shouts and their laughter. He allowed it soak over him, but as time passed it seemed to become less like laughter and more like screaming, the sound of feral cats squalling in the night. He felt their screaming rise from the house and float into the valley, the hills shaking and absorbing the violence of it, the trees taking their fill and bloating with the ugliness of it. He drank more as he listened, the whiskey scalding his throat as he thought of the beautiful rivulets slopping slowly down to Lough Gorm, and those rivers drinking in the bile and hatred of their howls, carrying them down to the lake, infecting everything until the water festered and boiled with their malice.

The longer he watched and listened, the more it felt just plain wrong what they were doing. What right had they? Who were they that they could go wherever the fuck they wanted? Did they not know anything about where they were? Or did they know, and just not care? He felt a deep anger stirring up in him.

He went to his door and opened it, and stood watching the house from the doorframe. A short lane sloped down from his house to theirs. He'd be there in only a few steps; just a few dozen large strides down away from his own house and he'd be in theirs. He'd put them right. He took a last, huge gulp out of the bottle of whiskey. It gave him strength.

He was into the cupboard under the stairs within a few seconds, and came out with the shotgun. He'd check on them, just to see what they were doing, if they needed help maybe, or if they were doing anything illegal. If they were fucking with anything they shouldn't be. He threw on his coat and went out into the black night. He walked down the steep hill from his house to theirs, sliding slightly on the wet stones, the long gun feeling light, almost joyful in his hands.

When he reached the front gate of the Lodge he paused. He supposed he knew it was wrong, but he was outside himself, watching himself. There was music coming from inside, and it was only to have a look, so he lifted the latch and plodded down the five stone steps onto the gravel patch, then he crossed over the stones lightly until he came to the window, and looked in.

They'd turned off the lights and left candles on the mantel. The fireside flickered, the room glowing yellow. In a doorway towards the back of the room, the short, pudgy girl drank steadily from a large glass of red wine. The other four sat around the room, looking to the pretty blonde girl who was up by the fireside, dancing slowly, her eyes closed and going all soft.

They sat in the gloom, watching her dance, their heads inclined. They were so young, all of them, their movements uninhibited and free, each of them so full of energy and booze and life. He wanted to join them. He wanted to sit with them and drink with them and laugh with them, and even if he didn't speak that would

78

be okay. He wanted to sit at their table and watch them, be about them as they moved around him and the room, as they hit and nudged each other, and held their young, skinny bodies in their arms, how they smiled so easily. Then he remembered he was old, and that he lived by himself, and before he knew it he was walking to the door and hammering on it with his fist.

Lucy

When she came back downstairs, the party had started up again. JJ was necking pint glasses of water and Red Bull to wake up and the rest were gathered round in front of the fireplace. Lucy watched them all from the doorway into the kitchen. The booze had hit her in a strange way and she saw them with a sense of detachment, as if her eyes had blurred and she could no longer distinguish between each person, but saw them instead as a moving, dynamic fuzz, a fuzz that was ignoring her as she stood alone in the doorway.

They listened to blues and jazz, making fun of country music. They smoked their cigarettes indoors and blew big, billowing half-rings towards the ceiling into the light bulbs, trying to achieve the ambience of an old-style saloon or a poker game from the 1950s. They turned off most of the lights to see if they could get the right gloom, and when that was a bit too dark they lit tea lights and put them on the fireplace and the mantelpiece.

They enjoyed the shadows they sent flying around the room with their movements. They got bored of trying to understand and appreciate the jazz that was on; they tried trad music but no one could get into it, so they knocked off the vinyl, and used Cath's laptop to send tinny music round the room. Merc started a press-up competition with himself. The darkness was finding its way into the room quicker than she expected. Someone was at her shoulder.

—Lucy? Lucy? You okay?

Lucy shook her head to knock the cobwebs out. Cath was by her side, asking after her.

—Yeah, Cath, I'm fine. I'm just taking it all in.

Cath smiled and went back to the couch. Lucy's eye was drawn to Steph.

She was dressed in tight black jeans and a see-through skin-colour top with a black bra underneath, sexy and understated at the same time. She got up in front of the fireplace and started to dance slowly to a song coming from the laptop speakers: 'Back to Black'.

You could see the outline of her hips and her flat stomach through her top as she moved under the candlelight. Merc watched her. JJ watched her, pretending he was watching the flame burn down on his spliff. Cath was fawning on DanDan, who was also watching Steph. Cath got close to him, nestled up to him on the couch. She rubbed her face on his shoulder.

DanDan lurched up from the chair, barely giving Cath time to steady herself. He rose and grabbed a can and toasted the party.

—Bless this house and all within. *In ainm an Athar agus an Mhic agus an Spioraid Naoimh. Amen.*

And all responded.

—Amen.

—And bless the dancer.

—Bless the dancer.

The song dragged along and Steph kept dancing as DanDan watched. He was surely a good soul, a man who could be trusted. Cath had her hooks in him but who could blame her? He was an honourable man. JJ was sitting on the ground smoking a cigarette. Merc had tired of his push-ups. No one had noticed that Lucy had withdrawn from them and was watching from the doorway. She went to cough, to interrupt their fucking song, when next thing—

BANG.

Lucy jumped as a sharp knock came blasting from the front door.

She didn't move.

BANG.

BANG.

Their heads all turned to the noise like gazelle. Lucy looked to Cath, who hissed.

—Shh, everyone shut up.

They hushed like children, like people who were in a place they shouldn't be, trespassers. No one said a word; all that passed between them was the dead silence that creeped and was made all the more empty and dark for the thin music coming from Cath's laptop.

The knocks sounded again.

BANG. BANG.

A man's voice, a real man's voice came from the door.

–HELLO!

—Shhhhh.

There was fear in Merc's eyes. DanDan was standing frozen beside the couch. Lucy had something stuck in her heart and stomach. JJ stubbed his smoke out on the ground and rose to his feet. She didn't know where Steph was. Cath approached the door. She called back softly.

—Hello?

Every sound was magnified in the small room, every click and scrape leaped in her stomach. The door handle chuckled as it turned. She heard rubber scraping on the tiled floor out of sight.

—Hello?

The first she saw of him was his muddy boots, though she could barely pay attention to any one part of him. She didn't move. All she could see after the muddy boots was the shotgun, the barrel pointed slightly towards the ground. She watched the solid metal, the unpolished wooden stock, the hand it was resting in, the clean hand with slightly dirty knuckles, tobacco yellow on the insides of the fore and ring fingers though the nails were clean and neatly clipped, the fingers splayed over the trigger cover and the face of the side of the gun, the other hand wrapped protectively around the barrel. It looked so heavy in his hands. And there was a man behind the gun, a huge man in a great big black coat. He stood in the room, in their room, in their space, taller and bigger than any of them. She could smell him, kind of warm,

82

clean, she didn't know. She heard him speak but couldn't quite make sense of it.

—Who are you?

It was said accusingly. There was a man behind the gun somewhere. He was massive. He seemed from somewhere else, a different world or planet, like he was a force that existed in more dimensions than them, thicker and bigger and more real than anything she'd ever seen. Cath moved towards him ever so slightly; she approached him slowly, her hands raised.

—I'm Catherine. I'm Tara Rourke's daught—

She was interrupted by a screeching noise, a sharp scrape of dull wood on cracked tile that jumped them all, as Merc pushed up out of his seat to his feet. He knocked the chair over behind him and barrelled through the room towards the back. It was ridiculous how late his reactions were. The man turned slightly and watched as Merc crashed by the table towards Lucy. She shrieked as he elbowed her out of the way from the doorframe. He elbowed her so hard she stumbled and almost fell. She managed to grab at the doorframe on her way down and shove her body against it so she got herself upright. Jesus Christ. She steadied herself. The man took a step forward but Merc was gone; he'd barged right past her and out the back door.

A thin silence was left in his wake, but his movement had broken whatever it was that had been holding them in place, what had sucked the air out of the room and kept them dead still. Cath coughed, breaking the silence, then spoke to the man very gently.

—I'm Catherine Blake. I'm Tara Rourke's daughter. We're just here for the weekend. I have keys.

The man took a step back and let the shotgun relax down by his side. Lucy began to be able to see bits of his face. He was old, his face wrinkled and worn. He looked like he'd been carved out of the side of a mountain, like he was an Easter Island statue.

—Rourke? Jesus Christ, what's wrong with you? You need to tell me you're here.

The moment he spoke, Lucy began to recognise that there were things in the room again: there was a table in it, and music playing. There were cans of beer everywhere and the ceiling was above them, the floor beneath, but for the life of her Lucy could barely remember how'd she'd gotten to where she was. She didn't know where she came from. She couldn't remember much of anything, who she was or where she was. Her hands were not her own, her life not her own, and Lucy was as far as she could possibly be from whoever she thought she was. She couldn't breathe. Lucy couldn't breathe, she needed air. Fuck. The fuck.

Cath stood up slightly in herself, held herself straight as the man let the gun dangle by his side.

—I know, I'm so sorry. You're Malachy, are you?

—Yes.

—I know, I'm so sorry, I meant to call you. My mam gave me your number earlier, I just forgot. I'm so sorry.

—It's fine, gave me a bit of a scare.

He was gentle in his words as he looked about the room, though he kept returning to stare right at Cath, examining her face. He was beginning to look a bit frail without the gun pointing at them, which was seeming smaller by the second, hanging by his leg.

JJ was in the room.

—We gave you a scare? Christ almighty, I almost just fucking died.

Malachy looked at the ground.

—I'm sorry, sorry about the gun, just, you never know.

—I almost had a fucking heart attack, lad. I'm way too young for fucking heart attacks.

JJ sat down. Then he laughed.

—HA!

He laughed loud and hard, the relief coming out with each howl.

—HA HA HA HA HA!

DanDan sat down. Lucy supported herself on the doorframe. Malachy kept going.

—Sorry, now, sorry. I meant no harm, was just looking after the place.

Thank Christ Cath was on the ball; the rest of them might never have spoken again.

—No, no, we're sorry, we meant to call you. Thank you, thank you for looking out for us.

—Have to be careful, you know.

—I know. Sorry.

—It's okay, it's fine.

His presence suddenly became inappropriate, if it hadn't been before. Suddenly he was an old man in the company of twenty-year-olds. He knew it, and they knew it.

—Do you need anything?

—No, no, thank you, Malachy, thank you. Do, do you want a drink or something? Tea?

—No, no, I'll be getting back.

—Yeah, cool, fine, thanks. We'll be here another day or so, I'll call up when we're leaving.

—Yes, fine.

—Okay.

He turned to go.

—Catherine, is it?

—Catherine, yeah . . .

Malachy paused just before he left. Lucy was only beginning to notice just then that his jacket was actually blue, a bright sky-blue. Why had she thought it was dark? It barely reached down past his waist, in fact, and he was wearing spotless boots; there was only a bit of dirt on the very bottom sides of them, fresh mud he'd walked in. His face had lines and etches in it, permanent ones, lines that remained even when his face was perfectly still. His farmer's cap looked oddly small over his big ears, and she could see the sides of grey hair poking out under it. He coughed a bit, just before he left, a clean one at first, three neat little hacks, but the last one hinted at mucous underneath. He seemed embarrassed by his own parting remark.

—Hope I didn't scare the other lad too much.

—Who?

—The lad, your man who took off there.

—What? Oh, no, he'll be fine.

—Grand. Good luck.

—Bye.

And he was gone. The door snapped shut behind him.

JJ grabbed his vest over his heart.

—JESUS CHRIST.

Then everyone started to join in. Even Steph was doing it.

—FUCK me, oh fuck me, my heart.

—Jesus Christ, holy mother of fucking God. Motherfucking
Christ. Mother of God. Christ fuck me.

—Where the fuck did Merc go?

—What?

—Everyone okay?

—I'm about to die of a fucking heart attack.

—Go on then.

—I'm going to fucking die right now.

—DID HE REALLY HAVE A FUCKING SHOTGUN IN HIS
HAND?

—Yes.

—DID EVERYONE ELSE SEE THE GODDAMNED
FUCKING SHOTGUN?

—Yes.

—Where's MERC?

—Who gives a fuck?

—WHERE'S MERC?

—I don't give a fuck.

—Did that actually just happen?

—Heh.

—Heh heh.

Lucy grabbed JJ by the collar of his vest, bunched it up in her
hands and shook him.

—Don't laugh! Don't you laugh!

She shook him hard. He grabbed her wrists and tried to calm
her but she wouldn't let go, only kept shaking him. Lucy felt
herself shouting at him.

—What the fuck is wrong with you? What's wrong with you?

86

—My heart's going the clappers.

—Oh shut up, shut up, you prick!

—Calm down, now. Calm down.

—Dickhead! Cunt!

She tried to shove him against the wall but he pressed back against her and she couldn't shift him.

—Calm it, Luce, calm it.

—Fuck you, what's the matter with you? Fuck you.

She let go of JJ's collar and he dropped her wrists. Lucy had been holding back the tears but they came now. She walked to the wall and slid down until she was sitting. She tried to calm herself but everything was bubbling up in her. She tried to think on what'd just happened. She'd barely gotten a good look at Malachy. The only ones who'd spoken in the room the whole time had been him, Cath and JJ. Their interaction had felt like it was in its own world, and Lucy was just watching it from the outside. But now Malachy was gone, and suddenly she had to keep going, keep going on, dealing with it.

All by herself. All alone, the tears came hot and quick down her cheeks. She didn't know why. All she knew was that JJ was an arsehole. He was an arsehole and a prick and he didn't appreciate any one of them. Not a single one.

Steph kneeled down beside her.

—It's fine, it's fine. You're in shock.

—No, I'm not.

DanDan went over and sat next to Lucy on the ground. She pushed her face into his shoulder and felt her snot soaking into the fabric of his shirt as he rubbed the back of her head. Her face squeezed against his shoulder, she could see nothing, and she tried to hide herself there, but she heard Steph speaking calmly, almost proudly.

—Stay sitting. Where's Merc?

—He bolted, that's where he is.

—Yes, JJ, but where did he bolt to?

—I dunno, don't ask me.

—Here, I'll go look for him.

—I'll go with you.

Lucy was left on the ground with DanDan, where she wanted to be. She could feel his arms around her. She didn't want to have been the wuss, but God, Merc had run out, so she wasn't the worst. DanDan was warm and close, she could smell him. JJ had left with Steph. Cath waited for a minute.

—Are you okay, Luce?

—Yeah, I'm fine.

She couldn't see anything – her face was buried into his shirt – but she was aware of the world outside herself, and she could feel DanDan giving significant looks to Cath and the silence of a returned nod.

—Grand, I'll help look for Merc so. Eejit.

She heard Cath leave, then it was just her and DanDan like it was meant to be. She started to cry into him and couldn't stop, couldn't stop. It felt like it was more than what had happened, more than just the incident. Floodgates, wasn't it?

Malachy

He saw himself do it. The PVC gave a little under each knock, the metal knocker banging back with the whiplash of it. It sounded like he was trying to bash the door in. He shouted Hello but got no answer.

Then, he wasn't sure why, but he had put the shotgun into the crook of his arm and was turning the door handle. He just wanted to be inside, to be warm maybe, he didn't know, but his foot was over the threshold and his body was in the house. Things were happening ahead of him, decisions made for him that he just followed, trying to keep up. It felt like someone had slowed everything down, that everything was moving at a fourth the normal pace. He came from around the passageway of the door, and stepped into their presence, his shotgun in his hands.

They were scattered around the room, frozen, the lot of them, looks of panic and terror washed into their clear, bright faces. His warning shout had given them enough time to stand, but not enough to do anything else, so they just stood there, unmoving. There was music playing, some kind of soul music coming tinny and artificial from a laptop on the table. He'd broken it, whatever warmth had been about the room, and though it had seemed to glow when he had watched them from outside, now it just seemed squalid. The place was covered in ashtrays and broken cigarettes and empty crushed cans and it stank of must and stale beer and what he presumed was dope. Malachy spoke first. He pretended to think they were burglars, and he knew they believed him, as they shrank away from his gaze, until the leader, the brunette stepped forward to explain.

Then a chair banged. The athletic fella jumped up out of his seat and bolted for the back door, shoving the pudgy girl with the wine out of his way, sending her staggering. He crashed through the door, leaving his friends in another shocked silence. It jolted Malachy out of his stupor.

He was in a room he shouldn't be in. Christ, what was he doing? He coughed, then the girl explained. They were allowed in the house. Her name was Catherine. She was Tara Rourke's daughter. Fuck.

Mona and Billy's granddaughter. Just looking at her he could see it, the thick brown hair, the snag tooth. Christ. It began to make a bit more sense to him, now, what had been going on. He apologised and he saw them looking at him and at his gun and he made sure to show them that it wasn't cocked and he wasn't pointing it, and they apologised and he apologised and he backed slowly out the door and away from the house.

His feet slid on the stones up to the latched gate, and it was only when he got through the gate and was safe again on the roadside that he breathed. He was cold and could hear his breathing. He stood by their front gate and felt so stupid, so creepy and foolish. His heart hammered inside his chest, and the gun in his hands seemed so heavy that he felt he could barely lift it. He turned on his heel and carried himself back on up to his house, as if he'd never been there, had never been spying, had never entered the house. As he left he could hear them squealing at each other, but he didn't look back.

He entered his house and closed the door behind him, then went straight to his chair, hoping that before he could think or do or say anything, he might erase what had just happened, that by refusing to dwell on it or even acknowledge it, if he just continued to stare at the house, as if he'd never left his chair, it might go away.

His heart thumped away. He couldn't sit still. He tried to feel for the shotgun in his hands and found nothing. He couldn't remember where'd he'd put it. He heard the people calling down the way. They were walking down towards the back garden wall of the Lodge, looking out towards the overgrowth, trying to light their way with the screens of their phones, throwing tiny blue flashes out onto the soggy grass. They were calling out. Maybe their friend who had run away had not come back. Their lonely, desperate shouts were all he could hear. He didn't want to be seen by them, not any more, not any chance of it.

He was drunker than he thought as well. His face felt warm and red. He stumbled into his bedroom. Erase it, get rid of it. He crashed into bed, and closed his eyes.

Cath

A light rain began to fall as they searched for Merc. The field out the back of the house sloped down fifty metres to a stone wall and beyond that was a tangle of trees and hedges. It was dark – the golden light from the house only reached so far down – and the ground was sodden under their feet.

—Meeeeeeerc.

—Meeeeeeerc.

—Merc, lad, it's grand, come on out.

JJ squelched on ahead with Steph.

—My fucking shoes.

Steph seemed in no mood for him.

—Shut up about your shoes, let's just find him. MEEEERC.

—MERC!

Cath was just very, very happy that it hadn't been her that ran. She'd dealt with it, she'd taken responsibility. Her heart was settling, and a deep, warm sense of pride was filling in the gaps where the tension was leaving her. She could feel it glowing, growing up inside her. She'd always worried what kind of person she'd be under pressure, and now she'd found out. She hadn't run, she hadn't screamed. She'd been more grown up and responsible than anyone else in that house. She felt a broad smile coming over her face, and she was glad of the dark, that they could barely see each other's faces in the light that was left.

—Meeerc.

They reached a low stone wall that marked the end of the garden. It was stacked bit on bit and stopped their path. Where could he have gone? Beyond the wall, the darkness seemed to rule everything, the trees and hedges, but was afraid of trespassing in the garden. JJ shivered in his T-shirt.

—Fuck him, like. He ran off on us.

Steph glared at him.

—He did not, he just got scared.

There was a hint of desperation in her voice, like she was trying to convince herself more than JJ. Whatever had been going on with Merc and Steph throughout the night, surely it would go a bit skew-ways now, what with Merc bounding off into the darkness like a terrified bunny. He wouldn't react well when they found him, Cath knew that much. What was more interesting was how kind Steph was being. Though she retained her sharp edges when talking with JJ, there was a sneaking tenderness in her voice, a softness to it. Maybe something had happened between her and Merc earlier, or even in the weeks before now, to cause that tenderness. Or maybe she just wanted to give him a break. Cath didn't get along all the time with Merc, or even with Steph. But, if Steph could see the human side of it, if Steph could give him the benefit of the doubt, then Cath might as well too.

She decided to back her up.

—Yeah, JJ. Maybe he went to get help or something, you don't know.

Cath tried her best not to shiver, her feet sinking more and more into the dank, squelchy mud. The lights back in the Lodge were dancing. It looked warm inside. They stood in silence, turning their heads this way and that trying to spot Merc. It felt like something had broken on them. As if they'd been under a spell for over a year, and now it seemed to be wearing off. She didn't know these people, did she? They seemed so small to Cath. There seemed to be a smallness to all things, now that she felt so big. She needed to keep them focused. She laid out the possibilities.

—So, he might have got to here and what? He either turned left, or right, or he hopped the wall.

JJ seemed nonplussed.

—Maybe his da sent out a helicopter for him. Maybe he's back home already with his da, drinking brandy and scratching people.

—Shut up, JJ, it's not funny.

—Just saying.

—So, did he go over the wall or not?

—If he did he's fucked. Doesn't it just go down to the lake from here? Only going to get wetter, and there's no houses in that direction.

—So what, think he went left, crossed the river?

—Why should I know, Cath? I stayed in the room.

—Stop it, would you.

Steph tried one last time.

—Meeeeeeerc. It's fine. MERC. Meeeeeeerc.

Her shout drifted to nothing. Cath was about to suggest going back inside to get proper shoes on, and coats, and find a torch or something, to do a search properly, when she heard a rustling a few metres away.

They looked for the sound. Just beyond the wall, four or five metres up a tree, Merc's head popped out from between some branches.

—Guys?

—Merc!

—Is he gone?

—Yeah, he's gone.

—Sure?

—Yeah.

—Who the fuck was that?

—It was Malachy, the neighbour. He lives up the way. Was just checking in.

—Fuck sake.

He stayed up the tree, gazing down at them. Cath couldn't see the rest of his body. The light from their phones threw barely enough light on the tree to find him, but she could see he had a large muck stain across his face.

—Come down, Merc, it's grand.

—Kay.

He hopped down, his feet making a sucking sound as he landed in the mud, though he raised his hands high over his head as he

94

did, like he was a gymnast completing a perfect landing. He looked straight ahead, as if waiting for them to remark on it.

—Have you no shoes, Merc?

—What? No.

He stood there in the muck gazing at them, as if he didn't know what to do or say. There was something awkward in the air, and the low stone wall separating them seemed to add to that, like he was in a different world to theirs, he'd crossed over some-how, and they were looking at each other beyond a divide they couldn't bridge. He seemed to know that once he was back over the wall, he'd have to account for himself. JJ spoke in a breezy tone.

—You just in your socks, so?

—Well, I didn't have time to lace up my fucking runners, did I?

Merc seemed to hit upon a tone he liked, and he marched towards them confidently. He planted one hand firmly on the rock wall and hoicked himself over. As he landed he affected his gymnast's landing again, then strode right by them towards the house. They followed him, trying to keep up. He took large, stretching strides that covered over a metre at a time, as if he was trying to measure the back garden. He retained his authoritative tone.

—Was going to go off and get help. Didn't know who the fuck your man was. The rest of you were frozen like fucking statues so I thought I'd go and get help. Wrecked my fucking feet running over this. I'm frozen as well.

Squelch, squelch, squelch. His socks were coming loose at the end, riding low on the ankles, his feet no longer occupying the toe parts which were covered in mud and swinging about, slap-ping him on the soles of his feet and around his ankles as he walked.

—Then when I got over the wall, I heard talking, and a bit of shouting, but it didn't seem that bad or anything, so I thought I'd wait it out. If things started to go off I'd keep going on for help. But if it was fine I was gonna go back. I didn't hear anything anyway after a minute or two so I thought it was alright, I was down by the base of the tree at that point. Then next thing I heard the door scraping again and thought he might be coming looking for me, so I climbed the tree.

He reached the back door and they could see him better in the light. His arms were covered in scrapes, his front smeared with mud and grime. He'd obviously fallen down on his way out, and scratched himself while climbing the tree. He turned on them and squared his shoulders, gritted his jaw. His tone was harsh and clear. Planned.

—You lot have no idea how to act in an emergency. First thing when you see a gun is what? Run. Yeah? Run. Bullets can't hit what they can't see. Are you thick? Ha?

He was breathing heavy. In his backlit glow, Cath could see his hands trembling, shaking violently. He kept moving his fingers, gripping and ungripping his fists, trying to disguise it, but it was as if the shaking was coming through his whole body; every muscle in him was showing it. Steph spoke first.

—I know, Merc. We're clueless. I just stood there like a deer in the headlights.

He nodded at her then looked straight at JJ, whose back was suddenly straight. Steph's arm brushed ever so gently off JJ's as she moved by them to go inside. Her touch seemed to wake something in him.

—I know, man, we froze. It happens.

Merc could see his advantage.

—Fucking eejits.

JJ nodded his head to him, bowed it almost, sent his eyes down to Merc's chest. Merc puffed it up grander than before. His hand shaking, he did a violent, purposeful shiver.

—Fucking hell it's cold out here. We going inside?

—Yeah.

Steph, who was waiting by the door behind Merc, nodded. She turned to go in first, followed by Merc, JJ and Cath, who still hadn't said anything. They filed in after her. Cath saw them just a second before Steph shouted.

—SNARED!

The gently kissing couple of Lucy and DanDan were sitting by the door, his arms around her, one hand on her back and the other on her chin, while her hand fumbled through the back of his hair, and her other hand cradled his knee, and they went in to each other and out, their lips merging and separating, flashes of tongue between. They split when Steph shouted. Lucy hopped up straight away.

—Drink?

She pushed by Cath into the kitchen. DanDan leaned back in his sitting position, and held himself up on his palms, a small smile on his face. He grinned, then rose with the rest of them to get a drink.

Steph

Steph sat at the table taking her shoes off and watched Merc sucking on a spliff by the fireside with JJ. JJ kept glancing over the back of the couch trying to catch her eye knowingly, like they were both in on a shared joke.

Everyone was watching everyone else. All the eyes of the room winked and pinched at each other, except Merc, who kept his eyes to the ground, or focused on the spliff in his fingers, the smoke rising lazily to the ceiling. He seemed aware he was being watched, his back tense as he sat cross-legged by the fire. Occasionally he would try to catch someone's eye, though, and glare at them, staring them down.

DanDan whispered quietly to Lucy. Steph didn't know where to look, so she just took interest in the ornaments on the wall.

The room looked different, on a skew since the hours before. It seemed to grow larger and stranger around her, the objects in it more apparent; the glints and little strikes of light bouncing off objects dazzled more; the chips off the frames and fading paint and mismatching furniture seemed more obvious now, more in the open. The odd combination of all the bits of half-loved curiosities and broken things, the sewing machine in the window alcove, the table tennis racket on a high shelf shedding itself of its red rubber cover, seemed more odd now, less a part of the house and more an accumulation of uncaring. The scuff marks on the tiles, the yellowing maps on the wall. They all seemed to close in around her. Merc coughed.

—I'm putting on some tunes.

He rose slowly from the fireside and pressed play on the laptop. The next song on the playlist started up, Lesley Gore singing 'It's My Party'.

JJ snorted and Merc went to sit back down. Steph couldn't get it squared, why the rest of them were being cold to him. Yes, he'd chickened out. They all knew that. But were they perfect? Was she perfect? Of course not. Coward was such a strong word. Such a loaded one. He'd been afraid. It wasn't selfishness that took him outside, it wasn't a deep lack of caring towards his friends. He'd just been afraid.

And not one of them had fought Malachy. They'd all frozen. Merc was the only one who had managed to even run. Steph had frozen. Did that make her a coward? Of course not. JJ was preparing an extra powerful spliff, layering it on really thick and rolling it, readying it for when Merc finished the one he was on.

Merc grimaced and took his last drag on the joint. He tried to throw it into the fire as JJ lit up the new one, flaring it with big puffs and blowing the smoke into Merc's face. He offered it to Merc.

—Here, this'll do the job.

—What job?

—Any job you need it to.

Merc nodded and accepted the yellowing joint from JJ. He looked pale and miserable, though he was acting like JJ's gestures were meant as adulation, admiration almost, like he was laying tribute down at Merc's feet. He sucked on the spliff in great, exuberant slurps.

JJ though, he seemed to be really enjoying himself. And she knew what he was up to. He'd score no points with her by getting Merc blitzed. Maybe he was hoping that Merc would be so fucked he'd collapse in on himself and not be able to go to bed with Steph. Joke was on JJ, though. The Merc thing was a one-time only. She'd had sex with him only a few hours before, but it seemed so far away now. Malachy bursting in had placed a black bar right down the middle of the night. Now there was only before it and after it. And after the black bar, she didn't sleep with cowards.

No. No, he wasn't a coward. He wasn't. Who were they to start throwing words like 'coward' around, when none of them had ever shown bravery? Who the fuck knew what a coward was, much less the lot in this house?

Steph poured herself more red wine, glugging it all the way to the top, then looked around for someone to share the bottle with. Cath's glass was empty. She was standing over by the fireplace, looking deep into the flames. It was strange. The music was so loud, and no one really talking, that it seemed almost like silence, like they were in some odd sort of vacuum where suddenly the need to make noise, to make conversation, was taken away, and they just floated by each other.

Then it hit her. Cath was only pretending to look into the fire. She was actually watching DanDan and Lucy, who were sitting on opposite ends of the couch, though their feet were touching. Their gazes kept catching, twitching with odd smiles. They thought they were being sly and subtle and putting everyone at ease by not mauling each other openly, but really they were making everyone in the room complicit in their little deceit. Cath was beginning to shake, swaying on her feet, as DanDan's knee brushed Lucy's outer thigh. Better to get her away from there.

—Cath? Wine?

It took Cath a while to answer, her voice shaky.

—What?

—Wine. Do you want some wine?

—Yeah, sure. Yeah, yeah, sure.

She walked to Steph and held a glass out to her, like a child putting her hand straight out for a smack. Steph poured the wine for her, going past Cath saying 'When' and filling it to the top. She put down the bottle, and looked into Cath's eyes as she clinked her glass.

—Cheers.

—Cheers.

You didn't have to be highly sensitive to spot that level of distress in someone's eyes. Cath was mangling inside. It was in her oddly wrinkled nose, in her furrowed brow and the mascara too fresh under her bloodshot eyes. She'd probably sucked the tears back by tilting her head up and blinking. Steph wasn't great at the whole emotions thing, but this wasn't some silly thing that was hurting Cath. It wasn't her holding back tears because her boss had been mean to her, or she was stressed out and needed a cry; this one was hurting her badly.

—Smoke?

Cath sniffled.

—I don't smoke.

—You do now. JJ, I'm stealing some fags, okay?

—Yeah, sure, we've enough here.

—Cheers. Come on.

Cath followed lamely out to the back. Steph made sure the door was closed properly behind them. She lit a cigarette for herself, then lit another one for Cath. Steph took a long drag and felt it coat the inside of her mouth, infecting her tongue, grazing her teeth. Cath sucked at hers every two seconds, hardly even inhaling. Steph looked at Cath.

—You okay?

—I'm fine, yeah.

Bollox she wasn't. It wasn't her job to weasel stuff out of Cath. She wasn't going to keep chipping away at her the rest of the night. She was there to listen if she wanted, but she wasn't there to indulge her.

—Fuck off, you're not. What's up?

—I dunno.

—DanDan.

—No, it's not that.

—DanDan and Lucy. You like DanDan.

—Me and DanDan are mates, sure. It's not like that.

—Then why are you upset?

—I'm not upset.

—You are. Listen, drop it and tell me.

—It's not DanDan. I dunno, Malachy just scared me.

—Scared everyone, but it's not Malachy.

—You know there's a thing in psychology called misattribution of arousal. Basically in times of high danger or stress, people are more likely to fall for each other.

—You know I hate psychology.

—Find each other more attractive, almost.

—So, DanDan and Lucy got stressed out and started scoring.

—Something like that.

—So it is DanDan upsetting you.

—I DON'T LIKE DANDAN, OKAY?

Cath's jaw was jutted at Steph. Mother of God. Steph had had no idea that this was such a big deal. They'd talked about it before, about her and DanDan, and Cath had always denied it, though Steph'd had her suspicions. Watching her face tonight though, when Cath saw them kissing, Steph knew it was there. She'd seen the hurt in Cath's face, the little jerks in her cheeks, how her smile twisted and shook in on itself. She must have been carrying it a while, and carrying it hard.

—Do not shout at me.

—Sorry.

—If you shout at me I won't talk to you.

—Sorry.

—So you don't like DanDan.

—No, I've told you. But then I was thinking about Paddy. Or, the fact that I wasn't thinking about him.

—What do you mean?

—I kind of broke it off with Paddy earlier.

—What, why?

—I don't know, I just wasn't feeling it. But all this happened and he never once crossed my mind. So I just felt guilty, I suppose, for not thinking about him. So I don't know how I feel.

—Look, Cath. We're not Americans, yeah. Not every feeling is the opposite of what it actually is. If you don't like him you don't like him. You've had a shock and you're just being weird.

—I know, I'm over-thinking it. That's why I didn't want to tell you. Afraid I would sound stupid.

102

—It is stupid, you are being stupid, but it's better you tell us these things, so we can correct you, tell you you're being fucking stupid.

—I suppose.

—But I can tell you, you were getting upset looking at DanDan as well.

—Was I?

—What, you weren't upset about him eye-fucking Lucy on the couch with everyone watching?

—Ha. Maybe a little.

—That's what they're doing. RIDING each other with their eyes.

—Haha, watch the hands.

—WATCH THE HANDS THERE. Like remember when we were in the Gaeltacht and they used to spray you with bottles of water if you were scoring a fella?

—Happened to me more than once.

—*STOP É SIN.*

—*CÁ BHFUIL DO LÁMHA?*

—*UISCE! UISCE!*

—Shh, shh, they'll hear us inside.

—You shush.

They laughed. Steph could feel Cath loosening.

She took one last drag of her smoke and threw it out into the grass. It was a nice night. Nice night to climb a tree, ha. No, she shouldn't joke.

—So, you're okay then.

—Yeah, thanks.

—Anyway. Why do we always have to talk about lads, ha? Can't we talk about motorcars or tits or something?

—Haha.

—Feeling good?

—Yeah, Steph. Thanks.

They opened the back door and stepped into the kitchen. Steph felt calmer now, having talked down Cath, like she'd done something good, but she still needed an outlet of some sort. She needed to do something fucking mischievous.

—Here, Cath, shh.

—What?

—Here, give us a hand with this.

—What?

—The big pot, here, turn on the water there.

—What?

—Like in the Gaeltacht, we'll pour this over them.

—What?

—Pour it over them. That'll separate them.

—No.

—Yeah. Come on.

She grabbed the big cooking pot, put it in the sink and turned on the tap. Cath had a look of horror on her face but she grew more excited as the tings of the water landing on the metal cooled away and were replaced with the noise of it rushing and circulating around the pot. Cath started to giggle a bit, nervous.

—No. Not here.

—What?

—What about the couch? We can't just throw a load of water on it.

—It's only water, sure. It won't stain anything. And it's right beside the fire. It'll dry out in a minute. Here, give us a hand.

Steph turned off the water. She grabbed a handle, and Cath grabbed the other. Jesus, it was heavy. They carried it down by their knees, bent over with the weight of it. They shuffled quickly from the kitchen into the main room.

DanDan and Lucy were still on the couch, their heads turned. They were whispering something to each other. JJ was in front of them by the fire. He spotted Steph and Cath coming and raised an eyebrow, but saw quickly he was to do nothing. Merc was nowhere to be seen. They were getting close. JJ coughed and drew Lucy and DanDan's attention.

—Hey, did you ever see this party trick?

He put his hand in his pocket. DanDan and Lucy leaned forward to see. Steph and Cath were just at the back of the couch,

104

right by their heads. JJ took his hand out of his pocket, empty, except for a clenched fist and a raised middle finger. DanDan snorted.

—Very good, JJ.

She nodded to Cath and they brought the pot up and tipped the contents onto the back of Lucy and DanDan's heads.

—AAAAAAH.

Steph had been hoping for more of a kind of dumping effect, where they turned the pot upside down over their heads and the whole thing hit them at once, but the pot being so heavy they just managed to tip it and the water slopped out of it at first and then streamed out, like a dam breaking, and poured right down over their heads and the backs of their necks.

—WHAT THE FUCK.

DanDan jumped and managed to struggle out of its way before it was finished. Lucy started at first but as the water came over her, splashed up over her shoulders and went down into her lap and the back of the couch and sloshed everywhere, she seemed almost to lean back and allow it to happen. JJ cracked his hole laughing.

—HAAAAAAAA!

Lucy turned around and looked to them, soaked, almost in wonder, like she didn't know such a thing could happen. DanDan had a look of quiet outrage on his face, which he relaxed into. They drained the rest of the pot onto Lucy and threw it down, big smiles on their faces. Steph screamed at them first.

—HANDS TO YOURSELVES, YOU TWO, *NÁ BÍ AG SHIFTÁIL IN THE HALL.*

Cath joined in.

—HANDS TO YOURSELVES.

—Fuck sake.

DanDan began to wipe the water out of his eyes, ignoring JJ's roars as they filled the place.

—HAAAAAAA!

But Lucy leaned down and looked at the floor.

—You okay, Merc?

Steph looked over the couch and saw that Merc was at the base of it, curled up, soaking, and clutching his stomach, his hair wet against his forehead. He writhed and looked up at them with a pure viciousness in his eyes. He was livid. DanDan, laughing, looked down at him.

—Ah here, man, I'm sorry. Didn't mean to stand on you there.

Cath's mouth was still holding the laughter but her eyes were starting to drop as she noticed Merc was not taking it well. Merc shouted.

—GODDAMMIT.

Everything stopped.

—What the fuck? The fuck is wrong with you? I'm fucking passed out on the floor and you fucking throw water on me and fucking stamp on me?

JJ was doubled over from laughing so much, and was not helping matters.

—HA! AH HAAAAA!! HAhahahahaaa. HO! HO!

DanDan tried to speak but Merc cut him off.

—Merc man, we didn't mean to—

—Fuck didn't mean to. Fucking arseholes. Cath, why the fuck did you do that?

His shoulders were jerked in weird places and all jagged, and Steph could see he'd been harbouring this one for longer than when the water hit him.

—HO!

JJ slapped his knee. Merc glared at Cath and seemed to square up to her. She retreated backwards, afraid. DanDan rushed to get between them.

—Ah now leave Cath out of this, man, it's no one's fault.

—Bollox no one's fault. It's fucking Cath and Steph's fault. Why the fuck, Cath, ha? Not getting enough attention, is it? Told you, you were fucking needy, you fucking—

—MERC, calm the fuck down, it's fine. Don't talk to her like that.

—HO! HO!

—JJ, SHUT UP!

Merc raised himself up, made himself big.

106

—AH FUCK YOU. FUCK ALL OF YOU. That your idea of a joke? I'm fucking going to bed, and you can go fuck yourselves.

—HA! HA! HAAAAAA!

Merc glared at each one of them in turn, then stamped upstairs. None of them said a word until he'd slammed the door shut.

They looked at each other in embarrassment, except for JJ who was bent over the couch, wheezing with laughter. Cath looked on the verge of tears.

Steph looked around at DanDan, who shrugged his shoulders. Lucy scrubbed her soaking hair with her coat, then rubbed the side of DanDan's arm.

—Why do you always take things too far, Steph?

She took DanDan's arm and put it around her. He seemed vaguely uncomfortable but allowed it, not looking at Cath. Lucy led him away. The two of them went upstairs together, and the bedroom door slammed shut.

Cath looked sick as a dog. Steph went to touch her but she shrugged her away.

—I'm going to bed too.

—Don't mind him, he's just being a prick.

—I'm going to bed.

Cath left to go upstairs by herself. All of Steph's work to get her to cheer up and here she was, even worse than before.

JJ was just getting over his giggle fit and was looking about like he'd come up for air.

—Jesus Christ, that was too much altogether. Christ almighty. Oh my God.

Steph had had enough of this.

—I'm off to bed as well.

—Ah here, is that the night over then?

—The fuck do you think?

Steph left him and went up to the spare bedroom. Too fucking stressful was all of this. She slammed the door to the room behind her. It was dusty and dark inside. She collapsed onto the bed and closed her eyes. Things would be difficult in the morning, but she couldn't worry about anyone, not any more. It was all fucked.

Day 2

Malachy

The shame in him, in his cruel and useless mind, had not faded with sleep but multiplied, piled on top of itself until all he could do was bury his face in his pillow and try to forget who he was. He had not dreamt or thought of them, the young folk down the way, but of himself. He saw his body entering the house over and over, and he appeared old and wild with the gun in his hands. He kept trying to play it back, to rewind himself back to the door, and there, when he placed his fist over the handle, make himself stop, let go, and retreat back up the hill. But he could not stop what happened.

Normally he never remembered the dreams he had during the night. He had dreams but forgot them, or he just never dreamed in the first place. Either way, he woke fresh each morning as if his mind had simply gone blank for hours.

But morbid, horrible dreams he'd had the night before. All that night, repeating over and over in his head, he'd thought of entering the house, shocking the young people. And then he dreamed of the Rourkes and Elaine and the lights on the hills. He'd turn in bed and was back in the Doon Shore with Elaine, floating in the water, and then she was leaving, walking away, and Billy was lying under him, sighing hard and Malachy beating him and Mona was crying and his father was dying and then it started over again, and Malachy would jerk awake, then he'd slip back into a dream again and it'd start over again, and again, and again.

When he woke properly, the last of sleep leaving him as sunlight shone through a gap in the curtains and warmed his clammy face, he only knew that this was not something he could change. He'd

111

not done anything like this before in his life, anything so uncontrolled and stupid. Perhaps the only other time he'd come even close was when he'd seen to Billy on the road to Carrig, left him bloodied in the dark. This was different. With Billy he'd been setting something right, he was delivering justice; at least that's what he had thought he was doing. Those down the way, though, they hadn't done any wrong. They'd committed no crime or vicious act, but he'd gone in all the same, on some strange impulse that he couldn't explain or reason away.

Malachy didn't want to dwell on his dreams, or think any more of the people down the way. They were nothing to him, and he was nothing to them, and if he left them alone they'd leave him alone. He felt the whiskey in him still, on his tongue, but knew to get up and fight it. Walking it off usually worked, so he was up, into his clothes and out of the house, no shower that morning for him, before the yellow sun could warm the dew off the grass.

DanDan

He creaked down the stairs wrapped in his blanket, his bare feet sticking slightly on the wooden steps. At the bottom, the clay tiles were cold, but he liked the freshness of it. The room stank of ashtrays and gone-off beers and dust and burnt toast. He could sense the heat of JJ passed out on the floor by the couch. He padded his way to the door, feeling the dust and tiny pebbles under the balls of his feet, and stepped outside.

It was that beautiful, gorgeous, fresh early air that made every worry evaporate and float silently away. Dew on the grass, everything looked like it was being seen through crystal. It was cold, and the gravel was wet on the path through the garden. He stepped off and felt the wet, dirty grass under his feet and it made him shiver. It reached up past his ankles and tickled his calves.

The morning was so bright and glistening and beautiful. He could almost feel the great tilt of the world, the white moon curving upwards in the pale blue sky. There was something in the day, he could feel a change in it. It was in the wind, in the earth maybe, in the river nearby. He stepped back inside and stood in the living room.

It was coming out of the fire grate. It was rising up out of the stack of briquettes and sods of turf. The whole room almost seemed to hum, and gurgling in the pipes of the house, in the toilet bowl upstairs and deep in him, deep down and bubbling slowly in his stomach and his chest and his balls, there was something bright and keen.

DanDan felt an erection coming on. Shit, there it was, warm, stuck between his thigh and his boxers. Memories of Jess came

113

surfacing up out of him, roaring through his head, specific memories he'd not thought of in ages, secondary scenes that didn't come up as first thoughts of her or at all since they'd finished: her running away from him to jump in the Irish Sea, and the time he told her he loved her and she bit into his shoulder, and the smell of her jumper, sour apple perfume mixed with sweat, that still made him want to jump out of his seat whenever he smelled it on someone, and he thought of those things and he didn't cry, and there came a smile from him. He looked to the guitar case in the corner, and that seemed like it was humming too. In the black cloth case there was a lovely, varnished guitar that was begging to be played. He'd play it later. He was going to be okay.

The world was feeling fresh and good again. For the first time in ages, DanDan felt that the world was settled. No longer at an angle. He could feel the sun shining through the window onto his body. It felt good. Like he was Superman getting his powers back. He climbed the stairs, returning to Lucy.

Merc

Merc woke early on a dusty mattress in the table tennis room. His first thought was Fuck Them. Fuck them all. Arseholes. He'd been nothing but nice to them. Nothing but fun and civil, and where had it got him? Drenched with water in the dead of night and DanDan stamping on his stomach. He was all for pranks and that sort of thing, but you didn't mess with people when they were sleeping.

He'd been conked out at the bottom of the sofa, trying to let DanDan and Lucy have their private time, and next thing whoosh, fucking soaking. Then bam. DanDan's big fucking size thirteens came thundering down. Might have really hurt him.

He got dressed quickly and went downstairs. He needed to walk it off. JJ was conked out on some cushions put down on the floor, absolutely stinking of cigarettes, one hand down his jocks feeling his balls. Fucking JJ. He'd rolled those joints way too strong, gotten him absolutely baked. Completely stoned. He did it only because he was jealous of Steph. Of him and Steph.

If nothing else, Merc could at least take that from the weekend. He'd ridden Steph. They'd done it right up against the rocky side of the house. She'd enjoyed it. He'd done that and JJ hadn't and so JJ was being a prick.

With JJ lying on the ground, though, almost exactly where Merc had been lying, he thought, why not get him back now? Soak him with water and they'd be even. He went into the kitchen and started to fill the same pot that'd been used to soak him. He watched it churn slowly to the top. He'd go in and tip the water over JJ, maybe give him a kick or two, and it'd be over. Evens-Stevens. They'd forget about it and move on.

He carried the full pot, heavy thing, into the living room. JJ was still asleep, his right arm covering his eyes. The pot heavy in his hands, Merc raised it up and prepared to pour it all over him.

Then he noticed there was a drawing on JJ's hand. He lowered the pot, and went to check it from a better angle. The palm of JJ's right hand was turned awkwardly as it dangled off the end of his arm covering his eyes, but Merc could see quite clearly what was drawn on it in pen. A stick figure with a gun, and another stick figure holding onto a tree like a koala bear. There was a speech bubble coming from the mouth of the person up the tree. Inside the bubble it said, 'Save me Mario! I'm a little princess!'

He stood over JJ with the pot of water, and felt like smashing the whole thing down on his face. Murder the bastard. Merc burned up with absolute fucking rage.

What did JJ know? JJ had just fucking stood there. What did any of them know? It was a reaction, he'd been going to get help. He remembered his run from the house the night before, pure cold icy fear in him, stumbling out into the garden and falling in the darkness, slapping through the muck and tumbling over the wall, scratching his face as he climbed the tree desperately, not even once looking back. He was going for help. He had been. Maybe he didn't know he was, but he was. And how had they dealt with him after? They'd fucking spurned him, tipped water over him and kicked him in his sleep. That was no way to treat friends. That was no way to treat anyone. They were boring and useless, every last one of them, and there was no more point in Merc being there, in being friends with them.

He brought the pot back into the kitchen and threw the water into the sink.

He was leaving. Fuck the lot of them, he was leaving. Right now. They could go to hell. He'd walk to Carrig and get the first train back to Dublin.

Only he'd too much to carry. His bags, and his booze, he couldn't carry the lot. He didn't want to bring the booze. But he'd be fucked if he was leaving it for them to drink for free, guzzling it back while they toasted him gone. No fucking way.

He found a screwdriver in a kitchen drawer, then took his slab of unopened cans from the bottom shelf of the fridge. He brought the slab out to the garden and threw it down into the grass. He went down on his knees, and with the screwdriver he stabbed a hole in every last one of those cans through the shrink-wrapped plastic. They crackled and fizzed as the beer sprayed out of them. Then he took the slab, the cans still held in place, and fucked it at the side wall of the house. The cans made a bursting, clumping sound against the gravelled wall before dropping to the ground fizzing. That felt good.

He went back in and found his bottle of sambuca and started to pour it into the herb garden. He watched about a shot or two glug out before he thought the better of it and took a swig from it. It burned his throat and made his head feel weak. He went back into the living room and poured a big load of it into the fireplace, on top of the ashes and everything. Fuck them. Then he walked about the house with the bottle of sambuca, spilling and splashing it on everything, on the curtains and on the rug and on the furniture, to really stink it up. When the bottle was empty he went around to the side of the house and flung it at the wall, where it shattered and burst into hundreds of tiny pieces. Broken glass glittered on the wall and on the ground.

He wiped his mouth. Now that it was done, it didn't feel that great. There was a hollowness in him, like a sense of loss or futility, he didn't know. Maybe because he'd wasted the sambuca without drinking more.

He went in and looked at JJ still sleeping. The floor was slippery and the place stank of sambuca. He looked down at him, his arm still covering his eyes and his hand down his boxers, his thin white body all bones and sinew. He yearned to kick him in the stomach but thought better not. Better just to be dignified, and leave.

He stamped upstairs and packed his bag. On the way out he passed the bathroom. He went in and turned on the shower, the hot water on full blast, and left it running. See how they liked not having any hot water when they woke.

He stomped downstairs and stood in the fusty room. He allowed himself a moment, as he stood there, to reconsider, to think about his decision. Should he go? Was there something he was missing, or not considering? Would he regret it?

Fuck it. No. He wouldn't. He was right and he shouldn't spend another minute around these bastards. He spoke loudly, to the whole house.

—Fuck this.

He kicked the table and left without another word.

JJ

The first thing he heard was Merc plodding down the stairs. JJ opened his eyes slowly and looked over. Merc stopped by the oak table and put his bag down on the dusty floor. Maybe he hoped someone would have been there to notice him. JJ was there. But he didn't give a shit.

Merc looked around, and scratched the small of his back.

—Fuck this.

He kicked the table, shouldered his bag and walked from the room, slamming the door after him.

Why should JJ care? Cowards fled. That's what cowards did. Merc had proved it by actually, literally running away. Then he couldn't handle it. Got all pissy about the water. Like that's what it was really about. Fooling no one. And now he was running away again.

JJ rose from the cushions wrapped in his blanket – a touch too airy below the knees, but what harm? – and went to the back door. He stepped outside.

He watched Merc walk from the house, away across the gravel car park and towards the road to Carrig. Once Merc got to the rock wall marking the start of the shared road, he turned slightly. JJ could sense that Merc was watching out of the corner of his eye to see if anyone was going to run after him, ask him to stay. But no one did. No one was calling his name, and no one was going to call his name. He waited a moment or two, then he turned away and started walking again. JJ watched him disappear out of sight.

The herb garden smelled earthy, of thyme maybe, or rosemary. He opened up the blanket and pissed in it. There was something really satisfying about pissing outside in the mornings. He finished up, the dirt mulchy from his urine.

JJ yawned and went back inside. He really should tell the others Merc had left. But then, if they ran after him and asked him to stay he'd only tell them to go fuck themselves, and it'd show them that he was right. Nope. He'd tell them later. Better to let the fucker walk away.

Steph

She heard Merc leaving. She listened to him cursing at the door and watched him from the bedroom window as he shuffled away. More than any kind of guilt, she felt an unsettling kind of queasiness at the fact that he had been so transparent, that he'd laid his emotions out so readily for them all to see. The tiny amount of pretence he'd shown, the half-gamble of trying to say he'd been going for help, made him seem all the more stupid and out of control. If he'd just admitted that he'd panicked, and that some kind of fight or flight response kicked in, if he'd told them, yes I ran, and yes I'm embarrassed and it won't happen again, they would've taken his apology and said don't worry, pal, it can happen to any of us, then it wouldn't have been mentioned again. Instead, he'd pretended it hadn't happened.

What bothered Steph was not that he'd run, or that he'd tried to cover it up; it was that he'd done it so badly. His complete lack of awareness was the problem. And surely he'd known that once he walked out the door, he'd be walking out on any chance that they'd believe him.

It also reflected badly on her no end. She'd been with him. Everyone would know soon enough. And it wasn't like she could shrug it off like, oh I was with him once, and another time he ran out on his friends then had a hissy fit. They were interlinked, the two of them. They would be paired in people's heads, the first event and the second, Steph and cowardice. That thing about conditioning, about causation and correlation – just by putting two events side by side people think that not only are they related, but that one caused the other. Steph and cowardice. Steph equals cowardice. Steph causes cowardice. Christ, she'd only been with him once, quickly, and it hadn't even been that great, it was just one of those nights, and now there were a whole load of other things to think about.

JJ downstairs for one. He'd been triumphant when it all came out. Him and Merc had been at each other all day, the whole thing had been coming to a head. Steph had felt it, knew it was going to happen, and couldn't help but think that somehow again she was involved. JJ might have a bit of a thing for her. She didn't want to admit it, but he did. How was that her fault, though? She hadn't encouraged JJ. She'd shown loyalty to Merc even though there'd been no need or responsibility on her part to do so. And yet she was going to get stuck with the consequences of all of it.

This whole situation was exactly the kind of thing she'd been hoping to avoid. She'd just wanted a few days away, some time to herself without all the petty arguments and things, and within the first few hours something major had happened. This would be all they would talk about now, on and off, for the next age.

Hang on.

DanDan had shifted Lucy.

DanDan and Lucy had gotten together. And they hadn't stopped, had they? Well no, they'd separated, but they didn't go their separate ways after . . . They'd gone to the same bedroom. Had they done filthy things together?

It'd take the heat off Steph if they had.

Actually, that was an idea. Maybe if this sort of thing continued, if dirty sexy things kept happening in the group, they could just dismiss the whole trip as one weekend when everyone had gone a bit mental and did things they shouldn't have. They could agree to forget about it, or just refer it as 'that time things went a bit mad'. This was perfect.

All they needed now was for Cath to do something scandalous. Something to put them all on a level playing field.

JJ and Cath. That was the only way for it. If JJ and Cath got together, then that would be everyone. Everyone had shagged.

Everyone was culpable so no one was, and it'd make Cath forget about DanDan as well. Ha. Then they could all go off and ride into the sunset after one big, whory weekend down the country. Everything would be fine in the end.

She decided to go for a run, get the plan straight in her head.

Malachy

He left the house and started down to the lake, taking his fishing gear with him. The sky was bluest in the mornings, at its freshest and coldest when the moon was still visible high up before the sun got to it. He passed the Lodge on the way and noticed they'd left the front door ajar. Condensation clouded the windows inside and the front of the house was littered with butt ends and empty cans. Malachy kept his pace, though, continuing past the church and down towards the lake.

It was not his business. He'd been watching over the house his whole life. People had come and gone and not once had he been able to change the nature of what went on within its walls.

The sun was up by the time he reached the Doon Shore. The lake spread out before him, the few square kilometres of water reflecting the sun, making it white and hazy. He took his fishing gear to the end of the pier and cast out. Far off on the lake he could see the rowboats already out, the locals practising for the trout competition.

It calmed him, the fishing. It was quiet and still, and he was also putting himself to use; there was a point in it. He could study the water and the sky and the islands out in the lake and still feel he was doing something useful. His mind could wander as it always did. His attention would catch something, like the weight of the rod in his hands, how it exerted an unbalanced pressure on the side of his forefingers, and pushed back against the palm of his right hand, or the look of the black fishing line coming from the top of the rod, striking out diagonally towards the water, appearing to cut a line through the blue sky behind, as though it

124

might slice open the sky itself like a sack of barley and the darkness would pour out and fall into the lake, and as he focused on just that line and on the weight in his hands, it seemed that whatever was in front of him disappeared and he almost went blind. The lake water shushed gently on the shore and he felt peaceful.

Lucy

She felt it deep in her chest, right down inside her. Excitement. Falling. There was something there in her, right inside her for DanDan. Even when she said his name in her own head it felt special. He wasn't in the best place, she shouldn't come on too strong, she knew that, but she couldn't help herself smiling when the thought of the night before circled back again and again through her head.

It was an amazing thing, was love, well, not love but sex. It was an entirely separate way of communicating. Touch a spot there and listen to the noise it makes, grab that and see what happens. How to interact with heat and cold and different textures and all weird sticky bits as well. You were communicating with another person in a way you could not even fathom normally, how your body went on instinct but was also guided by small movements in muscle and weird grunts and *oh* meant good but *oohhhh* meant better and stay there doing that, how the whole thing seemed suspended in its own logic and timeframe and rules, and how weird and raw you felt afterwards as well as warm and open. How could anyone go back to talking as a way of communicating when they had such a thing as sex?

And there he was asleep next to her, his strong back pale under the sheets. She leaned in close and listened to his breathing. She said his name.

—DanDan.

He didn't hear. He was breathing too smoothly. She got up, hid herself in her covers, and snapped on her knickers.

When the others had gone off to look for Merc she'd been upset. The gun had frightened the life out of her and she just needed a bit of a sit-down. Then DanDan was there, he'd caught her, he'd found her and looked out for her. When the rest were looking for Merc he'd put his arms around her and let her cry. She'd heard his voice in her ear.

—Shush. Shush.

She'd felt his breath in her ear, and his voice so loud it might as well have been in her head.

—Shush.

The air warm, and she could hear the tongue sticky in his mouth. She'd uncovered her head from under her arms and looked up around her. The room was quiet. All she could hear were the calls for Merc in the distance and her blood thumping in her ears, and as she looked about, the room seemed still, like it knew nothing of the fright she'd been given, and then she looked at him, and he was looking at her. His eyes flicking, snapping from side to side, looking into her eyes. Genuine concern in his eyes for her.

—You okay?

She'd looked at him.

—Yeah.

—You sure?

—I'm fine.

She'd nuzzled his neck, then worked her way up until she kissed his cheek once, twice and he'd come away and looked at her. Then he'd leaned in, or had she, AND THUNDERBIRDS WERE GO. It started soft and all a bit teary but then she'd gotten into it and he'd grabbed her and then the two of them there were just mauling on the floor. His hand was slipping down her knee and she could taste the wine off him, his hands were drifting, he was kissing her neck, then came back up to her mouth when next thing,

—SNARED!

She'd detached herself from his face. There was Cath and Steph stood in the door. Steph with a big smile on her face.

They'd separated for a while. Lucy'd jumped up off the ground and gone for a drink, Steph smacking her arse as she passed, saying 'naughty', and DanDan had stayed and for a while at least, they'd kept away from each other, for decorum. But every time he'd looked over at her she'd felt sex in his eyes, and she tried to put out sex in her stance to him, how did you communicate that? She didn't know now, not in the morning, in the bright air, but certainly she'd known then, because of the booze maybe, exactly how to angle herself at him. It felt good having him watch her. And they'd drawn closer in the night, speaking again without language, holy fuck what a world existed she'd never even been aware of.

Until the water came over them, shocked the two of them together, and DanDan stamped on Merc, and he'd shouted at them. And with everyone in uproar, Lucy saw her chance, and they went off together, into the room, and that was that. They'd knocked against each other standing up in the dark. Just them in a small room, still soaked with water, and when he'd pushed her towards the bed, she knew she wanted to do it, only she wanted him to be gentle with her, so she'd just kind of briefly, when he started to slide on top of her, whispered in his ear, 'It's my first, be kind, be kind.' And he'd stopped kissing her neck, and looked at her in the dark, as if to say, 'Really?' But then she'd kissed him full on the mouth, and in between said a few more times, 'I want to, I want to, just be kind.' And he had been, and they'd done it, THEY'D DONE IT.

She stood over DanDan, looking at him in the morning light. She'd heard that watching people sleep, lovers, like, was this grand big romantic thing.

Doing it now, though, watching DanDan, it was just fucking boring. Was she expected to just hang around waiting for him to wake up so that when he rolled over she could be all dreamy and be acting like she'd discover the secrets of the universe in his eyes? What the fuck? She stood over him.

—DanDan.

He made a noise, a mucky snort. It was maybe a little bit cute, but mostly it just made him sound like a piglet.

—Mwuh, huh?

—Shhh, back in a minute.

—Humm, yeah, sure.

128

He rolled back over. She checked outside the door. No one in the hallway. She had her knickers on and she pulled a T-shirt over her head. If she was caught nipping to the jacks it wouldn't be called being sensibly dressed, but no one could accuse her of flaunting herself all the same.

Where had Cath slept? Her and Cath were supposed to share the bed but obviously sex took precedence.

She went on tiptoes to the bathroom. She turned the handle on the bathroom door.

—OCCUPIED.

Shit. She ran back to the bedroom and waited by the door, her blood pumping. At least her head wasn't all that bad, considering. It was probably all the exercise she'd gotten. All the sex, the actual sex she'd had. She understood now, the big deal about it, though that's what people always said happened the first time. The reaction to losing your virginity was always either, 'So what's the big deal?', or, 'Ah, now I know what it's all about.' But she did understand, it was fucking great. It was great fucking, ha.

He'd been inside her. Like, *actually* inside her. No, that wasn't it. He'd been *inside* her. A part of him had been in her. She'd helped it in, and then it was all warm and any movement she made changed the feeling of it and sometimes for the better. Then better and better and then they were done. But wait, actually he hadn't been done. Just when she'd thought he was going to finish, he'd rolled over onto his back gasping, and she'd thought, shit, is that what it sounds like, a low groan like a tortured animal? 'Cramp,' he kept saying. 'Cramp, cramp, fuck cramp.' And she'd just waited there holding on for his cramp to go away. Then after a bit of stretching he'd rolled back onto her and gone again.

She worried that in the future she might think the whole experience had gone badly, just because he'd apologised so much about the cramp. She worried that she'd reimagine it as bad sex or uncaring sex. But he had cared. After the cramp went away and they'd finished for real, he'd turned to her and said, 'Okay?' except with his eyes she knew he was asking like, 'Okay for the first time, how are you feeling?' He could do that with his eyes,

DanDan. 'Fine,' she'd said, and used her eyes back and a little head nod to confirm.

She'd lain there after with her head in the nook of his arm and had felt glad. She was glad she'd waited that long. That was her best memory of the whole thing, lying in his arms after, warm and secure even though she was sore, knowing it had been the right choice. She hoped that that was the memory she'd hold onto, not the cramp memory.

She'd thought about things then. The past mostly. That was a funny thing. Lying there thinking about it, she hadn't thought so much about what might happen in the future, how DanDan would be the first of many, but of what had happened before him. She went back through a list of all her crushes, her boyfriends. Who would she have preferred to have been first?

She couldn't name anyone.

Then she'd asked herself, was she glad she'd done it. She was. Despite all she'd heard, all the horror stories and how sex was filthy and they'd be full of disease and babies and boats to England, she didn't feel ashamed or embarrassed. It hadn't been shameful. It had just been kind of lovely. There it was. She was glad it had happened, and she was glad it was DanDan. Suddenly she was just sorry she couldn't go out and lose it again.

She noticed she'd left the bedroom door open. She swung the door shut, but just as she did she caught a sight of Cath coming from the bathroom, her head held low. They got a quick pip in just before the wood slammed between them.

—Hi.

—Hi.

She had enough time to see something weird in Cath's posture. A bit too hunched or something. She didn't actually mind, did she?

No, too early to start thinking about that. She needed DanDan to wake so they could have another go, practice was the way forward. She bounced from foot to foot. Christ she needed to go. She nipped quickly to the empty bathroom, closed the door and finally got to pee.

130

She washed her hands and went back to the bedroom, jamming the door shut. The noise shook DanDan awake. As he turned around to check who it was, she jumped in next to him, wriggled into bed so she was facing him. His hand went onto her hip.

—Well, good morning.

—Morning to you, handsome.

He was a bit more lucid. A bit more Lucied, what. He had morning breath. She took his hand and put it up under her T-shirt. She felt the warmth of his hand on her chest.

—Last night was nice.

—Yeah.

His hand massaged her a little.

—Think it was a mistake?

—No.

His hand wandered a little more, down her body,

—We could always go again.

—If you say so.

HOW BRILLIANT TO BE SEXY.

Malachy

Malachy fished until past midday, though he caught nothing. His back was beginning to hurt, and his mood was changing quickly. He could feel himself getting darker, his mind forcing itself back to the people in the house. He felt old, helplessly fucking old. He could barely remember what it was like to move about without something hurting him. The calmness of the blue morning was long gone, and now all he heard was the rustle of discarded plastic bags in hedges, and the throbbing motor of the barge tour taking American tourists around the lake. The day was getting polluted. Malachy cast out one last time. He should leave before anyone else came down.

Nothing was grabbing on the fishing line, and his head was pierced from the whiskey the night before. He shouldn't even be fishing. Swimming on the shore had been banned five years before when some dogs died after drinking the water. It was due to a toxic algal bloom, something about plankton and mussels. The town had gone into an uproar, protesting about the danger, the loss of tourism, the death of their summer holidays, and they blamed the council and the government and anybody they could think to blame. But it was their fault. Every house in the area pumped all their sewage to a local treatment plant, which in turn sent it on down into the lake. Filled the water with shit and left it to foul in the sun. And people bathed there every day. They went down to the shore and washed in it, wiping their terrible bodies clean in it, then they stood up and got out, and left the lake rank, like left-over bathwater, until it killed any creature that drank from it.

The ban had been lifted only recently, when the algae had cleared and the water tested clean, but Malachy knew it would come back. The first time had been a warning shot. The poison would come back, only it wouldn't be dogs it killed this time but people. Some children, a little girl and tiny boy, would cup the water in their soft, curled hands and drink. A strong, handsome father would splash his wife in it, feel her fleshy, white body and dunk her head playfully under the water, then go under himself, and while they kissed sweetly in what they thought was God's blue water they'd drink in that same poison they'd helped create, and late that night they'd put their children to bed, and sleep themselves. The house would feel death that night, and their cold bodies would feel nothing by morning, only the bed springs would creak as the boy and girl and mother and father breathed their last, and sank deeper into their mattresses.

His boots were hanging off the edge of the pier. One untied shoelace dangled down, trailing in the water. Billy Rourke had drowned in that water. A few years later he'd kissed Elaine in the same spot.

He couldn't stop himself thinking on her. She was the first and only one he'd done a line with. She only lived a few miles down the road, so they used to go out walking together, all around the valley. He was always quiet, kept his thoughts to himself, but she laughed and joked with him. She dragged him out of himself, made him talk about his father and what he wanted in life and what he had planned for the future.

One night, they walked longer than usual, and he grabbed her and kissed her up against a rock wall. They kissed so hard they shoved up against the wall and knocked half of it down, the rocks tumbling away and rolling into the field behind. She told him she wanted to go to Dublin, start a career. He said she'd get a job in a week and put his hand up under her coat, and she whispered in his ear, come on, come with me, this way.

She led him down the sloping road to the Doon Shore. They kissed by the water's edge. Then she took off her dress and tossed it down onto the sand, so she was standing there in her slip, and she waded into the lake water. He'd thought they'd just have a talk by the shore, but then she was standing knee deep in the water in just her underwear, her hand stretched out for him to join her. He followed, numb. She led him farther in until they lost the ground beneath them. She held him close in the cold, black water. She kissed his face and his eyes and she told him she loved him.

Though Malachy remembered it clearly now, he'd no idea how he'd felt bobbing with her in the water. He knew he touched her, but he didn't know where exactly. He just knew it was soft, the feel of her warm under his hand. She put her head into his neck and said she wanted to wait. Not till marriage, she said, but just a while longer. She wasn't going to get trapped in their town. Wait, wait, she whispered in his ear. And then, come with me. We'll go together. He was so cold there, though she was warm on him, and he was all numb and gone, he had no idea where he was or what he was doing. Come away with me. He kissed the hair on her wet head and said yes. Yes? Yes. She kissed him in the cold water, and they floated together, he couldn't remember how long for, until they began to shiver and she breathed icy vapour on him in the black night, and he pulled her gently ashore. Her teeth clattered as he put his coat around her on the sand, and dried her wet body for her with his bunched up shirt.

And what had happened to her, in the end? Up and married a dentist, from what he'd heard. They moved to Mullingar for his practice. He passed her once, on the main street in Carrig, a few years later. She'd put on weight and was dragging a small child behind her, a little boy. They were back for their holidays, he supposed. He kept his stride and walked on past her, and she didn't even notice him, or she did, but didn't realise it was him. He walked right on by and didn't look back, though he'd wanted to, desperately. Even if she had recognised him, she would not have known what he was thinking, how every thought clawed at him to turn and look at her, to watch her face. He just kept on walking.

Malachy reeled in. He wondered whether he should warn the people in the house about the water, if he should call in and let them know not to go swimming there. Maybe it would be better just to let them go on ahead, let them drink the poison. They thought they were at home in the land, they went about acting like they owned the place. Maybe best to let them take all that that entailed. Let them drown each other in it.

No. He'd not warn them, only because there was nothing to warn them about. It was clear, the lake was clean and no longer dangerous, and they were free to enjoy it whatever way they wanted.

It was time to go. He got to his feet slowly, painfully, and left the pier where it was.

Cath

She pulled at the weeds in the herb garden by the back door. It was overgrown with parasites. Useless things that sucked all the good out of the ground. She used her bare hands. She dug her fingers down deep into the earth, felt in under a green weed to get to the root, got a good grasp on it, and twisted it out of its place. She threw it behind her at the wall of the house, where it hit the painted gravel and flopped down with a little pat onto the growing mound below.

She didn't bother to wipe her hands before she went in searching for the next one. She dug in under its roots then yanked. A few limp petals came away under her iron grip. She pushed her hands right in again and forced the rest of the bulb out. The dirt caught in under her nails and she knew there was muck on her nose, her hands were fierce dirty, but it was soothing enough doing it. She'd seen her mother do the gardening when she was stressed, when her and Cath's da were fighting again, and she'd never fully understood it. Now it made sense. It wasn't planting and cultivating, not growing life and all that New Earth kind of thing. It was destruction. Deadhead the flowers, rip out any common plants, tear away any outsiders, swiftly cut down anything that was growing too big or unwieldy.

DanDan and Lucy. The entire idea was ludicrous. Lucy an alcoholic and DanDan supposed to be grieving. He needed protecting, and so did Lucy. Lucy needed protecting from herself, and DanDan from Lucy. Cath had been at hand to counsel Lucy whenever she made shit out of any possible relationship she might have had. A lad would score her one night and then text her or not text her or use the wrong word, then Lucy would scald him with some insult she could never take back, or just shift one of his mates, and then he'd call her a bitch and she'd spend five days crying. And now she was going to bring that shit into DanDan's life. The two of them kissing. His hand on her tit. Her mouth on his . . .

No.

Fuck, no. Gardening gardening gardening. Her mouth on his cock.

Stop.

She dug her fingernails in; she was getting quicker at it, better. She could feel something in her eye.

Her mouth on his.

Shit, shit.

It wasn't fair. It wasn't. It just wasn't fair.

Why her? Why Lucy? Why had Lucy done this to her? And why had DanDan agreed? What about earlier that night, what he'd said to her? Had he forgotten? Or had she heard the wrong thing? Had he known she'd ditched Paddy? She hadn't told him . . . But still.

She wasn't sure what was what any more. She smelled dying sage, she must have pulled some up. She couldn't distinguish what she wanted to keep, what she should throw away.

She saw one last long nettle hiding in under the dirt. She grabbed it.

—OW.

The sting and tender throb of pain was immediate.

Fuck.

She sat back on the ground and held her hand. AH. Why had she done that? She'd known it was a nettle. But she'd grabbed onto it anyway. Christ, her hand. It felt like needles were boiling in under the skin, trying to break out through the surface. Oh shit, oh shit. She just sat, looking at her hand, feeling it pulse, her jeans getting mucky.

The garden looked as if someone had gone at it with an axe. The ground was chopped and ragged. Bits of green leaves were scattered in and around the muck, and by the wall were brown-stained green bulbs of weeds and plants and flowers and herbs, sweet-smelling things and beautiful things that'd done no wrong. There were still bits of weed in the patch, and, looking at her hand and taking stock of what had happened, and what was to come, she knew she couldn't leave them lying there. Any trace elements would just spawn more. All the work and sweat, and the pain she felt squeezing her hand tight, would be for nothing. They'd grow back in days and would be worse than before. She had to, now, while she was still aching with the sting of the nettle, uproot all of it, herb or no, crisp petals or not. Any one bit left behind would fuck everything. She'd have to destroy the lot of it.

She pushed herself to her feet.

What would she say to them when they came down? Congratulations? Go to fuck, it'll end badly? Ignore them? Give them a high-five?

She walked around the back of the house to the shed. She tugged the bolt on the door across, the metal screaming and squealing with rust.

It smelled like warm manure inside the shed. There were Frisbees and bits of Lego strewn across the ground, with old pots of paint and bottles containing mysterious liquids on higher shelves. A broken lawnmower had pride of place in the middle. Propped in the corner was a rolled-up badminton set, an axe and a hoe. She took the hoe and retreated, holding her breath.

She walked back around the house to the herb garden. Aside from unlocking the door she'd made little to no noise in the last hour, and there she was, walking under the first-floor window where she knew they were sleeping. The room she was supposed to sleep in but couldn't because they were inside, fucking. She'd slept on the mattress on the floor in the table tennis room, listening to Merc snore and mutter in his sleep. And the faint call inside of sex, the creak of the bed where the screws holding the thing together weren't tight enough. Excited whispers, and a little moan but only for a second. Then she'd heard nothing else, and even that made her angry. Why wouldn't they just wake up the entire house with their screams, their shouts of orgasm and pleasure and OH OH OH FUCK ME FUCK ME – why did they think they had to keep it down? Was it because they didn't want Cath to hear? They thought that loud sex would make her upset? That was just fucking arrogant and completely insane. They could fuck each other's brains out and scream the house awake for all she cared.

And then earlier when she'd come from the bathroom and seen Lucy, bare-legged in her underwear, in the same room as DanDan. What had that meant? That she'd been down to her underwear at least. And the T-shirt meant no bra. But then, that might just have been sleeping. Maybe Lucy had made him sleep on the floor while she took the bed.

Had they actually had sex then? Lucy was always very weird about sex. She'd never really told Cath anything about what she'd been up to. She always said something vague about going home with a lad or him turning out to be a weirdo, but she spared her the absolute details. Was it because she had some kind of weird fetish? Some weird fetish that she showed DanDan? What if he'd thought it was weird and said no and they'd just slept beside each other then and hadn't had any sex at all? What if he had the same fetish and they stayed up all night doing it, whatever it was, the fetish? Too many things to keep track of, and it was none of her business, she knew that, but the pressure, the burning need to know and not know, to know exactly what happened but to then have that not be what happened, to find out they only spooned together, and be certain that that was the truth, she felt it running in her stomach over and over, though she knew that's not what happened, and she wanted to kick their door in and scream at them till they dissolved into puddles by the floor of the bed.

All the same, she kept quiet passing under their window. She looked up, hoping to see something to confirm or deny what she knew anyway, but there was nothing. She just saw the wooden boards of the ceiling and the light bulb dangling from the wire, no lampshade, and the bulb dead.

She turned the corner, and there was the garden waiting for her. Maybe she was too late and the weeds had already dug in. She needed to be ruthless. The hoe in hand, she pulverised what was left. She scrambled and scooped the dirt up over the side and sent it flying. She hacked away everything until she was sweating and grunting with the effort. The weeds could make their own life in the wilds beyond, they could have all they wanted, but not in her garden. She poked and hassled and dug the earth again and again and again until she'd dredged up and thrown away almost half a foot of topsoil. The path and the walls of the house were sprayed with muck. Panting, she dug and dug and hacked again until the smell of turned soil rose in her face and her back ached.

She placed the hoe up against the wall of the house, her hands and clothes covered in soft muck. She tried to calm her heart rate, breathing sharp, cold air into her lungs, blood thumping in her ears.

Then it came to her, almost as if it had not existed before, or as if her ears were completely incapable of hearing it earlier, the rush of the river nearby. She could hear the cascade and the trickle of it, what had been going non-stop for years and would go on many more, streaming down over green rocks to the blue lake at its end. It calmed her.

She looked over to the church and the car park to see Steph bouncing back from a run, skin-tight Lycra on her and her hair in a ponytail, earphones in, coming steadily back. She didn't even look tired. And in that moment Cath loved Steph so much, how single-minded she was, how able. Despite all the drama and the hangovers, all the shit with Merc and DanDan and Malachy, she could still force herself on a morning run. Cath put her hand up and waved, and got a quick one in return, before Steph changed direction, running back and forth in zigzags, warming down.

She wiped her hands, and went inside to wash up.

Merc

By the time he reached the main road he was already wrecked. He carried his bag over his shoulder, but the straps were digging into his fingers and his hand was starting to go numb. It was red and splotchy where the flesh was poking out through the gap between the two straps. He switched hands, switched shoulders. It would take him another hour at least to get into Carrig. The road stretched out miles in front of him.

All he'd wanted was to go off and have a bit of a boozy weekend away, get stoned and mess about. And they'd ruined it. A deranged fucking farmer came in waving a shotgun, and they'd all turned on him. He thought he'd known them. He knew them now, though. At least that was one thing he got out of it. Couldn't trust anyone in this world. Not a soul.

His arm was wrecked, the bag heavy as fuck. His breathing was coming hard. His back was soaked with sweat. Fuck it, he should've brought the sambuca. He thought of how he'd walked away from the house. If only they'd caught him as he left, shouted after him to come back. If he'd just heard his name, from one of them, any of them, he'd have come back and they'd have forgotten the whole thing. But they hadn't, and he'd kept walking, and now there was no way he was just going to stop, turn on his heel and march back. Why should he? It wasn't even his fault.

He reached the town by midday. There wasn't a train for two hours, so he sat in a greasy spoon, ordered a coffee and waited with his bag.

He had a headache. His shoulders hurt. His phone was out of charge.

He tried not to think.
He couldn't shut off his head.
Hours till his train.
Couldn't stop the thoughts.
He felt sick.

DanDan

He put the shower on full blast. It was freezing, all the hot water gone, but it didn't matter. It woke him up. The jets of cold water made splattering noises on his body. He was awake, like he'd just surfaced from a long dive. Sounds came to him clearly; he could see farther, smell everything. Twice of a morning. Sex twice in the morning light. It wasn't just the sex, it was the freeing feeling of moving on. Of having someone else and finding it surprisingly familiar, and wonderfully different.

Quite funny really, the whole thing. He had no idea how it had started. Guy with a gun, next thing mauling. They were interrupted. Waited a bit. Merc had a hissy. Spontaneous shifting.

He sang to himself in the shower. He knew all the words to 'Tomorrow' from *Annie*, though he didn't know why. He belted it out, listening to it sound off the tiles and echo around the room. He didn't care who heard.

There was that thing Brian Keenan said when he came back from being kidnapped in Beirut. DanDan hadn't read the book, but he'd watched that clip of him on *Reeling in the Years*, when he gets to his front door after hugging his family. He's been released from captivity after four whole years and he's surrounded by his friends and loved ones and crowds of people from the area, and the reporter says, 'What'll you do next, Brian?', and with this big teary look on his face he says he's going to visit every country in the world and eat all the food in the world, and drink all the drink in the world and make love with every woman in the world. DanDan felt that way now, as if he'd been released from something, and was now full of love and desire for the world, and it was a tight, warm and wonderful feeling.

143

He finished up showering and dried himself. He pulled on his old boxers. He had fresh ones but they were in the other room and Cath might be in there. He had a feeling he might be in a little bit of trouble with her. She was always a bit weird about Lucy. She thought Lucy needed some kind of protecting, but fuck it, you couldn't protect everyone. Lucy was responsible for herself and when they'd gotten together she wasn't altogether drunk, in fact he'd been drunker than her, so technically, technically it was on her. She'd even made the first move.

He could still hear the noises she'd made in bed, the noises he'd made her make. They weren't exactly noises of the uninvolved, or disenchanted. Actually, they'd both made a fair bit of noise. He thought about apologising to Cath for the whole thing but it would make it more awkward. Best leave it.

Plus, should he have to apologise? No. He found no solid reason to. Though, somewhere, lurking, ghosting about him, he felt a shiver that maybe he might.

He looked at himself in the mirror. He was tall and he liked being tall. His jawline was visible enough. His right bicep was larger than his left. They said that was to do with the wanking, but he preferred to think it was due to playing the guitar. Altogether, he was alright. He left the bathroom, leaving the wet towel on the floor.

He passed down the corridor, opened the bedroom door and stepped in. Lucy was dressed. She had made the bed and was lying back on top of the covers, her wet hair spread out under her. She looked pretty fantastic, the mouth newly lip-balmed and delicate. It had been on him. Christ, he was getting horny again just thinking about it. She put her hand out for him.

—Hi.

—Hey.

He flopped down beside her. She snuggled up to him. There was still a faint smell of drink off her breath.

—So, what now?

He didn't know, he actually didn't, but for that moment, he didn't mind not knowing. He'd a great feeling of not giving a shit, of believing that everything would just work out.

It seemed strange, though, seeing her dressed. For as long as they'd been under the covers together, or rolling around, or spooning, naked or half-dressed or switching positions, or murmuring sleepily in each other's ears, they weren't themselves. He wasn't DanDan and she wasn't Lucy. But now, with her dressed, in her regular old clothes, with her hair drying, it felt like the life that had been separate and apart and completely of its own was gone, that now he was DanDan lying down with Lucy, and he didn't have a clue what to talk to her about.

—Dunno. We just go downstairs, and act like everything's normal.

—Is it not normal?

—I dunno. I mean, just like, don't draw attention to it, y'know. Just say, 'Good morning, hello hello, how are you.'

—I don't know.

He put his arm around her and held her to him. That would get it back maybe, that would bring them close again, put them back in their strange world where downstairs didn't exist, not in any real sense. He kissed her lips.

Nope. Didn't feel good. She tried to kiss him harder but he pulled away. Maybe kissing was a bad idea now. He didn't want her to think they were going out. They definitely weren't going out. His life was open two minutes before, when he was in the shower – he was ready to go off and travel the world and make love to everybody – and now he was trapped with Lucy in a small, dusty room, her latching on to him like they were soulmates. They were not going out. He should make that one clear.

Lucy nuzzled his neck.

—I enjoyed this.

—Yeah, Luce.

Eugh, saying her name like that, didn't work for him. It sounded forced. She put her hand on his face.

—Did you enjoy yourself?

—Course I did . . . You're not going to get insecure, are you?

—How do you mean?

—It's not going to get a bit weird and you think that anything I say from now on is like a veiled insult or suggestion.

—No . . .

There was hurt there. Defensiveness.

—I mean, like, God, I'm not saying this well. Just, just don't do the whole girl thing where you think it over too much.

—What do you mean, think it over? Like overthink it?

—No. Yes, no. I mean like don't start making it into something it's not.

Her shoulders stiffened and she looked at him.

—What do you mean, something it's not?

—I don't know. We had a good night together, a great night. But like, I don't want this to be a huge deal.

Her voice was clipped and harsh.

—No. Okay, fine. No, not a big deal.

—You know what I mean.

—Fuck sake, DanDan, I haven't started drafting our wedding invitations just yet. I'd had a great time up until now. I think you've overthought it, not me.

—Sorry.

—Yeah, you're sorry.

She turned away from him. He waited a few moments and thought about the best way to go forward.

—I didn't mean it like that.

—No, come on, you seem to know exactly what this is, what the whole thing is – what exactly is this?

—I don't know.

—Come on.

—I don't know, it was just, two mates had a good night together.

—Mates?

—Sorry, friends. But if I say friends it sounds weird. It sounds like, I dunno, like I'm trying to say it was a mistake.

—Was it?

—No. Of course it wasn't. And if it was, it was the greatest mistake I ever made.

—Don't try to sound fucking cool, DanDan, it doesn't suit you.

—Sorry. I'm not saying what I'm trying to say.

—No, you're not.

They were silent, looking up at the ceiling. How had he managed to fuck that up? She lay beside him, her arms tucked in front of her, protecting herself, her chest, or her heart, he didn't know. Her face was going from one that was wet, wounded and soppy, to one that had a glint of danger in it. She was steaming, her jaw clenched. He tried to speak softly.

—What do we do now?

She didn't say anything for a long time. Then, without looking at him:

—Nothing. I'll see you downstairs.

He understood. She was fuming. He got up and dressed, tugging on his jeans from the night before. He found his T-shirt thrown over a lampshade and put it on.

—I'm sorry, y'know. I don't know what the fuck I was saying. We okay?

—We're fine.

She didn't look at him the entire time. He pulled the door shut behind him. He listened to see if she made any kind of noise. Nothing. There he was in the corridor, in his bare feet. Couldn't go back in.

No choice but go downstairs.

His stomach gave a little jolt.

He'd still gotten the ride.

Malachy

He got back in the afternoon, when the sun had disappeared through cloud and mist and the valley was grey again. His legs ached and it'd taken him longer than usual to get home.

On the way back he passed the Lodge and spotted her, there in the garden, pulling up plants by the root and tossing them over her head. The girl, Catherine. Christ, she looked like a Rourke, now that he thought about it. All that fucking sadness on her. He watched her tear up all the plants from the herb garden with a fury. She looked different to the girl he'd seen just yesterday, who'd run in and out of the house organising things with a manic smile on her face, rounding up her friends and telling them where to go and what to do. Now she was just a sad, solitary shape in the back garden, like her mother and grandmother before her.

When he got in, he undressed and put away his fishing gear. He stalled in the corridor outside his kitchen for several moments, in his underwear and grey T-shirt, refusing to enter for fear of seeing the Lodge through the screen door, like the very sight of it might kill him. He took two deep breaths and entered the kitchen. He imagined himself with blinders on, keeping his gaze away from the window and the screen door as he walked straight to the kettle and filled it from the tap, his old, wrinkled fingers wrapped around the handle, feeling the weight of the water as it gushed down the spout and settled bubbling at the bottom. He brought it towards the base plate, his arm giving in under the weight of it. He shuffled forward quickly to place it down before it fell. He was tired.

He watched the kettle boil for some minutes, waiting for it to rumble and shake. When it was ready, he just stared at it some more. The thought of going for a teabag, a cup, the milk, seemed useless and made him weary beyond measure. He looked up from the kettle, and for a tiny moment, glanced out the window towards the Lodge.

Catherine was gone. The house was the same, the walls of it still dull white, the roof still on. Nothing happened when he watched it, no one rapped his knuckles, no voice boomed down to keep his eyes to himself. He moved from around the counter and stood by the screen door to see it better.

It was just another house. There was nothing special about it, nothing unique that made it unlike any other house. He breathed out, and put his hand against the cooling glass of the screen door. He was fine.

Only he needed to sort a few things. He'd entered a home without permission, and waved a gun about that wasn't technically legal for him to own, having let the licence lapse. Maybe he could go down and talk to them, smooth things out. But, they'd have their wits about them now, without the drink in them, and if they asked him questions, about why he thought they were burglars, or why he'd come down and brought the gun without just phoning someone, they might get suspicious. And he wasn't a man suited to lies.

He also didn't want to see them or face them again. He didn't want to be reminded of the fear he'd seen in them. He wanted no more material that could be reworked into dreams and nightmares and rolling thoughts. Plus, the girl, Catherine, was Billy and Mona's granddaughter, and he wanted no reminder of them, he didn't want to see their faces in hers.

If he couldn't confront them, then he'd just have to tell someone else. He'd spread the news before they could. Go into the village and tell his side first. It was usual for him to go into town on Saturdays anyway, to the Riverside Hotel for his weekly drink. The thought of more booze churned horribly in him now, his stomach iffy. It was not often he took to drinking two nights in a row, but it was needed. No one seemed to be moving inside the house, though the lights were still on. He turned away, and went to the cupboard for a teacup. He'd wait a few hours, then he'd dress and walk out to the Riverside.

JJ

He thought all hell would break loose when DanDan came down. He was getting stuck into a rasher sandwich when he heard the stamp of his feet on the stairs. DanDan was taking it slowly, announcing his arrival, the steepness of the steps making each footfall heavier.

DUSH, DUSH.

Steph was drying her hair by the TV. Cath had her feet up on the table, squeezing at a sting in her hand.

DUSH, DUSH, DUSH.

Down came DanDan, the *brrrrriiiiiiiiizzzzzhhhh* of the hair-dryer meaning Steph couldn't hear. Her hair was flying out behind her like she was in a shampoo ad. Trying to drown out the noise of her shame in Merc probably.

DUSH, DUSH, DUSH, DUSH, DUSH.

And he was down, his hair damp, a wet stain on the front of his T-shirt where he'd not towelled properly.

Cath squeezed her hand like she'd discovered an infection in it and was trying to force out all the poison. She was totally focused on it, squeezing till it went red, and then a bit blue. JJ chewed his sandwich.

—Howdy.

DanDan looked a little bit stunned. JJ winked at him.

—HOWDY, I said.

DanDan nodded at JJ.

—Howiya.

DanDan looked about the room, like he was seeing it fresh for the first time. There was a certain glow off him. He was wearing the same clothes as the night before. The dirtbag.

He might've had a bit more tact around Cath, who finally turned and looked up at him, square in the eye.

—Hey.

Then she went back to her hand.

Steph's hairdryer was still going. *BRRRRRRIIIIIZZZZZZZ-HHHHHHHH.*

JJ shouted over to her.

—STEPH.

She cut it out and once it died down the room felt deathly quiet. Steph spoke up.

—Hey, DanDan.

—Hey.

—Hungry?

—Ha?

—There's rashers there, if JJ hasn't eaten all of them.

—I haven't eaten all of them.

—Then there's rashers there anyway.

—Cheers, Steph.

—Sleep well?

Steph let it echo in the room. Ha! The bitch! He didn't know anyone else who'd have the balls to say something like that. Sleep well. Ha! DanDan spoke in a breezy tone.

—Yeah, grand. I might just get some cereal.

—There should be milk there.

—Cheers.

She was a mad yoke. Mental.

JJ needed a bit of action. This kind of languid lounging didn't suit him. The day was beginning to stir up in him. It was already past one o'clock. They'd all slept in. Well, almost all of them. DanDan and Lucy might not have slept much.

Cath squeaked as she gave up squeezing her hand.

—You okay, Cath, your hand?

—Yeah, it's fine. Was just gardening earlier.

—Where?

—The herb garden.

—Oh, okay.

Shiiiiiiittttt, did she know he'd been pissing in it?

DanDan stomped through into the kitchen, and Steph made a noise. Kind of a *chizzk* sort of a noise, like, 'check out the scandal'. Cath tsked, so JJ baaaaed like a sheep. Just to fill it out.

The air in the house had turned sour. Everyone was fresh and washed, in cold water no less, and he had twice the normal amount of Lynx on, but there was something dirty and unclean about the whole thing. No one had mentioned Merc yet.

They probably needed to mention Merc.

Were there any Red Bulls left? He leaned back in his chair. There was a can in the window alcove behind him. If he leaned back on his chair, on the back legs juuuuuust enough he could reach it.

He tilted back, his arm stretched out behind him, his eyes rolling back with his head looking out over the back of the chair. His hand was getting there, just a little farther, but he'd need to tilt the chair more. Everything in the balance, he was reaching the tipping point, he could go for gold or go home. Cath caught him doing it.

—JJ, no.

—I'll get there. I'll get it.

—You've had too many Red Bulls regardless, your heart is liable to give out.

—I'm gonna make it.

He hooked his foot around the side of the table leg to give him a bit of stability. He could feel his whole internal balancing mechanism going wild as he tilted farther and farther back, almost there, almost there. Then. Crack.

—FUCK.

In a single tilt too far he knew he was fucked. The chair leg slid on the tile. His steadying foot on the leg of the table wasn't able to hook him back in time, and the chair collapsed under him.

His head bounced off the tile.

Pain. Pain. Pain. Ahhh. His elbow smashed the tile as well. He lay there holding himself.

—Oh, my elbow. My elbow. Shit, shit, shit.

A numbness shivered through him that he knew came before pain; he needed to move around quickly before it started hurting, but no, no it was too late, it was coming up.

—Aaaahh.

He groaned to himself before the very air he breathed was filled with squawks from Steph.

—AHHH, AHHH, AHH, AHH, AHH!

She was bent over herself, her chest jagging back and forth. He'd never heard her laugh like that before. She looked ugly when she laughed. Her mouth was screwed up and twisted around her face and teeth, completely asymmetrical. Maybe that was why she didn't laugh usually. And the noise of it, like a donkey.

—HEEEE HAW. HEEE HAW. HEE HEE HEE HEE! HEEEEEE HAAAWWW.

Christ almighty. Before long there was another sound – Cath, who was shrieking at him.

—HA HA HA HA HA HA HA HA.

And his elbow, Christ his elbow. The pain started exploding out of him in waves.

—Ah, shit. Shit, my elbow. Christ. Christ.

The two of them laughing at him. He rolled off the floor and got to his feet.

—Yeah, yeah, laugh it off.

—HA HA HA HA HA HA.

—HEEE HAWWWW, HEEE HAWWW.

—HA HA HA HA HA, AHA.

—HEE HEE HEEEEE HEE HEE HEE HEEEE HAWWWW.

DanDan shot his head back in from the kitchen.

—What's going on?

Steph was still laughing but Cath calmed herself quickly.

—Nothing. JJ fell.

—Okay.

DanDan looked around expectantly, and . . . nothing. He looked bewildered, then he smiled, a big white grin spread over his face. Holy shit, JJ hadn't seen him smile in so long. Well done,

DanDan. He'd sucked the energy from the room, though. Cath went back to squeezing her hand, and Steph floated out her hair in her hands.

Cath looked miserable, sitting hunched in her chair. When had that happened? When was Cath morose and DanDan cheerful? It was as if DanDan had passed on his sadness to Cath like a relay baton.

JJ grabbed the can of Red Bull. Enough of that kind of business now. He righted the chair and sat back down.

—Right, you've all had your giggles, we can move on.

DanDan went back into the kitchen and Steph wiped her eyes. Why had she taken so much pleasure from that? Was she not concerned about him, his health, his head, his elbow?

Cath looked over at him. There was a determination in her eyes.

—JJ?

—Yah.

—Can we take pills later?

—Serious?

That wasn't like her now, bringing that up. Was she upset, or bored? He'd always suspected the DanDan thing, but he just used to enjoy teasing her like the rest of them. Same as he enjoyed teasing DanDan about it. But now with Lucy, it seemed like that would stop, and she'd be glad of it. She didn't seem glad.

Steph added her little contribution.

—Oh JJ, trying to take advantage of poor Cath, are we?

—What? She asked me.

—Oh right. Sure. Sure, you sly dog.

—JJ, can we take them later?

—Yeah, of course.

—That's right, get her nice and high so you can have your wicked way with her.

—I'd like to take them.

—Fine, okay then. We'll do it.

—Ho!

155

—Steph, don't even act like you're not joining in.

—Oh, of course I am.

—Well, thanks for asking politely.

—Ah, get off the high horse, you've been looking for this for a while.

—I've an idea.

—Now, Cath has an idea.

—She does.

—Tell him, Cath.

—Can we take them and go swimming later?

—Well yeah, I s'pose.

—Now look at you, JJ, see her there, trying to get you skinny-dipping. Oh, I see what's going on now, I see what's happening between you two.

—Feck off, Steph.

—Calm down, only making fun.

—You up for it, so?

—Yeah, I s'pose.

—Are you able to take pills and then swim?

—No rules against it.

—There wouldn't be a chance of drowning or anything?

—You'd have to be pretty stupid to do that.

—Kay.

—We'll do it then.

—Alright.

—Steph?

—Fuck it, sure, why not. Last night.

—We'll walk in to Carrig. Have a few pints, then later take a pill and go swimming.

—Look at Cath getting all adventurous. You're leading us down a dark and lonely path to drug addiction and desolation, Miz Blake.

—Miz Rourke-Blake, if we're being formal.

—Nah. Fuck double barrels.

—I guess I'm just bored.

—Same, I'm getting a bit stir crazy as well. JJ?

—Yeah, plan.
—Right, fuck it.
—One thing, though.
—JJ has a point of order.
—We need to talk about Merc.
—Fine. Get Lucy down, we'll have a go of it.

Lucy

She stayed a while in the bedroom before coming down. She did her make-up, not too much, she wasn't dressing up for him, but she was looking well all the same. When she came down the stairs, Cath was standing at the bottom. She barely even looked at Lucy.

—Hey. We're just having a chat, if you could sit down.

She saw the rest of them then sitting around the table, all looking at her. DanDan glancing over, JJ with a little smile in the corner, and Steph looking bored as always. Her stomach gave a twirl. Why were they sitting there like she was going to the principal's office? She tried to look calm.

—Okay.

She sat down beside JJ. What were they going to say to her? Was it about her and DanDan? It must be, couldn't be anything else. Had she said something bad the night before? Had she insulted anyone? She remembered the noises she'd made with DanDan. They'd all heard her. JJ spoke first.

—So, Merc has gone.

What? Was that it? Sure, that was hardly a big deal.

—Where's he gone?

—He's gone home. Took off this morning. All his stuff is gone.

—Christ, really?

—And he made a point to wreck all his cans before he left so we couldn't have any.

—You serious?

—Yeah, he smashed them all against the back wall.

—Why would he do that?

—Cos he's a prick.

Cath interjected.

—JJ.

—What? He is. He had a fucking hissy fit and then he took it out on us.

—He was embarrassed.

—He took it out on you.

—No, he didn't.

—He did. He shouted at you.

DanDan caught Lucy's eye and did something with his eyebrows. An 'I'm sorry, Lucy' look, maybe. He did look sorry. Maybe he hadn't been so bad after all. Maybe it could still work out, if she just made sure not to give in too quick to him.

Cath started again.

—Well, anyway, he's gone. So, I dunno. We could call him, ask him to come back, or just let him go.

—Let him go.

—JJ.

—No, he made his decision, okay. He did. So we leave him go. He's a stubborn fella. He wouldn't come back even if we asked him. I'm not saying exile him or anything. Just, we can make it up when we get back.

—What does everyone else think? Steph?

—Why you asking me?

—DanDan?

—Don't care.

—Just like that? We leave him go?

Cath let her eyes settle on Lucy. Why was this Lucy's business? She hadn't soaked him, she hadn't kicked him or stamped on him. Lucy shrugged.

Cath sighed.

—Well, okay then. We'll leave it. I do think we should get out of the house, though. You know?

Lucy nodded fiercely.

—That's a plan, Cath. Get out, have a laugh.

They all nodded or shrugged around the table, DanDan keeping his opinion to himself. Good. Let him hold his peace. Lucy wanted to get out of the house. Get rid of DanDan. Go out and meet some people, go out and see the world, get chatted up. She'd had enough of this small room, of these people.

Steph

Her and Cath sat drinking tea in silence. Cath had barely said a word all day, except to ask JJ about taking pills. Cath was not a risk-taker. If she was talking about pills, then she was definitely, definitely in a state. Poor fucking woman. She needed distraction then. And what better form than in JJ.

Steph knew the best way of going about it, how to weave the beginnings of love in someone's mind. It disturbed her how she might know this. But it just made sense to her. Nudge them along.

She just needed to make things VERY obvious to JJ, make insinuations he couldn't possibly miss. And then say nothing about it to Cath. Let her wonder what was going on. It felt weird, but she just knew that's how it would work. A female friend of Ferg's had done it to her on the night they first kissed. The sly bitch.

It was in their best interests. JJ was a good fella. And Cath deserved to be happy. She shouted out for JJ. He was somewhere in the house.

—Hey, JJ!

His voice floated in from somewhere.

—Yeah?

—Give Cath a hand with the washing-up.

—Sure thing.

Cath looked at her, and spoke softly at her.

—What are you doing?

—What? Nothing. I don't fancy helping you is all.

Cath frowned at her and drained her tea. JJ swept in and started to grab the plates up, looking at Cath, smiling. Too fucking easy.

JJ

He smoked the afternoon away. He was giving himself some time, just for his thoughts, today. He'd earned it after being good, doing the washing-up. He'd chatted to Cath, made her laugh. They were just silly jokes at the sink, but it'd felt like they were coming close together, like there was something there between them.

There was a pressure looming in the day and night ahead. Ever since Malachy had come in and threatened them, he'd been feeling a curious pull on him. A man with a gun, an actual gun, had burst in, and then like in those apocalypse films where the end of the world is announced and people run about screaming and couples fall into each other's arms and ride in a closet, DanDan and Lucy had gone at it. They'd seized life and sex first chance they got. Merc had run for his life, he'd wanted to live. Cath had dealt with the threat in front of her, showed her quality.

What had he done? Nothing. He hadn't been particularly scared, or distraught that his life would end. He was just shocked by the sight of the gun. Once Malachy left and they'd found Merc, he'd poured himself a drink and had a smoke. He'd gone straight fucking back to being how he was, how he'd always been.

This new line of thought troubled him. Made him anxious. What if he had nothing worth saving?

Earlier that morning, he'd laughed to himself when Merc left. He'd looked forward to when he could go back to Dublin and see Merc in the street, or in a bar, and look at him. Without flinching or showing regret, look right at him and nod hello, or even wave and shout at him and Merc would have to look away. And JJ would just stand there and smile.

He didn't feel like smiling now, though. With all the dust in the room, his head hazy and his nose filling, he felt a darkness creeping into his mind. His dark days were coming. He knew they were. Maybe this was the hangover he was owed, the one he thought he'd magically avoided. Maybe he was on the brink of coming down, wallowing in his own murky, silly thoughts. Maybe it was just the truth. He was an arsehole. Making himself feel better by what, by imagining his friend was worse off than him. He had acted just as childish. He'd been just as petty. He'd wanted Merc to say he was wrong, to apologise for scratching him, for getting competitive about Steph. For trying to intimidate him with his body, for slagging him in front of everyone.

He'd wanted to humiliate Merc, shame him even further. What kind of person did that make him? What bullshit was that? His friend had left the house and gone home alone. He'd let him. But now, he was alone as well. And outside of Merc, who was he friends with? What had he done with himself besides mess around with Merc for the last year? He'd just spent time alone. He'd been alone for a long, long time.

He knew it was the truth. It hurt but it was true. He thought of making amends. He'd ask Cath later, maybe. Across the way, she was sitting by the table scrolling through her texts, holding her head up on her fingertips. She was pretty. Very pretty.

Her hand brushed through her hair. There she was. All pretty.

Lucy

She was holding strong, not talking to DanDan. They'd moved off to various places around the house, mixed between drinking and not drinking, talking and not talking. Where did she fit in the whole thing?

JJ was lying on his back across the wooden dining table, looking up at the ceiling and trying to smoke a fag out of the corner of his mouth without dropping ash into his face. Lucy tried to play a hand of gin around his body with Steph and Cath, though none of them seemed very into it, not least when JJ kept knocking over their deck of cards with his shoe.

—JJ, stop.

—I am booored.

—Yeah well, saying it isn't helping.

—What will help, Cath?

—Yeah, JJ, what way could you help Cath?

Cath seemed bewildered. And Lucy was confused. Were they just messing? But JJ was kind of being overly affectionate with Cath.

—Will we go soon?

—Soon enough.

Was their centre JJ then? Considering they were all literally playing around his body, around this solid mass on their table? Lucy would have thought at one point that Merc was the centre of the group, somehow, maybe just because he was the best-looking of them, except for Steph possibly, and you automatically looked to people like that as central to the group. But here they were, playing away, existing away, and Merc gone. Maybe Lucy was the centre?

—Here, it's getting dark, can we head in to Carrig soon?

—Yeah, why not. Start getting ready, so.

Merc

He stood alone in his kitchen with his bag. His folks were away. His mam had left him a note about going to a spa. Merc put his bag down in the middle of the floor. The kitchen was quiet and it was dark outside. All the other lights in the house were off. His clothes smelled like beer. His hair was greasy.

He'd been travelling all day.

He was alone and wondered how. He could barely even trace his reasoning. A black rage had come over him and he'd found himself gone. He thought of all their arguments through the night and how he'd acted. Maybe he'd walked away too soon, too easily.

He kicked the fridge.

JJ

The afternoon had passed by quickly and the darkness had come down on them as if from nowhere. Between half cleaning the house and making lunch, and various people ignoring each other wandering about the living room and the garden, and then him trying to talk to Cath while the girls got ready, they'd fucked the whole day away. Eventually, they'd started on the walk to Carrig, taking some drinks with them for the road.

Cath led the way with JJ beside her. She guided them on the road to Carrig marked by stone walls. There were long gaps between street lights and often the only light came from a mist-covered moon and DanDan's small torch as he walked behind them. JJ enjoyed being at the front of the group with Cath, like he was setting not just the pace, but the tone for the night. He decided that that tone was going to be dirty. It was time for him to get the shift. He hadn't thought so much about it before that day, but the night before he'd sat downstairs listening to DanDan and Lucy in bed, giggling and moaning, and he'd felt a stir in him.

He could feel heat in him, in his loins, begging, commanding him: fuck something. He knew it was vulgar. He knew it was against his more civil nature, but it was there and it spoke, implored him, in a dark red voice, Fuck. It didn't say embrace or be intimate. It didn't whisper love or kiss. It said Fuck. He looked at Cath walking beside him. Still pretty.

His ma had always told him he'd end up with someone pretty. She'd insisted on it. More than any of the rest of his brothers. She'd always come in to see him when he was going to sleep, and tell him, you'll get a beautiful girlfriend one day. And he'd sleep well. The last time she spoke to him, having already said everything she needed to say over weeks and months of hospital visits, about love and growing up kind, she gave him her final advice in slow, weak breaths. She told him he had a brain and a heart, and she didn't want him to stay at home and let them go to waste. He had to go away, she said, and never stop learning. He had to take chances and love as many people as he could. Then she shouted it to him, for all the ward to hear, way too loud because she had been saving her strength for it, so he could hear her. She roared.

—The women will eat you alive!

He laughed and she smiled at him. It was just like her. He could see she'd thought it through, that she wanted him to remember her properly, as she was: fun. She laughed and fell back on the pillow, closing her eyes. He held her hand till she fell asleep, and she didn't speak to him ever again.

Cath bumped into him on the uneven road, steadying herself by grabbing his arm.

—How you feeling, Cath?

—Good, yeah. Up for a party.

—It's a lovely night.

—Yeah.

—The stars and that.

—It's why I like coming out here. With my cousins, anyway. My mam never comes out. Did you bring the pills?

—Yeah, of course. Bit early to take them, though.

—I know, I was just checking.

—Later though, yeah?

Lucy came up and walked with them. DanDan and Steph trailed behind. Lucy's voice was confident, all sing-song.

—This night, this night is gonna be massive, Cath. Yeah? JJ, do you have the pills?

—Yeah, Christ, I have them. Stop talking to me like I'm a dealer or something.

—Grand, just checking. Cath? We going to get the shift tonight?

Cath looked at the ground, but responded quickly.

—Yeah, we'll see. See what happens.

—We'll get you the shift.

—We'll see, we'll see.

A silence settled over them. They kept walking into the darkness. They listened to the sound of their feet on the worn and muddied road, the scraping of it, the uneven tread they were making. JJ went to say something to Cath; it seemed to him as if something was developing there, so he should be interesting, entertaining. He opened his mouth to speak, then . . . Nothing.

He couldn't.

He couldn't pull anything out of his head. All current events fell out of his mind; any kind of possible context of that weekend went blank.

Cath was quiet beside him. Had he any stories?

Fuck, he had no stories.

He could talk to her about Dublin maybe, people he'd met there, funny things that happened to him. But then he thought, fuck, all he'd done in Dublin was walk. Smoke and walk and play games online and fuck about.

He thought of how he'd spent the last year. He'd done nothing. He'd used his time for fuck all. He'd barely seen his old friends, and not made any new ones. He'd stopped going to gigs, only smoked his time away at home or fucked about online. He'd not watched any films or helped out at home or talked to his family. He thought of his ma, and what she'd said to him. It was a lie. If it wasn't a lie when she'd said it to him it was a lie now, he'd made it into a lie. He'd let his mind go dull, his heart fucking empty. What good had he done for anyone?

The black night stretched out above him and in front of him and beyond him, and he felt regret. What a waste. What a complete fucking waste.

He felt it wrench in him, and suddenly he wanted to sit down in the road and scream. Lucy and Cath were still walking beside him. He should speak, but he was afraid he might cry.

—My shoes are getting fucking muddy.

169

The minute he spoke he had to stifle a wet cry from coming up in his throat. It was dark so they couldn't see his eyes steaming up and his nose starting to run. Lucy nodded along.

—It's muddy alright.

A sigh escaped him but he gasped to disguise it. His breath went out ahead of him in great unwinding fogs. He felt a can of cider pressing up against his ribs inside his jacket. He took it out and cracked it open. It foamed and he drank it, long and warm, until it melted down his throat and the rim clinked against his teeth, and he squeezed his eyes against the tears that were coming.

Lucy looked over once then turned to Cath.

—But yeah, shift tonight, Cath? Reckon I might try to get one myself.

—Yeah?

—Yeah.

—We'll try the two of us, so.

JJ slowed down, looking at his shoes.

—Go on ahead, I've to fix my shoe.

Lucy forcibly linked arms with Cath and they walked ahead. JJ slowed down. He stopped in the road. DanDan and Steph were coming up behind him. He kneeled down and pretended to look at his shoe. As they passed him Steph asked him was he alright.

—Grand, just fixing this fucking thing. Go on, I'll catch up.

JJ let them walk around the corner and out of sight. He stood, his shoe firmly tied, and his fingers covered with mud. He'd no idea what was going on. He pinched himself on the middle of his arm. Nothing. He looked to the sky and into the hedges, and turned around looking up and let the stars swoop around him.

—Fuck.

Steph

They were on a dirty, unlit road cut into the valley. On one side was the rock face of the hill, cool, hard, green-grey rock with overhanging ivy. On the other side there was a sharp drop where the hill continued down, though the tops of dark trees rose up above the road. Every so often a gap in the trees gave a view of the lake and the valley all around, but mostly the rock face and the trees just kept them trapped in, wrapped up in darkness.

She fell into step with DanDan. As the house lost itself from view around the curve of the road, she started to pull the heads off various flowers as they passed the hedgerows behind the stone walls. She grabbed the middle of a stem between two fingers and pulled up, the petals coming off into her palm. Then she threw the petals ahead of her. Gave her something to do while DanDan looked at his feet.

Eventually, he cleared his throat and spoke at her.

—Right then, what do you think?

—About what?

—About tonight.

—Nothing, really. Go in, get pissed, enjoy ourselves, I dunno.

—Cool, yeah. Yeah, yeah.

She went quiet again, but DanDan pressed ahead talking.

—Okay, so, would you rather . . .

Steph knew forced conversation when it was shoved in her face.

—Are we playing this?

—Yeah, we are.

—Fine.

Ahead of them, JJ was walking awkwardly beside Lucy and Cath. Steph should be up there, trying to sow seeds of attraction between the two of them, scraping their faces together like flint to see if any sparks flew.

She sighed and slowed her pace. Every minute she spent with DanDan, alone like this, she could feel herself liking him less. There was something oily about him now, at this hour of the evening. She knew it was to do with Cath. Cath was hurting, and though Steph knew it was none of her business, and that Cath would probably defend him to the death, she knew it was DanDan's fault. It wasn't just that DanDan had shifted Lucy; it felt like something had happened between Cath and DanDan that Cath wasn't saying. And judging by the awkward, cloying remarks from DanDan, she was probably right. He started off.

—Right, would you rather . . . Vagina for a nose or nose for a vagina?

—Nose for vagina.

—Shit out your nose or piss out your mouth.

—Ew, DanDan, no.

—Answer it.

—Jesus. Piss out my mouth.

—Okay, would you rather . . . Live the rest of your life alone on an island, or . . . live happily for ten years and die.

—Alone on an island.

—Really, Steph?

—Yeah. Why not?

—It's just, Christ, really?

—Yeah. I mean. I don't believe in the afterlife or whatever, so live as long as I can.

—But the quality of it.

—I like my own company.

—Yeah, but come on. You need other people, don't you?

—Not so much.

—I don't believe you.

—Believe it or not, it's true.

172

He huffed. What she really meant was, she didn't need him, the stupid grinning face on him. Whatever way she was looking at him seemed to register with him, and a slight frown came onto his face.

—Fergus said you were like that, alright.

—What? Fergus like my Fergus, my ex Fergus?

—Sorry, that's none of my business really.

That remark, it was fucking planned. He'd meant to say it. Like he'd deliberately pulled it out of the back of his throat and placed it slimy on a plate in front of her.

—He said what?

—Forget about it. Shouldn't have said that.

—Shut the fuck up. What did he say?

—Ah, he just said you don't really need other people.

—When did he say this?

She looked intently at the side of DanDan's head. It was as if she was seeing him fresh for the first time. He was a fucking villain. He walked away from her, at an angle, towards the mucky side of the road, along the drop down in the trees. She followed. The drop at the side of the road loomed as she came closer. Imagine falling down that. Imagine pushing this greasy fuck off.

—A while ago.

—How long a while?

—Few months or so.

—Hang on, like after we broke up?

—Yeah.

—Why were you talking to him?

—Well, y'know, we still kind of hang around a bit.

—*What?*

She glared at him and he shied away. She was ready to hit him, ready to drag her nails down his face if he didn't give up this stupid fucking game and stop messing with her. DanDan pretended to play with the sleeve of his jacket.

—Yeah, I dunno. After the two of you broke up he asked me to go for a pint. I felt sorry for him, so I met up with him. Now we just kind of go out every so often. It's not a big deal.

173

She stopped in the middle of the road. He walked a few paces ahead then stopped as well. She thought she might actually deck him.

—Why didn't you tell me if it wasn't such a big deal?

—There was no point, like. Anyway, it was you broke up with him.

—Yeah, but I'm your mate, DanDan, not him. You don't just go around behind my back.

—Hang on now, you don't own mates, Steph. I'm free to do what I want.

—I know you are, but you thought, you obviously thought that I wouldn't like it so . . .

She switched argument mid-sentence.

—But, hang on . . . What did he say about me?

—I'm sorry I've been meeting up with him, Steph, but I really shouldn't tell you what he said.

—Fuck off, what did he say? Tell me.

—Ah, we were just having a pint, you know, and he kind of said that you didn't really need other people. He said you were happiest not needing anyone. It wasn't that big a deal, Steph. I'm sorry.

—Word for word, what did he say? . . . What did he say, DanDan?

—He said you pretend you're different but really you just don't give a fuck about anyone.

She started walking again. She just wanted to be away from him.

—Fuck this.

—Sorry.

—Fuck it.

She didn't want to spend another minute with him. She needed to think. DanDan called after her.

—I was only messing.

She strode away quickly to catch up to Cath and Lucy, and put on a brave face. Couldn't let anyone see DanDan had gotten to her.

She wasn't happiest not needing people. She just wasn't needy – had that been what Fergus meant? Had that been what he actually said to DanDan, or had DanDan twisted the words? She could sense him watching her, his oily gaze on the back of her head, and it felt like she'd discovered a snake, a little reptile, had been living with them all this time.

Malachy

He squeezed and rolled his toes inside his boots. The Riverside Hotel was a dark, warm place. The barmaid, Sheila, always spotted him coming and had a whiskey ready and the paper fresh.

There was a fire, still, in the hotel bar, and it gave him warmth in the legs that had forced themselves down the main road. The five miles he was used to walking, every Saturday evening, for his whiskey and his paper.

Sheila scrubbed a clean bar with a dry washcloth. The lights above the mirrored bar behind her filtered through the dusty green bottles and the unused bottles of novelty shots, Mickey Finn's with congealed red about the caps, Jägermeister with purple crust. Thirty years at least she'd worked behind that bar. He wondered how she stuck it.

Johnny Redmond sat up at the end of the bar, his elbows on the edge and his head drooping between his arms, humming softly to himself.

Malachy let him hum away. Better than having to talk to him. He'd lost his wife and taken it poorly. Gone to the drink, humming and weeping himself to his grave. If Malachy ever tried to talk with him he'd just slur about times gone past, about things that leave you forever and you can't get back.

Malachy flicked his paper up and felt the sound of it fade in the empty bar. The place had been a lot livelier a few years before, just like everything else. They'd had trad sessions at the corner tables, the local musicians playing with any visiting ones, the drunks at the bar shouting at each other and waving bits of betting slips and talking nonsense about oil prices and world politics, the

176

younger crowd sitting in the snugs in their own private worlds. Sometimes there'd be a fight, or the local sergeant would have to bust the place for serving after hours, and they'd go piling out the back door, jumping walls and disappearing into the night, only to continue on to someone's house or down the Rockadoon Shore where they'd light a fire and shout at each other some more. But that was over now. The young had moved away to Sligo, or Galway, many to Dublin, for work or adventure. The old farmers didn't make the effort. The drink-driving ban forced them to choose between a five-mile walk or a night alone. It was only the likes of Johnny now stuck in the town as it filled with ghosts and the streets chipped themselves down under tractors and ruined the axles of everything else.

The walk in was getting harder. His legs were slower on the hills, though he felt more and more urgently the desire to come in, just to be around people. Sheila was absentmindedly smoothing the bar with one hand, flipping the pages of a newspaper with the other. She was his best option of spreading what happened. He could tell her what had occurred while still casting himself in a good light, beyond suspicion, and as she was the source of much information in the town, his version of the story would be spread, not any other.

He shook himself, his whiskey finished, and went up to Sheila. She shut the paper for him and Johnny mumbled something, his head resting in his arms folded on the bar. Malachy pushed his glass across the bar at Sheila.

—Double.

She clicked the tumbler up into the optic twice. The whiskey streamed out, measured pure and precise. She put it down and he gave her a tenner. She knew to keep the change. She turned back from the till and he spoke up.

—There's people staying up at the Lodge.

—Oh yeah?

—Group of them. Young folk.

—When did they get in?

—Just yesterday.

—Fair enough.

She went to turn away. She wasn't biting. Normally she had her nose in everything, so he pushed a bit.

—They gave me a bit of a scare, though.

That caught her attention. She turned back to him.

—What do you mean by that now?

—They didn't tell me they were coming. I saw lights in the house and went down. Thought someone was robbing the place.

Sheila leaned in over the counter at him.

—Did you take the gun?

—I had it with me now, but I didn't point it.

He coughed and sipped at his whiskey, though he could see her looking at him as he drank. He left her waiting a few moments. He looked into his whiskey and shrugged. She kept staring at him, using her soft voice.

—They didn't do anything stupid?

—No. No, it was fine. They weren't expecting me, though, I can tell you.

—Gave them a fright?

—I did, I think. Didn't mean to.

She raised herself back from over the bar and sighed.

—They should know better. Did Tara Rourke not tell them to ring?

—Whether she did or not, they didn't call.

Malachy sipped his whiskey. Sheila shook her head.

—I'd say they got a shock all the same.

—I think so.

—Well, you've nothing to be feeling sorry about. You were good now, to look after the place for them. The least they can be doing is letting you know.

He waved his hand, dismissed the thought.

—It's done. They know I'm here now, sure.

—And they'll know next time.

—Let's hope.

—Another?

—Have one yourself.

178

—Cheers.

She poured them both a small one, and they drank. She sipped and looked at him.

—Do you think they'll come in to town?

—Don't know.

—They'll go to Sligo maybe.

— I don't know, they seemed pretty well stocked up there anyway. They'd enough to last them. But they might want to get out of the house.

—We could do with the business.

—Couldn't ye all.

—We won't be the first to shut down, now. But we won't be the last either.

—Ah.

—Look at the place, I mean. If it wasn't for the fishing we'd be closed already.

She finished her whiskey and sighed. She started to scrub the counter again. Johnny jerked up from his arms, drank his pint, and hummed slowly to himself.

Malachy had done what he came to do. He nodded at Sheila.

—I'm going to head on.

—Good luck.

He turned his back on her and walked for the door, Johnny droning drunkenly as he left.

He could feel the whiskey burning, putting the heat into him. His job done, he almost looked forward to the walk home now.

He stepped out and it was a lovely spring night. The mist was down and the street lamps glowed through, setting the wet street in a hazy gloom. There were no cars parked on the road and as he walked he tried to spot anything that might give away the time, the year it was. He could find very little, only the ad for the mobile phone shop, but everything else, the dirty, cracked road, chipped concrete, the peeling shop fronts and the one pub down by the very end of the street, could be from any time in the last sixty years. It brought the street back, as quiet and still as it was, to a time he remembered from many years past. He imagined then that he'd stepped into the past, that he was himself, only decades younger, and he tried to think how he had walked then.

He'd walked quicker, almost certainly, and he'd been impatient with the road, for not ending, for always having a new curve to it, another bend he'd forgotten about that would add on another few minutes to his journey, keeping him from wherever he was going, to friends so they could drink in the fields behind the hedges, or to Elaine's house, where he waited outside on the cold road for her to emerge, tucking her scarf in under her collar.

It was only ever with her, out walking with her, that he could let some of his mind go. No one else had ever seen inside his mind, into his head, but perhaps they sensed it, the weight of the moods and dark thoughts he suffered, and that was one reason he'd been left by himself. Malachy had always assumed he'd been left alone by a swaying mix of choice and circumstance. Choice, the first time he stayed, when Elaine wanted him to go.

She'd kept mentioning Dublin after their swim together, pushing for it, asking him when was best to go, and talking about where they would live, and what they would do for work, and he'd listened to her and mumbled replies she couldn't make out, before saying he'd to get back to the farm. After a while he just stopped calling to her door.

He'd ignored her, avoided her until she called out to him one day, hammered on his door, and waited till he came down. She'd stood outside in the wind with her hands pulling her coat tight around her.

He'd stood in the doorframe, neither in nor out, and watched the wind catching stray strands of her hair and blowing them about her face, and said nothing. She looked him right in the eye.

—Are you coming?

In truth, he was terrified. Malachy had never been with anyone before. He'd not had that experience. It'd just been him and his father the whole time, away from the town, just their house and the Lodge out by themselves, and no real reason to go into town. And then all of a sudden he was being dragged around by this young thing. They'd not made love by the lake, and when that hadn't happened, the prospect of it ever happening again terrified him. She didn't want to wait, she said, till marriage. She just wanted to wait till Dublin. Why wouldn't she want to wait altogether, till marriage? What was wrong with waiting? And wait for what, to have sex, or to wait for what came from it? He'd never thought about children before, never thought he might have one of his own; all he knew was little Tara Rourke screaming inside the Lodge while Mona cried. Was that what Elaine wanted to wait for? What if she did that sort of thing all the time? What if she promised that to everyone?

And the way she'd taken her dress off before going swimming, leading him, it was as if she'd done it before, with someone else maybe. What if she'd been with someone else? Why else would she want to leave? Why else would she swim with him, kiss him, push her body against his? She wanted to take him away from his home, away from his father and from everything he'd known all his life. The farm, the lake, the Lodge. It was all he knew. She wanted him to throw it all away, for a life in a city she'd never been to and hadn't planned for.

He couldn't. He couldn't.

—I can't.

She stood square in front of him. She scraped the ground with her plain shoes, and pulled her coat tight again as she scanned his face, her eyes filling.

—I won't see you again.

And he paused a moment, before speaking.

—You won't.

She dropped her head and stood in front of him, silent. She took one last look at him before she walked away down the little hill, past the Lodge, her small leather shoes tapping and scratching on the gravel. She didn't look back, her braided hair swinging cruelly behind her, almost waving goodbye, and he thought he could just shout at her and tell her to come back, shout her name once, Elaine, that's all it would take, just once, Elaine, but each step she took away made it harder to speak, and a lump was torn out of his heart, not out of the fringes but out of the very centre of it, tendrils and tissue ripped out of him, and he wondered if then he'd cried, but he couldn't remember. He'd just shut the door.

Malachy tripped on a pothole and stumbled a step or two forward. His hands were stung with the cold and he realised he hadn't even put his gloves on. He'd been dozing while walking, and had walked on automatic out of the town. He looked to see where he was. He'd walked far down along the road without realising it. He'd covered at least a mile without even once thinking about walking, or about where he was or if he was taking the right path. His body had guided him while his mind ran circles in on itself.

Maybe in a few years he'd get to the stage where he might live his whole life that way. When he left the house he might walk straight to the Riverside, order a drink and chat with Sheila and walk back, without ever once coming out of his own thoughts, and he'd find himself back in front of the fire in his living room, pissed, having left the house for five hours and still not have noticed anything along the way.

He walked the length of the main road, farther and farther into the darkness, leaving the lights of the town behind, until he turned off on the boreen past the Rockadoon Shore. The road black, a car could strike him at any point, and he wondered would he mind. He felt strong in his body, the power of whiskey in him, and he felt that any car that hit him would instead feel itself hit, and he would remain unchanged in the middle of the road.

He heard their voices before he saw them coming around the bend. He'd counted six of them the time before. Only five this time, though, shouting and laughing at each other in the dark. One had a little hand torch barely lighting the road. The beam went this way and that and they were boisterous and loud, though he could make out their shivering through the mist. Malachy walked in the very middle of the road as they approached, and straightened his back, and made his boots stamp so they'd know he was coming.

He tramped towards them, and they went silent as he approached, their shoulders up, hunched. They shrank from him,

182

even though the light was on him, and he could barely make out their forms behind it. He stopped a few metres from them. He couldn't see their faces in the dark, just the outlines of their heads, the shape of their haircuts and jawlines and ears.

The girl, Catherine, stepped forward so he could see her better and spoke.

—Hi.

—Hello.

—It's a cold night.

—It is.

He could barely look at them now, how they were standing around. He could see in their stance that they still feared him, though they tried to seem jovial and neighbourly.

—We were just walking into town.

—Oh right. Mind yourself on the road. It's dark.

—Yeah. Yeah, we will.

They moved to go, and he started to take a step, before the young skinny lad, with the, what was it, a Kildare accent, asked him:

—Any good pubs?

He stopped.

—In town?

—Yeah.

—You might try in at the Tavern. But drop in on Sheila first at the Riverside, she'll sort you out.

—Cheers.

—Good night.

He walked from them, and as they set off he could hear them snicker, trying to suppress laughter. Their voices carried and stayed with him, long after he lost sight of them.

Then he felt the cold. He felt wet in his bones, chills. His arms felt weak and useless, like they were barely holding bones in them at all, and his back ached. He felt suddenly so far from home, and he imagined the walk, the road stretching out before him, all those turns he knew were coming, and his little house seemed so far away. He'd beaten Billy on this road. In the dark by himself. He tried to pick out the hedge he'd hidden in, the little bump of road where he'd tripped Billy's legs and crushed his face.

He stopped in the road, and looked about, and wondered if perhaps the sixth one, the athletic fella, was instead waiting for him somewhere, that that was what they were laughing at, the fact that he was walking into an ambush. They were taking revenge for the Rourke family. For beating Billy. For letting Billy take it out on Mona, and for watching and doing nothing while little Tara biked around in loneliness. It wasn't fear he felt, just tiredness. There was no more fight left in him. The idea of striking someone, of raising his arms and throwing a punch, putting his weight behind it, clawing at someone's face, or wrestling in their arms, was just too much. His limbs felt too weak, and he could barely even think about how tired he was, how fatigued, and wished that someone would just end it. Maybe this was how Billy had felt, why he'd put up no fight. The body he thought could withstand a car just minutes earlier felt exposed and numb, and his nose ran with snot and the back of his neck and his ears were cold, and he wondered if this was his last night on earth would he care.

DanDan

Even though it took them absolutely ages to reach the Riverside Hotel, and his legs were wrecked after it, DanDan was in a great mood. Their little encounter with Malachy along the way had made him giddy. He'd scared the shit out of them, creeping up like that in the dark. It was the last thing they were expecting. But after he walked away DanDan couldn't stop himself from laughing. It hit him so hard he had to bend over and hold his sides it hurt so much. Cath had told him to stop, that Malachy could still hear them, but he couldn't help himself. He'd gasped and giggled to himself all the way to the Riverside.

When they got into the hotel reception, the woman behind the counter almost jumped out of her seat, until they pointed at the sign to the lounge and she parked herself back down, disappointed. The lounge itself was pretty standard. A long, empty bar with some round tables farther back against the wall, and a fire in the far corner. A lot of red velvet and polished wood. The bar lady greeted them when they came in, and Steph went over and grabbed a table by the wall. DanDan went to the bar to order and noticed that no one was in a great mood to follow him. They all took their time arranging their coats around the table before coming over.

He could understand, maybe, why people were angry with him. He'd pissed off Steph. He shouldn't have said that to her about Fergus, shouldn't have told her they still met up, but everyone had been really pissy with him all day, ignoring him and giving him the cold shoulder, barely acknowledging him. He just wanted to get some kind of a reaction out of her. They were all so attentive to him when he was sad, but then, when he finally came round, and was ready to have fun and be merry, they all took off. It was like they only wanted to be around sadness.

They were all pissed off with him but his prospects lay in Lucy. He'd get around her anger. He was sure of it. All he had to do was wait till she got a drink or two in her, till she softened, then just grab her arm maybe and apologise. He didn't want her to feel bad, he didn't, and after all it was just a miscommunication that had changed the day for them.

He introduced himself to Sheila, that was the bar lady's name, and sat up at the bar drinking a pint and talking shit with her. She told him she'd heard they were in, and he said aye alright we are indeed and they made jokes here and there, while the others stayed back and looked at the menus. He was okay by himself there with Sheila.

After a while, they came up and ordered, and Sheila introduced herself and they introduced themselves, though she stopped at Cath, and made a comment about the Rourkes, and Cath said she was one of them.

—Oh right, now. You're in the Lodge?

—Yeah.

—I heard ye'd a bit of a shock.

—Yeah, Malachy came in.

— He was only looking out for it. The place has been burgled a few times over the years.

—Oh God, yeah, oh we know. No, he was very nice, wasn't he?

JJ nodded his head at Cath vigorously

—Yeah, he was sound. Sound fella.

Sheila nodded and served them drinks. DanDan remained sitting up on his barstool as the rest drifted between the bar and their table, taking turns talking with him and Sheila or huddling in around the table by themselves. At one point a family came in and ordered food at a distant table, and they kept to themselves. It was nowhere near as busy as they'd hoped, not exactly chock-a-block, but it was better than back in the house anyway. Everything was going grand, as DanDan got the drinks into him, never leaving his seat, until JJ came up and sat beside him on a stool. JJ rubbed his hands, looking down at the bar.

—How's it going, JJ?

—Grand.

—Cool.

JJ paused a moment, his face down, then he turned to him.

—No, I'm not fucking grand actually. Far from fucking grand.

—What's up?

—I don't know. I've just been thinking.

—Thinking's bad.

—Do you ever feel like you've been lying to yourself, or something?

—Ha?

JJ looked over his shoulder, back at Cath and the other two sitting by themselves at the table, then he turned back and started talking with his voice lowered.

—Like, have you ever found yourself lying to yourself, or avoiding something you already know? That you've avoided something cos you didn't want to deal with it, and then you wake up and you're just standing in this fucking mess you've made for yourself, and all this wasted time, and you've just been this piece of shit underneath.

—It's okay, JJ. I think everyone's pretty much good underneath. You just have to get there.

—But that's exactly what I fucking mean, though. There's all this shit you do that you remove yourself from, because that's not you, that's just you doing bad shit. What if all you do all your life is just try and distract yourself from that one simple fucking fact, that you're a piece of shit, you know? What if you're just a piece of shit?

DanDan sincerely hoped all this was just a bit, that JJ was just riffing. JJ went silent and looked at the bar. But DanDan felt something washing over him again, regardless of JJ's downer. He felt the exact opposite of what JJ was saying. All that awkwardness with Steph before hadn't fazed him, and neither had JJ's weird little speech. He had this new feeling of life and regeneration fresh in him still from earlier.

187

—We're fine, JJ. Look, we're good. Nobody here is a piece of shit, okay?

He could feel energy, a great happiness swimming up inside him, and now he just wanted to go out and do everything all at once. Fucking Brian Keenan all the way.

JJ held his face and spoke into his hands.

—Fuck sake.

—Ah, you're grand.

—Fuck, fuck sake.

—What's up with you?

—Nothing, nothing.

—Well, sure we'll get you some Red Bull. Jägerbombs, isn't it, the ones you're always trying to get us to do?

He called back to the girls at their table. They were leaning into each other, talking quietly.

—Hey! Hey, Jäger? Jäger?

Steph called back.

—Yeah, Jesus. Give us a minute.

He turned back to JJ.

—How about it, man? Jägermeister's your friend tonight.

—I might not be up for a mad one tonight.

—What do you mean, fella? We're going tomorrow. And we haven't even really gone mad yet.

—No, but like, why am I always the one, the one supposed to be going mad?

—What? No one says you're the one.

—Well, it feels like that.

—Sure aren't we going to take pills later? Aren't we?

—Yeah, stop asking me.

—What's up your arse?

—Nothing, I'm saying. Nothing. Don't feel great.

—Well, it's time for fucking Jäger then, isn't it?

He turned around on his stool and called again over to the girls.

—Come on, now! Come on! It's time for shots.

Steph shouted over.

—Okay, for fuck sake. We're coming.

They stood up and joined him and JJ at the bar. Sheila came over to them, nodding. Lucy put herself between him and JJ on their stools. With everyone leaning over the bar looking at the bottles at the back, he brushed up slightly against Lucy. He put his hand in the small of her back, feeling her spine through her top. He thought he felt a slight bit of resistance, her pushing back against his hand, as if to say 'forgiven'. She turned her head to him slightly, almost acknowledging it, then shifted away. He had her.

Lucy

What good did these hotel bars do for anybody? Why did they bother coming to this place? Just because Malachy told them to?

She was with Steph, the two of them left together as JJ and DanDan and Cath sat at the bar talking to the bar lady. Lucy just wanted to talk. Usually she went to Cath because Cath was a good, sympathetic listener, but with Cath and DanDan being such good mates and all, it seemed like there'd be a conflict of interest, especially since she just wanted to shout, to vent about DanDan, though she told herself she wasn't going to do that.

She just needed to tell someone, to let it out. Steph was sitting back on a cushioned red bench in front of a circular table. They were beside the window. A deep mist had come down on the street outside. It made her feel like they were sealed in. Up at the bar, DanDan clapped his hands and downed his pint, while JJ slapped him on the back. She made the first move.

—You know, I should probably tell you . . . I've never really told anyone this . . .

Steph leaned forward to her, her nostrils flared, like she knew she was about to get something juicy out of her.

—Told anyone what?

—That, y'know. I've not much experience, like. Experience with fellas.

—You've shifted plenty of fellas.

—I know, but I've never, you know.

—No . . .

—Like, fully, you know . . .

Steph was silent a moment, and her eyes darted over Lucy's face. Lucy could feel herself being measured up, judged. Steph exhaled, and spoke slowly.

—No, you mean like, never . . .

—No.

—What, like you've never . . .

Steph made a forward bumping motion with her fist. Lucy shook her head.

—Yeah. It's not that bad, is it?

—No, it's just, I'm surprised. You never really mentioned it before.

Lucy could trust Steph, she thought. She'd never blab her secrets, she wouldn't spread it around, would she?

—I was embarrassed, maybe. It bothered me.

—Why would it bother you?

—Cos I'm twenty, for Christ's sake, and shush, sorry, shouting. I'm twenty for fuck sake and I'd never been with anyone.

—Okay, well first, it shouldn't bother you.

—No?

—No, course not. But wait, *had* never been with anyone. Had? Steph's eyes gleamed.

—DanDan?

—Yeah.

Lucy nodded quickly. Steph's face lit up. She slapped her knee.

—HA!

—Shush.

—Sorry. Oh God. That's too good. HA.

—Shush.

—I mean, maybe you could've done better than DanDan.

—What's wrong with DanDan?

Steph paused and drank her whiskey.

—Nothing. Nothing at all.

—Okay, okay. Yeah. But that's not bad, is it, that last night was the first?

—No. It's not like you didn't have the chance before, is it?

—No, I'd plenty of chances.

—Yeah, and why didn't you?

—I dunno, cos they were all manky. I didn't trust them. Or, I dunno. It was less I wanted it to be special, and more like I wasn't sure if they'd be dicks about the whole thing.

—They often are.

—Yeah, that's what I was worried about. It just never felt right.

—Well, fine. So firstly you actually waited till you wanted to. That's far more fucking healthy than what other girls do. The ones who go off into the bushes when they're like fourteen or fifteen with some sleazy fella, because they feel like they should, y'know, or because their friends are pressuring them, and then they come out and they're fucking scarred for life, y'know.

—I suppose.

—So fair fucking play to you, lady. Fair play. You waited till you wanted to and you did it when you wanted to. That takes guts.

—I guess.

—You did want to, didn't you?

—Yeah, I did.

—DanDan wasn't pressuring you or anything?

This was why Lucy liked talking to Steph. Cath wouldn't speak this way with her. She'd never ask Lucy these questions about DanDan. She'd never raise her glass to her, the way Steph just did, for losing her virginity. Cath would have looked at her with concern. She would have put her hand on her arm, looked in her eyes and asked her how she felt and if she needed anything. But Steph was busting in with questions, she was laughing and squawking, giving her own opinions. There was no bullshit with Steph and that's what Lucy loved. Steph leaned in over the table, her fingers curled around her glass of whiskey, and signalled for her to speak. Lucy shrugged her shoulders.

—No, he was pretty good about it actually. I was letting it go where it was going, but he did kinda stop and ask if I was too drunk.

—And were you?

192

—Too drunk?

—Yeah.

—No, I was good. I got a real wake-up with Malachy coming in and giving us a shock, y'know, so I didn't even feel tipsy.

—Okay. Well, did you enjoy yourself at least?

—I dunno. When we were just fumbling around, I was enjoying that. Because I've messed round with fellas like that before.

—I know you have. Saw you giving head to Declan Moloney behind Coppers that time.

—SHUSH, shush shush shush. Ha, but yeah, so I was enjoying that. And then when we started to do it, yeah, it hurt a little, but when we got into it, like, I enjoyed it.

—Well, good.

—Like, it wasn't like, y'know, screaming monkey stuff.

—HOO HOO HOO HA HA HA.

—Shush, shush. But when it was done it was great.

—So you don't regret it?

—No, I don't.

—Good.

—Though.

—Though what?

Lucy had originally planned to just give Steph the basic facts, get a thumbs-up or a seal of approval or something, and then leave it there. Have a bit of class about it, not be one of those girls who goes blabbing, but fuck, Steph was looking at her, and why should she keep it to herself?

—He was being a bit of a dick this morning.

—DanDan?

—Yeah.

—Cunt.

Jesus. Cath would never ever say that about DanDan. Steph was awesome, it gave Lucy courage.

—Yeah, last night he was really cool about it, but just this morning he starts getting really bullish like, like, 'I'm not in love with you, don't start falling in love with me.'

—Eugh, prick. Not surprised.

—Yeah, but you know what, the more I think about it, I don't really care. Yeah, he was my first but it's not like we're teenage sweethearts. That's that done and now I'm mad to try it again.

—Woah, hold your horses.

—No, it's like, now that it's done I don't see why I was making such a big deal of it in the first place. Cos it's great, I mean, it's not that much different than fingering or blow jobs or whatever, maybe, I don't know. It's not this sacred weight around me any more, you know?

—Yeah, I know.

—So, I mean, I feel like I've been wasting all this time not doing it. Like I've been missing an important part of growing up, or going to college or something.

—Well, yeah, but it's new stuff now so don't just go off on a bender. Pace yourself.

—Of course. I'm taking it with a sophisticated degree of maturity.

—Well, good on you, then. Here, cheers, yeah.

They clinked glasses and Lucy knocked her gin back. She was way ahead of Steph on drinks but Steph drank slowly. It was one of the things that made Steph seem so much older than the rest of them, like she was from a completely different time or place. Still, there was something so cut-off about her, something behind her eyes that you couldn't quite get at. She was sort of I Am Woman Hear Me Roar, but in a real reserved, poker-face kind of way.

—Why are you looking at me like that?

—I'm not.

—You were looking at me.

—You're really fucking pretty, Steph.

—Fuck off.

—No, you are. I don't know how you do it. Even when you're not looking pretty you're still pretty.

—Oh cheers.

—You know what I mean. Wish I had boobs like yours.

—Let's not get into that.

—No, I wish had yours, I do. They're sexy as fuck. They're so big, but like, perky at the same time.

194

Steph looked down at herself and seemed to consider them.

—Eugh, I don't get what the big deal with them is.

—That's cos you have them.

—You have boobs, Luce.

—Yeah. Fucking bitty ones. Wonky ones. There's a weird curve to them.

She dropped her head and felt Steph watching her, then Steph moved a little closer in the seat. She lowered her voice like she was ashamed to be heard. But who'd hear them? DanDan, JJ and Cath were up at the bar, huddled together, getting into an argument about Jägerbombs, and now with Steph in the corner of her eye, watching her, Lucy felt even more conscious about her body, about the things she was wearing, about her make-up and her boobs, the boobs she'd always hoped would get bigger, or even just have a nicer shape, and never did. She needed a fresh gin. Steph's voice was low and soft.

—Luce, listen. They're a pain in the arse. Seriously. Fellas just try and fucking grab them all the time. And it's not like you get an hour into a conversation with a fella and he forgets about them. They can't stop gawking at you, no matter how many times they've had a sneaky look. It's weird . . . I dunno.

Steph hesitated. She began to speak, then stopped herself, her lip twisting in her teeth and her blonde hair falling about her shoulders. This was new.

—You know, it's just. It'd make you wonder, you know, about what we think we know about men, or, what we think we know about ourselves, or just. It's stupid.

—It's fine, go on. Go on.

Steph stared at a point on the table, not making eye contact with Lucy. Was she going to reveal a little bit of herself? She had always seemed so aloof to Lucy, so distant and cool and so much smarter and colder and more capable than her, that it felt like they could never be friends. But Steph had her head lowered now, her hand spinning the tumbler of whiskey on the table top till it rattled, her foot tapping the ground under the table.

—I dunno. I just . . . Do you ever feel that you can't really see outside yourself? That there's what you think is going on, and how you see it, and then there's what's actually going on, but you've never been able to see it, or even imagine it's there . . .

She'd never seen Steph fumble her words like this. She was talking pure shite. Lucy liked it and didn't like it. On the one hand, Steph was talking to her, telling her things like they were proper friends, not just acquaintances, or mates, but actual true-to-God friends and that was fucking brilliant. And how good was it that someone as tough as Steph could still get like this, could switch from being mad and funny and furious to a halting mess in a matter of seconds? It made it okay to be weak sometimes, for all of them. But on the other hand: No. No no no. Steph shouldn't be showing cracks like this. She was letting the side down. She was the tough one, or was supposed to be, at least. Still, Lucy wanted to know what it was that was chewing Steph, what was so important to get out there.

—No . . . but go on, Steph. Out with it.

—I dunno. Just thinking about it. Have you ever been in love, Luce?

She had to have a rummage in her head for that one. Had she ever been in love? There was that one lad in fifth year. Paul.

—Kind of, I suppose.

But Steph shook her head.

—No, not like, 'Have you ever had a crush, have you ever had an unrequited love affair?' Like, have you ever been truly, deeply in love with someone who loved you back?

—No.

—Well, I have. Or then, I dunno . . . Well, I was. I was in love with Fergus.

—The ex?

Steph was staring hard at the table.

—Yeah. I mean. Right, so when I was in school I didn't think I'd ever love anyone. I thought everyone was a fucking eejit, at least the lads I knew, all the rugby fellas or the GAA boys or whatever, you know. There were always lads going after me, but I never really felt any need to go after them . . . Then one night I meet

Fergus out with some friends. We get talking in the pub and he's charming and he listens to me. That's the big thing. He listens to what I have to say and we have a conversation, an actual two-way conversation. So later that night I shift the head off him, and he calls me the next day, and we go out, and talk and shift again, and then next thing, right, I have a boyfriend. But I'm happy with him, y'know. He's my first boyfriend so I've got that over with, and he's good-looking as well, so I'm happy enough.

—He was a looker alright. Abs on him.

—Exactly. So we have good craic. We go out at night and get pissed and we have sex, or we stay up talking, and he always listens to me. Then we go off to college and we're still going out and that's fine . . . But then, like six months in, he knocks on my door at the dead of night. I go down and open it out and he's standing there all excited and he tells me he loves me.

—Aw, that's nice.

—Yeah, it was. But I'm standing there, not really sure what to do, so I say it too. I say I love you. And I do love him. It feels great when I say it. So we keep going out but then I hear the stories repeated, I get to know the same ways he always reacts after everything, y'know, and the same sex. Anyway, he always calls me from college early in the morning or late at night pissed. He says he's just calling to tell me he loves me. And I tell him back. And it becomes meaningless. Like, I feel the same way when I say 'I love cheese' as when I say 'I love you'. If we're two days apart he calls and says he's dying to see me. And then I think like, yeah, but am I dying to see him? Do I actually miss him when he's away? And after a while I realise, no. I don't miss him at all. Then, he's saying, y'know, I always call you but you never call me. And it upsets him, and I feel bad, but . . . I don't really. I mean . . . Is that normal? I'm supposed to be in love with him but I don't miss him when he's gone. You wouldn't know, maybe, I dunno.

Lucy stayed quiet throughout the whole thing. Christ, it had gotten bleak. She was way outside where she wanted to be. She just wanted to have the dirty-chat, she wanted to talk about sex and lads, but this was heavy stuff. She tried to buy time.

—Yeah . . . I dunno . . . But as you said yourself, I've never been in love, so . . .

But Steph wouldn't let her away with it. She downed her drink and pleaded with her.

—I know, yeah. But can you imagine? At the time I thought it was normal. I thought I was normal. But then looking back I'm thinking, how fucked up is that? I tell him I love him but I don't want to see him. So either I never loved him but told him I did . . . Or I did love him but treated him like shit. And who does that? And how could he love someone like that?

—We love you.

—That's different. I dunno, Luce, I'm just trying to think about what kind of a person I am.

—You've a lot going on in your head there, Steph. You need another drink. Calm that voice of yours down.

—No, I'm fine. Don't get up, Lucy. I'm sorry, I dragged the tone down. I'm sorry. I just . . . I need to know if that's normal. How I behaved. I've always worried that I'm very cold, that people see me as this cold person.

—Listen, Steph. I'm getting a drink, do you want a drink?

—Yeah, please. I'm going out for a smoke though.

—Okay. You have a smoke, and I'll get you a whiskey.

—Okay.

Lucy got up from her seat and went to the bar. She took a look back at Steph, who was trying to slip into her coat without actually standing up. She looked so little, quietly wriggling into her coat. Good Lord. Only two minutes before she'd seemed like this kind of giant, unassailable colossus, a sort of sage philosopher who was miles ahead of them in everything, in how she thought and felt about the world, but now she was just some fucking drunk lady who moaned about her exes and couldn't get her coat on.

Lucy joined the others at the bar. DanDan was roaring laughing talking to the bar lady Sheila, who was leaning back, her arms on the counter, nodding her head at him. The door banged as Steph went outside.

Steph

Outside, the wet mist cloaked her and blew in wisps up the street. She heard a cat yowling far off in the night. Her hands were already getting cold. Her fingers slipped and trembled as she tried to get a fresh smoke out of the pack. She'd crushed it in her back pocket and they were all smushed together. She forced one out but it broke mid-way. Soft tobacco crumbled out and blew off in the wind. Fuck it, she threw it to the ground and went for another one.

Why had she talked to Lucy about that? She should be mortified. Lucy could be in there right now, blabbing away. Who knew how Lucy's tongue would be when she'd had a few drinks?

She put a fag to her lips and tried to spark the lighter but it wouldn't go. *Chick, chick, chick.* It caught once but the flame blew out. Fuck. Why had she spilled her guts like that?

She was freezing, and she could feel it especially in her ears, on her lobes where the hair wasn't covering. She turned around and hugged herself into the wall of the pub and made a shield with one hand and her body. Her thumb was rubbed sore by the flint wheel but she persisted. She managed to get one half of the circular tip of her cigarette to glow red, and then sensing her victory she sucked and sucked on it until the red spread to the rest of the tobacco, soft blue smoke starting to rise from the end. She felt it coat her tongue and her lips. She relaxed and moved out from the wall, blowing smoke up into the air to mix with the mist.

She'd loved Fergus. She had. Or had she? Shit, she didn't know. But when she'd been inside with Lucy just now something had clicked with her.

She'd been shit to Ferg. She'd treated him fucking terribly.

Click. Like a light going on. It was all she could think about, and she knew it was true. She even had a time and place she could pin down. She could actually put a location on her cruelty. Stephen's Green, their first time there and their last time there and every other time they'd been near that fucking park.

Normally she avoided it on her dates with Ferg. If they weren't going to meet somewhere to eat or drink then she preferred going walking. If they were going to have a chat or one of those long droney talks about life, with no drinks or distractions in the way, then she wanted to feel the blood going in her legs at least. She walked fast so it kept her heart rate up and also meant that Ferg wasn't looking at her every minute.

Her favourite was to walk up one side of the quays and back down the other. They'd see alcos getting in fights over cans and cyclists getting snotty shouting at cars. They'd walk by the Four Courts, past little hipster coffee docks serving ridiculously priced lattes and homeless guys with torn coffee cups. They'd watch the hen parties trundle by wearing L-plates and waving giant inflatable dicks. It gave her something to talk about with Ferg, something to point out if they ran out of things to say to each other. Look, Ferg, there's a baby on a leash. Oh look, a dead seagull.

Her hands were going numb, her nose starting to run; she didn't want to go back inside. She remembered Fergus with his chlorine-blue eyes lying on his side in Stephen's Green.

He'd taken her there once, insisted on it. It was a sunny April afternoon, the first hot day they'd had in months. They lay on the grass opposite each other, their faces inches apart. They were almost nose to nose and she wondered what the script was. What was it couples whispered to each other on hot sunny days? What were they discussing when they giggled and nuzzled? She had no clue, though Fergus seemed to have a good idea. He held her in his arms on the soft grass and looked in her eyes and in a quiet murmur he questioned her.

He asked about her family and her childhood. He asked about her fears and her loves and what she wanted to do for a career and where would she go if she had all the money in the world. If she had to give away all her possessions what was the one thing she'd keep? Did she want to marry at any stage and did she want children and how did she feel about her parents? Was she a happy child or not and what was her first kiss like? He asked her what her fantasies were, whether sexual or otherwise, and if there was anything she'd like them to do together.

She gave him short, nondescriptive answers, or she said yes, no, maybe. Have you ever wanted kinky sex? Not really. Bondage? Maybe. He looked hurt. He asked her did she ever want to sleep with anyone else, if she had sex dreams and if she believed in love at first sight or soul mates. No, maybe, I don't know. He told her she'd a problem with trust and she said it wasn't that, she just didn't have any real fantasies.

He asked her who she hated most in the world and who pissed her off out of all her friends and if there was one part of herself she could change what would it be, and all the while the only thing she could think of was how boring the whole process was. Getting interrogated about things that didn't matter, and him watching her at all times. She wondered how long she had to look at his eyes, how boring his lips were and how often she'd seen those ears and that forehead and those lashes. She closed her eyes and tried to remember what colour his were, but she couldn't. She kept her eyes shut and asked him, what colour are my eyes, and in the darkness his voice came, they're deep amber brown with a little hint of green around the edges. She said well done. He asked her what colour his were and she said blue, you have blue eyes. Then he insisted that they lock eyes again and every time she looked away or over his head at a cloud or a plane or something, anything to distract from the deep boredom of his face, he'd get concerned, and though he never said it, she knew he wondered, why is she looking away?

He asked her about her most humiliating moment and the last time she felt truly, truly happy, and she said she couldn't remember. He looked angry, frowning at her. Fine, then you go, she said to him, when was the last time you felt true, sure, unabashed happiness and he said that night we first met. I kissed you in the rain outside the pub and I knew then that I had someone, and I went home and told my brother, I met a girl tonight, and lying in bed that night going to sleep I could feel you on my lips and the things you said and the stories you told me in my ears and I just couldn't wait to hear from you the next day. That was the last time, he said, I felt true, pure happiness. She smiled and told him he was sweet. He told her he loved her. She kissed him, but she kept her eyes open when she did. She watched a part of his nose and his closed eyelid blurry next to her face. In that moment it came to her as a concrete thought, what she'd always worried about without ever voicing it, though it had been rooted right in her the whole time. I don't love you. I don't love you. I don't.

Once that happened, she knew she should break up with him. But she didn't. She kept letting it go on, drag out. She called him less and less, and he called her more. She dragged him along behind her, watching him rip and fall apart but she never let go. For months he grew more and more desperate for her, and she'd watched with curiosity how the worse she treated him, the more he wanted her. Eventually, she'd asked him to meet, then dumped him in Stephen's Green. It was not widely known as a place for dumpings. It was more of a place for young lovers, but at the time it had seemed like the best place to do it. It had the right light, it was public and spread out enough where they could talk without fear of being heard, but he couldn't go on shouting or making a massive scene.

They'd sat on a bench near a homeless man drinking from a two-litre bottle of cider. Fergus had leaned in to kiss her and she'd pushed him away. She told him she couldn't do it any more. She was done. His gaze dropped to the ground and he cried. He actually cried. He begged and begged and said that yes he knew they were growing apart and that he was more interested in her than her in him, but Christ, could they not work on it? They just had to learn to be tender with each other and he knew that she was her own woman and that's what he loved about her, he loved that she had her own mind and her own ways and that was the most

202

exciting thing in the world but they shouldn't throw what they had away. She said she was sorry and that it just wasn't realistic and that they should still be friends, though with snot in his voice he gave a little pah at that suggestion. She said sorry again and that she'd send Cath to pick up her things.

She left him on the bench and didn't look back. The homeless guy shouted after her that she was a bitch. As she walked away she felt nothing but sorrow and the horrible, desperate urge to run back and apologise, beg him to forget everything she'd just said.

But she kept walking. Then the minute she turned the corner and he disappeared from sight all she could feel was that she was free, free and away to do whatever she liked and be whoever she wanted to be, and she realised he'd been holding her back all along, that there'd been a world of people and new experiences kept from her because she'd been with him. And now, she just wanted to go out and live loud and run around and enjoy herself. The very first thing she wanted to do was go off to a sweaty club and grab the first foreign-looking man she could find, someone with an accent and stubble, and crush her face into his on the dance floor, have him put his hands all over her and then drag him into the toilets and fuck him up against a stall and not give a shit who could hear. But she calmed herself as she walked; they still had mutual friends and so she should at least wait a few weeks.

She waited the few weeks, then she set out on her new life and though she never did find a stranger and fuck him in the bathroom the way she'd imagined, she did plenty of other things. She smoked spliffs on rooftops and went to kick-boxing classes and got into arguments with total strangers. The first man she had sex with after Fergus was a guy she met at a yoga class. He was thin and flexible and looked a little bit like Jesus. They went for a drink after the class and when last orders came they kissed in the street. They couldn't find anywhere to go and she didn't want him to come back to hers so they walked around looking for a quiet spot. They found the rails of Stephen's Green. The gates were locked, so he gave her a leg up over the fence and he vaulted over himself. They ran to the playground and smoked a spliff sitting on a slide, then they had sex underneath the tyre swings. She remembered the excitement of hopping over the railings, of tumbling down a slide, high as a kite, and having sex in wet gravel, two tyres on metal chains swaying and squeaking above them.

Steph realised she was looking straight up to the black misty sky. Her cigarette was finished, though she'd not even realised she'd been smoking it. It had burned down to the filter and gone dead in her hands. Then she thought of what she'd said to Lucy inside.

She'd never loved Fergus, but she'd stayed with him and taken his love, and what kind of a person did that? She didn't know. She couldn't get her thoughts organised, she couldn't keep one mood straight. She should think on it, really give it thought, but she was cold, and her cigarette was dead. She pulled her coat tight and went back to the doors. She'd see this night through, and then she'd think on it, think of all the shit things she'd done. The warmth blasted her as she came in the doors, as did the laughter and the light, and she felt like she'd left Fergus behind again, shivering and sniffling outside in the cold.

Cath

—Cath, Jäger.

—Cheers, JJ.

—Take it easy, Cath.

—Fuck off, DanDan. Right, JJ, c'mon. One. Two. Three.

They bopped the bar with the bottoms of their shot glasses and threw it back. Fuck. She tried her best not to snarl or gag as it sent a queasiness rolling through her, deep down to her stomach. It seemed to bubble inside her. Made her feel like getting sick. She pushed the side of her hand to her face as her eyes teared up.

JJ drummed the bar and bounced on the balls of his feet.

—Again, again, again.

—No, Christ almighty, you'll have us killed.

—You're boring. BORING. THE PAIR OF YE ARE BORING.

—G'WAY.

—BOOOOOOORRRRINGG.

—Fine, okay. One, one more.

Cath leaned over the bar and looked down for Sheila, who was trying to be inconspicuous reading a paper down the other end. Sheila looked up at her and nodded, getting up from her seat.

—Hi, Sheila. Yeah, can we get another three shots?

—Jäger.

—No Jäger, JJ. Do you have . . . tequila?

Sheila nodded.

She measured out three shots of tequila and put them in front of them. JJ and DanDan elbowed their way towards the drinks and Cath had to shout to keep them in line.

—STOP. Stop, now. Be civil. We are guests in this drinking establishment, and we are going to be civil.

—Jesus Christ, Cath, you're pissed already.

—I am not, Jonathan James.

—That your name, JJ?

—Fuck off.

—I, am not drunk, Jonathan. I'm just trying to make sure we represent ourselves in the best possible manner.

—Ah fuck off and let's drink this.

—Alright. ONE, TWO, THREE.

She threw it back and it burned her all the way down. Gah. It was worse this time, the urge to get sick. She felt wetness at the back of her throat. The tequila was lingering there, dying to come back up. She put the back of her wrist to her mouth and her eyes watered. JJ smacked the bar.

—That'll put chest on your hairs.

Cath nodded. She smacked the bar as well, and gave a satisfied gasp. JJ put his hand on her elbow, the elbow of the arm with the hand that was put to her mouth.

—You alright?

—MMMM.

Hold it down, hold it down. Nope, no, gotta go.

She shoved her way through them and walked in a quick step to the bathroom. Once through the door, she bundled herself into a cubicle and over a raised toilet seat. Hovering over the bowl, she allowed her body to open up and gave herself over to any fleeting wave of sick that might come. She waited to burst forth, to spray hot black tequila all over the bowl and the floor, to have it scald her nose and drip down onto her top and to have to go out and grab one of the girls, call a cab and run off home. A relief surely, to have the weight of the night taken off. Not to have to commit to anything. But it never came. Bent over the toilet bowl, her head started to clear and gradually she felt fine.

She straightened up and left the cubicle. The toilet was a grubby little affair. The red tiles on the floor were cracked and rubbed black in the mortar between. The sink was a tiny little one with twisting taps and a mirror in front, stained with flecks of snot. High up, nailed to the wall, was a little font, like one of those holy water things in old people's homes. Inside was what looked like yellowing pot-pourri.

How exactly had Cath ended up here? This was not what she had wanted. She'd wanted just a nice weekend. She'd imagined them sitting round a couch and playing music, or doing spin the bottle or whatever, maybe getting in a few scrapes but nothing that ended too badly. She'd suggested it. She'd made the plans and done the groundwork, shoved them all into it. But this, standing in a decaying bathroom with a font of going-off pot-pourri, was not what she'd wanted.

There'd been no shortage of uproar at least. Malachy and all that. Merc had gotten a shock. Himself and Steph had something going on as well. And DanDan and Lucy, they'd gotten more than they bargained for. DanDan was in a better mood too, though she could barely bring herself to look at him now.

She was grateful to him, at least, that he'd tried to show tact. But he couldn't hide it. He held his head up now the way he had when he'd been with Jess. He was over her, or had stopped hurting, at the very least. Cath remembered how happy he'd been with Jess. At the time she'd told him it was brilliant, she was delighted for him, that she loved Jess and they were great together. But she could see it now, though, she'd burned alive when she saw them together. Cath had liked Jess, she'd been generally a great laugh, and good for DanDan, but she'd hated her so much as well. She'd go out for coffee with the two of them, pretending to enjoy talking and laughing with her, but really what she'd be thinking was you bitch, you fucking bitch, you bitch, stop kissing him, stop touching him.

And why was it only now, when Jess was gone and DanDan on the rise, that she realised how she felt? How had she possibly lied to herself for so long about something so fucking obvious? Something so blatant that people always pointed it out to her, or asked her directly did she fancy him, and that one time her mam told her she shouldn't be messing around with a fella in a relationship, and she'd screamed back at her, saying Ma we're allowed have male friends you know, it's not the Fifties. How was it she'd managed to convince herself it was anything else? Even now, so recently, she'd orchestrated a weekend to be with him, she'd wanted DanDan, and it was obvious to them all, except maybe DanDan.

If there was one thing that was good, it was that there'd been no public humiliation. There'd been no out-and-out denial of her. Only, the conversation between her and DanDan she'd obviously misinterpreted. When he said he was into someone close to him, he'd meant Lucy, not her. How stupid could she have been? How could she have deceived herself like that?

Her eyes were red in the mirror. She had to go back inside. Fuck it, just get it over with. No one could help anything. If they all went and got stocious and had a good night of it, they'd forget all the boring bits, the emotional bits. DanDan would get with Lucy, stay with Lucy, and he'd never realise how Cath had felt. Now that she knew she liked him, she could make herself not like him, and put it in the past tense, she *had* liked him. She'd grab Steph and JJ. They'd go to the lake and swim. They'd dance and enjoy themselves, and that'd be it. She fixed her mascara in the mirror.

She crashed back in to the rest of them. At the bar, JJ and DanDan were giggling away. She threw her arms around JJ and hugged him tight. He hugged her back. JJ never hugged back.

DanDan

They stayed in the bar another couple of hours until Cath suggested they head on. As Sheila wiped down the tables, Lucy left her seat for the toilet and he knew the time was right to make it up to her. He left a minute or so after her, turning into the corridor for the bathroom. He waited at the end of the corridor until he heard the door to the ladies' toilet scrape back, then he started his walk down. Lucy tripped out and he smiled at her as he approached.

—Hey.

—Hey.

She moved to the side slightly to let him pass, but he stopped in front of her. They stood opposite each other in the narrow corridor, barely any space between them. She was looking well in her top, though her face was flushed, and small beads of sweat brushed her face. DanDan started.

—So I just wanted to say, sorry about earlier.

—Yeah?

—Yeah, I'm sorry. I haven't been with a girl since, you know . . . So I didn't know what to do. I panicked. Sorry.

He reached out for her slightly, felt the edge of her elbow, which she withdrew.

—Are you just trying it on again?

—No, it's not that. It's not. It's just, I know I upset you, and I didn't want you to be upset, so yeah.

Lucy cocked her head to the side. He tried his best to look into the centre of her forehead so she wouldn't see his eyes drifting down to her top. She let him stew for a bit, then hit him on the arm.

—It's okay, you're fine.

—Yeah?

—Yeah, come here.

She brought him in for a hug, and held his face in her hair, her left hand stroking his back. He smelled sweat and perfume off her. He was right back in there, no matter what she said about friends. The night was going smoothly. Brian Keenan smiled inside him.

They broke apart and she patted his shoulder.

—Let's go back.

—Sure.

They turned and went back to the group, who were waiting by the door in their coats. Cath stared resolutely at an old Guinness poster, ignoring him and Lucy.

They left Sheila at the Riverside and started on the walk back. JJ sang songs and paced ahead with Cath. Steph was being awful quiet, though Lucy continued talking in a high, animated pitch. They left the village and when they rounded a bend, the main street disappearing from view, JJ and Cath stopped just under an orange street lamp. Steph and Lucy caught up in a few seconds and DanDan was the first to ask.

—What's up?

Cath nodded at JJ and he took a little plastic packet out of his back pocket.

—Ladies and Gentlemen, the time is upon us. Give us some light.

Cath pressed the light on her phone and held it out for JJ. He tipped the little packet and shook it until five small, pale blue pills fell into the palm of his right hand. He closed the packet, stuffed it back into his jeans, then held the pills out to them.

—Right, there's one each there now and more if we need them later. They're fairly weak so don't worry.

They all hesitated. JJ looked around the group.

—Ah, come here to fuck like, you don't need to take them if you don't want. I'm not Mister Peer Pressure. But I'm taking mine anyway.

He spaced the pills out around his palm using his forefinger.

—Only take it if you want.

Steph put her hand in and picked one out.

—Sure, what else is there to do?

Cath seemed distracted. Like she'd never considered that she might actually have to take a pill out of JJ's hand and swallow it.

—It's weird. I want to take one. I do. Dying to. But it's all this shit from school they teach you, about it being poison and all that, even though I know it's bullshit. Can't help but be weirded out by the sight of it.

JJ put his hand on the small of her back, as if to reassure her. When had they gotten all touchy? And she didn't take it off, or slap it away. What was JJ at?

—Listen, if you don't want, there's absolutely no problem.

—No, I do. It's just a weird feeling.

She took a pill out of his palm and held it up to the light, like she was appraising a jewel. DanDan reached for his one.

—Come on, so.

It was stupid to think too much of these things. He took one out of JJ's hand, followed by Lucy, who was the last and seemed to enjoy the moment for herself.

DanDan looked at each of them as they shuffled nervously and excitedly. Lucy had a cheeky grin on her face, Steph looked melancholic. Cath seemed to have reached a decision, her face growing calm, while JJ rubbed her back. He'd better get his fucking hand off her back. JJ winked at him.

—Right, so.

JJ tossed the last remaining pill in his palm into his mouth. He took another can of cider out of his jacket pocket and cracked it open. It foamed and he swallowed a large glug to wash the pill down, then smacked his lips. He passed the can to Cath. Cath smiled. She still had the pill in her hand.

—Sorry. I want to. I do. But, no. No, you know what, it's not me.

She gave the pill back to JJ, who clapped her on the back.

—Hey, that's fine. There's no pressure. There's no point doing it if you're not sure, because then you can panic on it or whatever. That's fine. Sure?

—Sure. It's not me.

—Then no more said about it. Feel like the right decision?

She smiled coyly and looked at JJ.

—Actually yeah. Fuck it. Yes, fuck it. I can still drink anyway.

She handed the can on and each of the others took their pill in turn. Steph placed hers almost sadly on her tongue and glugged the can. Lucy did hers with a deliberate air of grandeur. She twirled her fingers as she put it in her mouth and raised her little finger as she tipped back the can. DanDan was last. He put the pill in his mouth and washed it down with the warm bubbling cider before he really thought about the decision he was making.

JJ jumped up and down and took the can off him.

—Right, so. Half an hour and we'll be set.

Lucy leaned in on his shoulder and jumped with him.

—Can't wait.

—Right then, let's go, get to the lake.

They walked on towards the main road, the moon shining and the mist drifting as they shuffled places, switching positions and conversations, altering the pace of their steps and the volume of their chats until DanDan was left walking by himself at the back of the group, watching them all go ahead of him to the lake.

Malachy

Back in his kitchen he watched the Lodge for signs of life. All the lights were off, and it lay dark and quiet opposite the church, returned to how it had been for the last ten years. Malachy gripped the sides of his chair. His brain felt sick, like it was overheating. Then it came to him, fluttering down in him gradually over a few moments until eventually it came to solid ground and he knew it was the truth: he'd fucked it all up.

When Elaine had come to him and begged him to leave, he'd said no to her, too young and afraid. Then he'd blamed circumstance that he'd not been given another chance to do differently, that no other offers had come his way so he could go again, retake a life he'd lost. He'd waited for his father to die, to hand over the farm, as he was supposed to. Only, his father had held on too long, had been too strong despite growing weak. He'd spent his last years infirm and helpless, over-living until he'd eaten into Malachy's time. But his father had eventually died, and Malachy had gotten his chance again. He should've given the farm up then, thrown it away, only he couldn't. He'd waited so long for it, been through so much just to see his name on the deed. Next season, he said. Next year. Slowly, he'd just dropped it, the idea of being with someone. It had slipped away. He'd settled into his life alone too early, with too little resistance, assuming that it was just what had to happen. He was supposed to be one of those lonely fucks out by themselves in the valley. He'd remained doing his work on the farm, finding something romantic almost in tending to it himself, being one of those men who saw to the land all by themselves.

Then, out of nowhere, too late, he'd sold the farm, like it was nothing. Fucked away the thing that was supposed to have meant most. All that trouble and he'd thrown it away in the end. All that money and nothing to do with it. He'd left himself with no more work to do. All gone. Wasted away. And he had no excuse. It had just happened.

And he wondered now, even if the luck had fallen his way during that time, if another lovely young thing had come and knocked on his door then, asked him to come to Dublin, or to London or wherever, offering him love and companionship and children and sex, would he have taken that option? Would he have taken her hand and departed with her, or would he have told her where to go, and closed the door in her face?

It occurred to him now, as he sat watching the empty Lodge, that he might have taken the exact same action as he had the first time with Elaine, that he was trapped in himself, in who and how and whatever way he was. Too afraid to let go and move on, too scared to leave everything he knew. He'd always thought of himself as strong, and firm. Maybe it wasn't strength, though, but stubbornness and fear. It was just ordinary, his life, and he'd taken no steps to change that. Just a long-drawn life that could have been better once, happy even, but now never could. He'd missed his chance.

Everything was old and done, finished, and though it was too late to start again, he still had a lot left to go. Another twenty years, maybe. A little weaker every day, a little madder, a little softer, until all his strength left him and he'd just sit in his chair and wait to die like his father.

He sat and watched the house, the darkness flooding his mind, drowning it.

DanDan

He wasn't sure when the pill was supposed to kick in, but it didn't matter. The moon was hazy overhead through the mist and he could feel himself getting energy from it, he could feel the stars and the massive darkness around him and the mist off his breath and the fire in his crotch and having tumbled with another warm body in dusty sheets.

He felt energy in him, like nothing he'd felt in a while. He'd love again, live again, and an endless world of possibilities seemed to open to him. Christ, it was coming back all the time now. He was back. He was back and unstoppable. He was becoming Himself, he was fucking DANDAN!

Behind him Steph was talking to Lucy about Fergus.

—I was thinking I might call him, Luce.

—Are you mad?

—Maybe it's a bad idea.

He didn't want them to think he was eavesdropping, so he took out his earphones and put them in his ears, though they were attached to nothing, which let him eavesdrop anyway. Steph was having some sort of crisis about Fergus.

—I don't know, Luce, I don't know. What the fuck did I do to him?

—You need to forget it, don't think about it.

He wondered briefly if he shouldn't have just kept his mouth shut about meeting up with Fergus, about what he'd said about Steph, but then, nah, she'd been on his case for no reason, acting really stuck up, and maybe Fergus was right and DanDan was doing her a favour telling her those things about herself. He felt like he should care but didn't. He was on a national road at God knows what hour with friends and everything was going great.

They were turning off the main road now and taking the side road Cath had pointed out earlier, the one that went down to the lake. He felt the ground give way as the road led down to the shore, where their world opened out.

A long stretch of black water lay in front of them. There was a strip of tarmac for cars, and a few dozen square metres of dirty sand by the water's edge. A pier shafted out into the black lake on the right side of the sand. A series of posts with chains running between them curved around in a quarter circle from the end of the pier to the edge of the sand on the left side, leaving a protective little enclave for them to swim in. It was silly to think that the enclave would protect them in any way. The water pushed freely in and out under the chains. Yet it still seemed as if somehow the area inside the chains was cleaner, safer somehow. This was their place. It felt like it had been waiting just for them.

Steph, Lucy and Cath went down to the end of the pier to change. JJ turned to DanDan.

—We might as well just get the hard part over with. Get in and cold quick so we can start to warm.

—Yeah. Might as well.

JJ stripped down and dumped his clothes on the dirty sand. He stood in the moonlight doing little hip thrusts and flexes in his tight boxers. There was no fat on him. You'd think he was half-starved. You could see every sinew of his body, nothing between his skin and his bones. He started jogging on the spot.

DanDan pulled off his socks and felt the sand rubbing between his toes. He stripped down to his boxers then walked towards JJ. The air was cold and fresh and seemed flavoured by the lake and the moon and the single yellow street lamp farther down by the car park. He picked his way on the balls of his feet through the sand, bits of stray gravel and broken glass needling his soles.

On the edge of the water, JJ was psyching himself to go in. Out over the lake the mist seemed thin and the moon was high up above them. It seemed much bigger than usual. It was almost full,

216

a slight little shaving taken off one of the corners. It glowed bright and silver, reflecting off the lake.

JJ jumped up and down in front of him.

—Bit chilly, now.

—That's no joke.

—Do some stretches, warm yourself up.

DanDan held himself and rubbed the back of his arms. He'd more fat on him than JJ, more muscle, so why did he seem colder? How would Merc have reacted? Merc. Christ.

But he felt tall in the night air. The beach was littered with bits of fag ends and bottle caps, though the moon was shining on them and they seemed beautiful. As they jumped up and down together, he looked into the dark water a few paces down. It looked dangerously cold. The water lapped on the shore. He didn't know lakes had tides, but he looked at JJ and he felt a warmth in him, a rhythm almost, and he was so, so glad to be alive and single and free in this world, and he knew he loved JJ, even though he was terribly skinny, and JJ looked at him sideways.

—Hit you, hasn't it?

—Dern tootin'.

JJ pushed him towards the water, clapping his bare back.

—Come on.

—Okay, okay.

They backed up, giving themselves a run-up, then ONE, TWO, THREE they raced down to the lake's edge. They bulldozed into the water. They continued to run when the water hit their toes and on the next step the calves and the next up to the knees. JJ was the first to go down, his legs cut out from under him by his own momentum and the barrier of black water. DanDan lasted a pace or two more until the water hit his thighs and he went down, slapping the surface with his body, not even a little bit of time to make a fake dive, and then next all he knew was cold and wet over every part of his body, cold he'd never known, and holy shit, water in his mouth and his head wet and his body not floating but suspended and his hearing gone, he was drowning, he was drowning, NO! till he broke back out to the surface, freezing, his balls and his neck and his nose and his ears, and he thought he was blind, only he realised he hadn't opened his eyes yet. He opened his eyes and felt himself floating in the water, and there was JJ screaming, his head just having popped up from the water.

—HAAAAAAAAAA FUCKING FREEZING.

DanDan laughed and knew he was okay. His feet could touch on the bottom of the lake, and he leaned back. The moon was blasting silver his way, though the mist was still blowing across, and though cold, yes, so, so cold, he felt warm. Lucy and Cath and Steph appeared above him on the pier, looking down to him; he couldn't see their faces in the dark.

—How cold is it?

—FUCKING COLD.

—Well, that's encouraging. We'll be in in a minute.

JJ

Christ on a tricycle it was fucking freezing. He swam on his back and then again on his front and watched DanDan over the way trying to claw up onto the pier, reaching for the three girls who were standing shivering in the night air. Cath, Lucy and Steph looked down at DanDan, shaking their heads as he tried to grab their toes and their ankles, scraping his chest on the corner of the pier.

He felt his heart in his chest and his body in the water, the cold-ness of it rising up and down over his nipples as he bounced on his tippy toes. They'd never been this close to each other before, the group of them, never been so openly aware of each other's pres-ence, of their bodies. Surely this was what he had been missing, the sense of being part of something, of being present in some significant moment that would stay with him for years to come. He shouted over to them.

—Coming in?

Cath waved.

—We'll be in in a minute.

There was something with her and him, JJ and Cath. He was getting a weird creeping sense of it, of something growing with-out him pushing. Steph nudged Cath and shouted:

—Actually, we might not.

DanDan roared and splashed them.

—What?

—Yeah, we've changed our mind. Too cold.

—The fuck?

DanDan was too easy to fool. JJ splashed water at his head.

—They're joking, fella. They are coming in, aren't they?

Lucy bumped her chest with a fist then extended her fingers to him in a peace sign.

—Right on, brother.

—See?

They all moved to change at the same time. Steph peeled off her jumper and threw it down at her feet. Lucy wiggled off her bracelets while Cath bent down and slipped off her pumps. DanDan whooped.

—That's right, ladies. Off they go.

Christ, he would go and ruin it, wouldn't he? JJ did a stroke or two away from them, towards the chains that sectioned off the bathing area of the lake. Steph spoke to DanDan.

—We're not undressing for you. Turn around and fuck off over there like a good fella.

—Fine, fine. I was joking.

He pretended not to notice as DanDan splashed a few metres away. Probably going to sulk now.

JJ needed to get warm, so he rolled into a front crawl and swam towards the chain. He just focused on swimming. Hand over hand, right foot left. Swim your little heart out, you beast. He began to find his rhythm. With his eyes closed and his head crushed with the cold he kept his face down and reached up every fourth stroke for a breath. Splash, splash, splash, breath, splash, splash, splash, breath.

He felt he could swim like this forever, hard and fast, out from the chained enclosure of the bathing area and into the great lake beyond, past the submerged trees and the islands and the crannógs. He could swim up one of the rivers and go all the way upstream like a salmon. He'd swim up and up against the flow and force of the river along with all the other fishes, and all the people he passed would try and fish him out of the river. They'd float cans of Druids and pills and CDs, iPods and ham sambos with hooks in them, but he'd know better and continue on. He'd surge up through rapids and he'd jump over waterfalls, past fishermen and murdered bodies and secrets buried under silt. He'd go so far upstream he'd come up in the cool, crisp waters of the mountain, go to the very top, maybe to the highest peaks, and perhaps there locate a secret lake for himself where he could die, but then no, JJ wouldn't stop there, he'd be evaporated up, he'd lose his body as it swirled into steam and he'd be taken up into the clouds and float over the length and breadth of Ireland. He'd be beyond himself, part of something greater, part of the earth, and he'd no longer worry about where he was going or what he was doing or if he was wasting his life. He'd go up into the clouds and blow out to Kildare, and he'd swoop down to the family farm where his brothers would be sitting in their usual chairs, doing up their cars and drinking from big bottles of cider and picking on someone who wasn't him, because he was gone, he was a cloud, and his body would be a million, million little wisps of vapour and he'd come down and rust their cars, put water into the petrol tanks of the cars they'd spent much more time on than they ever had with him and then he'd go in and flood the basement where his dad used to send him when he'd acted up. He'd flood the whole fucking place and they'd scream at each other and there'd be no one to clean or mop and then he'd be back up into the sky. He'd turn around and come back, brush up the little streets of Carrig, make everyone who walked the streets feel cold and give them shivers, but leave off Steph and Lucy and Cath because they were good. Finally he'd go and rain himself back down into Lough Gorm, rain every last bit of him down into the lake where he could re-form his body and start his journey upstream all over again. Re-form the body that was freezing him now and his balls contracting up inside him, keep doing his front stroke, hand over hand over hand. But JJ was past the railings and the chain, into the lake beyond, still swimming. And he thought, why go back? Why go back at all? Why not keep swimming till his feet went cold and numb and he wouldn't go up into the mountains and swim upstream, he'd simply lose the feeling in his arms and sink under the surface, go down to the very bottom of the lake and drown and they'd never find his body. Just sink down, and down, and it'd all go away, but then Cath screamed.

—JJ! JJ! Come back. Come back. NOW.

He broke his head full out of the water for the first time, his lungs burning. Treading water, he turned and looked back. He'd swum under the chains and was about twenty or thirty metres gone beyond the rails. Cath was there on the pier down to her bra and knickers, and Steph and Lucy's heads in the water bobbing up and down. He considered keeping going. Just turn, throw another arm into the water and keep going. Keep swimming. He needed some time to himself. But Cath shouted again.

—GET BACK HERE NOW!

Such a simple request. So direct and honest. He turned, and realising how tired his arms were, did a sloppy breaststroke back. Then he was scared. The chains far away. His arms aching, and his breath laboured coming in gulps. The chains swayed, squeaking above the water. He inhaled a mouthful of water and gagged. Vomit rose up into the back of his nose and he felt water and bile flooding his nostrils. Just one stroke more, one stroke more. Get back to the chains. His legs could barely keep him afloat, they kicked weak and feeble. His left arm doggy-paddled as he left his right one stretched out before him, his eyes closed against the rising water that went at his mouth, trying to force its way in, trying to kill him.

He was almost down to his last stroke when he felt the chain slimy in his hands. He pulled himself into the post supporting the chain and spat into the water. He was safe. He pressed his cheek close against the rotten wood and tried to get his breath. Calm yourself. Christ. His arms like there was something dead in them.

As he gulped the burning air down, opening his lungs, he wondered if the others had seen him. But Lucy and Steph were in the water splashing each other, DanDan going argh like a pirate. They carried on noticing nothing. Grand. Grand.

He could see the outline of Cath on the pier. Beautiful she was. There was moonlight on her white skin. Painted her shining silver against the black water. Cath looked at him from the edge of the concrete shelf. It seemed like a moment between them. Something tense he couldn't explain.

Cath jumped into the water. Her body slapped as it hit and the black water swallowed her. Lucy and Steph screamed WAHEY and shouted for her to come on, play polo.

But when she surfaced, Cath was swimming towards him. A deliberate strong stroke. He'd already forgotten what it was he was feeling when he'd gone out beyond. Just a relief now, to be back.

Cath slurped to a halt beside him. He couldn't see the details of her face. Her hair was wet over her head and spread out floating around her shoulders in the water. She held on to the chain where it joined the mossy, green post at the top. He could see the outline of her nose and her eyes in the dark but not much else, and he tried to hide in the shadow her head was making. Water dripped softly from the end of her nose. She waited a moment then spoke quietly.

—What were you doing?

—Swimming.

—You went out.

—Just for a ramble.

Was he? Had he been? Christ, his heart was going so fast. He didn't know. He had no fucking clue.

—Were you?

—Course.

—You scared me.

—Sorry, I didn't mean to.

—Arsehole.

Cath was hugging him. Wrapping herself around him in the water. Her hair against his nose. Even in the freezing water she felt warm to him. He allowed her to hug him, and just a little, his left hand felt the curve of her back, his ring finger pressed the edge of her bra strap. She released him slowly and they bobbed together in the icy water.

Steph

Could the world stop beating? The world surely had a heart-beat. She could feel it thumping inside her, in the cold water, in the stars above and the mist coating them between. Her heart and the earth's heart beating as one. But if the earth had a heartbeat it could be stopped. It could be irregular, arrhyth-mic. What if it skipped a beat? What if the ventricles collapsed, the blood-flow to the world would stop, the beat inside all the trees and the lake and the islands and inside her would cease. Her heart would stop beating. Fergus's heart would stop beating.

Her and Lucy and DanDan were sat up to their belly buttons in the lake. Was something wrong with her heart? She stood up. Water dripped from her, flowed down her body, her heart beating. She stretched her arms and put two fingers to her jugular. She couldn't find her own pulse. Lucy laughed at her.

—Look at you posing there. Moonstruck beauty.

—My heart.

—What?

—My heart is going.

Lucy laughed.

—Don't worry, it's the pill. That is amazing, though. Oh my. I can feel it too.

Lucy banged her chest with her fist.

—Dun dun dun. I feel warm. Even though I know I'm cold, I feel warm.

DanDan reclined and looked up at the stars.

—It's all the love in your heart doing that.

She watched the twin heads of Cath and JJ swaying down by the railings. They drifted gently this way and that, anchored on the chains.

—Course you worry about being cold, don't you, Steph?

—What?

Lucy was looking up at her, her hair wet and sticking to her skin in places. She had a little bundle of puppy fat creasing on her stomach. Her face was visible from the yellow of the lamp farther down.

—You worry about being cold.

DanDan also looked up.

—How so, Steph?

The two of them, looking up at her. Why the fuck had Lucy said that? Heart, heart beating so, so fast.

—I asked you not to say, Luce.

Lucy waved her hand.

—It's nothing to worry about, Steph. It's not true so there's no point worrying.

DanDan pinched Lucy.

—This one ain't cold. This one's smoking.

Lucy slapped DanDan on the shoulder and he patted her hand. Then they both stared at her sympathetically.

She made to go back to the sand but Lucy grabbed her leg and hugged on to it. DanDan did the same. She tried to twist away.

—Ah stop now.

Lucy gnawed on her calf, and DanDan smacked her arse over her wet knickers. She knocked his hand away.

—Hey! Don't do that.

Lucy screamed.

—We want your warmth, Steph.

The two of them grabbed their arms together and she splashed back down, falling into the lake. Steph couldn't stop herself from laughing as Lucy crawled over her and hugged her close in the water.

—You're warm, darling. You're so warm. You're not cold.

—Ha.

—Warm warm warm, I could eat you up. I could snuggle you in bed like a hot water bottle.

—Ah!

Her heart was beating but it was warm. She could feel in her a lovely breath of love for the world and for Lucy and yes for DanDan, who was again leaning back on his elbows in the water, flexing a pretend six-pack. Life was still lovely after the whole travesty of the weekend. They'd fixed it, made up, and the world kept a strong and ready heartbeat and flushed warm, nutritious blood all over the planet, and the hearts in their chests beat as one with the beat of the world.

Lucy began to wrestle her, attempting to pin her down, so Steph tried to roll away. Lucy was too strong, though, and forced her shoulders back into the water. She loomed over her, her knees either side of Steph's body, breathing.

Steph looked around Lucy's body and saw DanDan lean towards them. His hand floated forward in the water, coming to rest around Lucy's ankle. She watched as Lucy's legs slowly stopped kicking. She lay silent under Lucy in the dark. She knew DanDan couldn't see her looking, but she could see him playing with Lucy's toes, until Lucy's other foot came over, drifted in the water, and scratched the side of his wrist with her big toe.

Lucy hiccupped, her head close by Steph's ear. She stroked the side of Steph's cheek with her hand. Then she leaned down and kissed her neck. There was a little punch of tongue in the wet kiss she placed right between Steph's clavicle and jugular. Lucy held it there a few seconds then brought her head up and watched her, her wet hair forming a dark curtain around them. She felt Lucy still scratching DanDan's hand with her toes. Lucy was leaning down towards her lips.

Oh Christ. Steph started laughing. She couldn't help it. It was absurd but with the warmth in her and her heart beating beating beating all she could do was laugh up and out to the night. Lucy laughed with her as well, either out of awkwardness or not, and then so did DanDan till all three of them were tangled together in a foot of water, all laughing in the night. She laughed till she could barely breathe. Oh dear Christ. Get out. She shrugged Lucy off and stepped out from the two of them. She got up and started to walk for the pier. Lucy splashed to one side in the water and immediately DanDan launched himself on her and pretended to drown her. Lucy faked and cried for help, shouting after her.

—HELP! A bad man is drowning me. I'm drowning! Steph, where you going? Steph?

She turned and spoke quickly.

—I'll be back in a minute.

DanDan put his head to Lucy's chest, and as Steph walked away through the coarse sand towards the pier, she heard him whispering to Lucy.

—Your heart is beating so fast.

—It must be love then.

—G'way outta that.

—Don't be rude.

—I apologise.

—Listen to my heart.

—I'm listening.

—Can you hear it?

—I can hear it. You're alive in there.

For fuck sake, had that just happened? She left them there. JJ and Cath were still down in the water. They appeared closer together, the two of them facing the same direction, both sets of hands on the chain over the water. They looked between their arms out over the lake with their backs to the shore.

She walked barefoot on the cold, scraping concrete of the pier. The pill in her, Christ, she felt something, she needed something. She found her jeans in their pile of discarded clothes, and her hand went into the pockets for her phone. It'd been a year. It'd been a year and yet she still knew his number off by heart. What was in her own heart, and what was in her head, and had she betrayed Ferg, she wanted to know. And she felt then that she loved him, that she'd made a huge mistake. She could feel him in her. It was Fergus that was in her, not the earth's heart beating, not the blood of the stars or the trees or whatever, it was Fergus, and she could see his face in front of her. Both sets of couples were moving closer to each other in the water, and Steph alone up on the pier. She loved Ferg and she should tell him. Yes, she loved him. He needed to know. She keyed his number in and dialled.

She felt the sweep of the mist on her skin, and the smell of the lake filled her as she hunkered out on the pier, and the phone rang.

Beep Beep.

Beep Beep.

She stuffed her finger in her right ear to hear better. And Fergus's voice came.

—Steph?

Oh God, his voice, she'd missed it so much. She spoke as gently as she could.

—It's late. I'm sorry. Were you sleeping?

—No. Yeah. What time's it?

—Late.

He had that groggy, just-awake confusion in his voice.

—What's going on?

—I knew your number off by heart.

—Oh right . . . Steph, what's up?

His voice was just beautiful like that. She'd always known and loved his voice. She was filling with love but there was also something under it, something sad and horrible, though she felt joyful now as she meant to say sorry. Everything was making such perfect sense to her, and there was a love in her that was strong if she could only get by her past actions.

—I'm sorry, Ferg.

—For what?

—For everything.

—Okay . . .

He sounded hesitant, wary. Like he thought she was prank-calling him. She loved that about him, she loved that she could still hurt him, that she'd hurt him so badly he wasn't even able to answer a call from her without fearing. She didn't know why that made her happy. None of it was making that much sense to her

228

any more, no words made any sense to her, like sadness or hurt or sorry, there was just one word that made sense and that word was love. She heard him breathing down the line, and she tried to speak in her softest voice, a voice so soft it'd melt him.

—I need to tell you something.

—What?

—I love you.

There was such a long silence on the other end that she thought the phone had died. She was getting cold out on the pier. Why wasn't he answering?

—Ferg.

—Yeah?

—I love you. I always loved you and I'm so sorry I hurt you.

—Where are you?

Again, she tried to get all the softness she could into her voice, to be that person who held and touched other people's bodies and was warm and friendly and loveable.

—We're in the country. Out by a lake. We took pills. I was thinking about you.

—You took pills?

—Yeah.

A horrible drop happened in Ferg's voice. His voice was quiet and cruel in the earpiece.

—You don't mean it.

—What?

—You don't mean it. You're pilled up.

—No, I love you.

—For fuck sake, Steph. You can't say that to me.

His voice was changing again. He was getting upset. She began to get frantic.

—I do. I love you. I love you. I do. I love you.

—You don't.

—I do.

—Why?

—What do you mean?

—Why do you love me? What about me do you love?

—I don't know. I just love you.

—What do you love, Steph? What exactly?

—Your eyes, I don't know. All of you.

—I can't believe you did this, Steph.

—What? I love you.

—You don't love anyone. You don't give a fuck about anyone but yourself.

—Fergus.

—Bye.

The phone beeped. He'd hung up. Why? What was that? Christ, no. She was still hunkered down by the end of the pier, and she was getting cold, really cold. Cath was out in the water with JJ, but she'd left her place by the chains now and was swimming away from him. DanDan was tickling Lucy on the shore, her screams carrying across the water. Steph didn't understand why, but she knew she'd fucked up. She knew by his voice, by the hurt in it, she'd broken something. What was wrong with her?

Cath

She bobbed in JJ's arms in the cold water. He'd scared her, swimming out like that. She'd watched him from the pier when Lucy and Steph jumped in screaming and splashing. She'd watched him go swimming out, his head down in the water and his arms going lap after lap over his head. He'd not even stopped at the chains, and there'd been a kind of resolve in his stroke that had not sat well with her. He'd not been heading towards any one point farther out, just swimming in a straight line into open water. It was only when she'd shouted and he'd started to come back that she'd relaxed.

As she hugged him she didn't feel any sort of romantic thing for him. Nothing of what Steph had jokingly been building up. She just didn't feel much when she went close and pressed herself against him in the cold water. No tingle. Nope. Nothing. Not on her side and not on his either. They floated together, and JJ seemed to recognise it as well. They broke apart and held on to the chain above their heads. JJ was the first to speak.

—How you getting on?

—Grand.

—Sure?

—Yeah. Why?

—You've seemed a bit down.

—What? No.

—You have.

—I didn't think anyone would notice.

—I noticed.

Cath looked at him by her side, and he gave her a little grin. She tsked.

It was strange to think it, but Cath realised that she and JJ had never once had an actual, properly honest talk together. She was beginning to see, only because of what had happened over the weekend, that she'd known these people at least a year and a half, yet had never had a direct, truthful conversation with any of them. So much of it was bullshit. They'd all been bullshitting each other. Lying to each other and lying to themselves. She didn't know a single thing about JJ's life, honestly. What did he know about hers? Cath had been surrounded by people she knew nothing about. Their minds were shut to each other. And yet she cared for them, was always concerned and worried about them. Why?

—Why are we friends, JJ?

—Ha?

—Have you not wondered, all that's happened, you know, why am I friends with these people?

—Well, cheers.

—Shut up for a second and be honest with me. Please.

JJ kept one hand on the chain and washed his other hand up through the water, cupping then releasing it through his fingers. He repeated this a few times then responded without looking at her.

—Thinking about that myself a little now as well.

—I didn't mean to insult you.

—No, I know what you mean. I don't know, to be honest.

—I mean, me and you for example. Are we friends?

—Course, Cath.

—But, really. Are we? I mean, what is it makes us friends? That we spend time together? But we never do that alone really. We never talk about anything.

—I tell you stuff.

—Not actual stuff.

—Fine. Well, I dunno. I think we're friends. But then I don't know much about you either. So, no. I'm not sure. I feel we're better friends now than before.

—Yeah. Me too. But what about the others?

—I'm not getting into a bitching session.

—God, JJ, would you stop being so wary. I'm just asking. Do you think about the others and what that means?

—Sometimes. Not till now. I mean, Merc. He was a dick. But we let him go so easily. I saw him leave, you know. I watched him leaving and I didn't try and stop him. I was sick of him. Wanted him to go.

—Yeah. Me too. He was mean to me.

—I know. I'm sorry about that.

—And the others?

—Why we're friends?

—Yeah.

—I dunno. I s'pose the lady-fella thing does come into it in some form.

—But when you take that away. Jesus, are we any good for each other at all, as a group? I mean, are we better people for being together, or worse? I think about everything that's happened so far and all I can think is that people are getting hurt and the more time we spend together the more bad things happen.

—Listen, you know. I'm not sure I should say this, but if we're not . . . If we're dragging you down . . . Cut us loose. I mean that. I don't care as much as you. It's fine for me because I'm fairly easy-going and I can kind of get on with anyone.

—I'm easy-going.

—You're not. Believe me, you're not. That's not a bad thing, mind. I mean that in a good way. You give a shit. You don't just fuck around and do whatever you want. You look after us. But it means you take stuff to heart. So I'm saying if you're taking care of us and we're not taking care of you, get rid of us.

—G'way outta that.

—No. I'm deadly serious. You're too good to have us drag you down.

She felt something welling up in her. She wanted to cry. Maybe he was right, but she had just one question for him, and then she'd know. She'd been too afraid of the answer.

—JJ?

—Yeah.

—Can I ask you something? Something personal.

—Sure.

—No. Personal for me. And you won't repeat it, and you can tell me, even if it hurts me.

—Yeah, sure.

—This is embarrassing for me, okay, so please just tell me the truth and don't make fun.

—I'll do my best. I'm not going to coddle you.

—Okay.

She could barely look at him.

—Did DanDan say anything to you about me and him, ever?

JJ sighed and rubbed his arms, treading water to keep him afloat while his hands were off the chain. Then he put his arms back up.

—This is not good talk when you're on pills. Drags you down.

—Please just tell me.

—Okay, okay . . . He did mention it last night. That there was something going on between you.

—Elaborate. What way something going on? As in something going on for him or for me?

—DanDan's a mate, right, but I'm looking out for you so I'll tell you.

—Go on.

—He said that he was sort of looking at women again. That he was getting round to the idea of it, of being interested in someone.

—In me specifically, or just interested in anyone?

—You specifically.

Cath let go of the chain.

—Did he say this to you before or after he was with Lucy?

—Before.

The son of a bitch. That's all she had for herself to think or feel. She turned in the water and started to swim slowly back to the pier. She was going to hop up but when she got there she saw Steph was hunkered down at the far end, speaking quietly into her phone, her head in her right hand and the phone in the other to

234

her ear. She swam away then, pulling herself along the wall so she'd reach the dirtied sand quicker, down by where Lucy and DanDan were rolling. Bastard DanDan. JJ called after her.

—Cath!

She ignored him. DanDan had known, then. All that day she'd been telling herself that she'd simply misunderstood him. But no. It was right there, confirmed by JJ. He'd suggested she ditch Paddy for him, which she did, and then he threw her away the minute Lucy looked at him. He just wanted to shift something, to fuck someone. He'd no preference really; whichever came first to him he'd take. What kind of bollox did that? And now there he was, rolling around with Lucy still, right in front of her, when she'd been telling herself she wasn't jealous the whole day. He was basically having sex with Lucy in front of her, not giving a single shit about how she might feel seeing it. What kind of a bollox . . .

Her feet found the bottom of the lake and she stood. The water was up to her waist. She waded hard as she could, the water rushing as she moved through. JJ was treading water back by the end of the pier, giving her her space, letting her go. She was coming out of the lake, displacing water around her knees. Five or six metres to her right was DanDan. He called to her.

—Freezing, isn't it?

And he fucking tickled Lucy as he shouted, who shrieked and splashed around him. Cath faced him. She was standing only up to her ankles in the water, and her knickers wet and soft around her, and the bra she knew was transparent. And she went at him. Loud and clear. She screamed it.

—FUCKER.

He splashed up onto his knees and she could see him peering through the dark at her, so she shouted again.

—FUCKER.

Bewildered, he spoke.

—What?

—You knew. You fucking knew.

She'd give him no more. She stomped out of the water, and climbed up onto the pier and started to walk down to where her clothes were. She knew it was cold but there was a fire alive in her bones and on her skin, there was wildfire burning up, and though she didn't look back she could hear DanDan get to his feet, and then it was Lucy's turn to half get up on her knees, and she called.

—Cath! What's up?

Cath turned again and there was DanDan, out of the water, standing on the dirty sand, his boxers tiny on his big frame, clinging to his junk, and Lucy in the water near him, so innocent, so very fucking drunk and innocent and stupid. She shouted at him.

—You absolute dickhead.

She stepped into her jeans and struggled to get them on, the water bunching them up on her. They scraped at her skin. JJ was calling to her from the water but she ignored him. DanDan was still ten metres or so away on the beach, looking about at what to do, bewildered still. And next thing Steph was beside her. Steph was already in her jeans and had her top on, her phone glowing in her hand.

—Cath, what's going on?

Cath almost choked saying it.

—I'm going back to the house.

Steph put her hand in the small of her back.

—Okay, I'm coming with you.

She didn't need pity. She didn't want it. She just wanted to be back and in a blanket. She wanted to be away from the absolute pig-fucker, her so-called friend who'd betrayed her at every turn and was still, at that very moment, looking to and from each member of the group, shrugging his shoulders in the night, looking for a reason why he was being called a fucker.

She finally got her jeans up, then she threw all three layers of her tops – the vest, the cardigan and the hoodie – on at once. She squeezed her feet back into her shoes. JJ swam up to her by the pier.

—You okay?

—I'm okay, JJ. I'm heading back to the house.

—I'll come with you.

—No. No, you're fine. I'm going with Steph. Stay here.

236

—I didn't mean to upset you.

She looked down to him. She could feel Steph looking at her.

—No, it's fine. Thank you for telling me. You were right to.

—I'm sorry.

—It's fine. Just give me some time before you come back.

—Okay.

She shoved her socks into her pocket and Steph steered her back down the pier. They walked by DanDan on their way towards the road. He stood aghast, dumb to all the world. When she reached the start of the pier with Steph, he came forward to talk to her.

—What's going on?

—Fuck off, would you.

—Hey! Don't say that, what's going on?

Cath marched right on by him. He went to go for her hand but she slapped him away.

—Stay the fuck away.

—Here, come on.

Steph helped warn him.

—No, DanDan. Leave us walk home.

Steph's fingers remained in the small of her back the whole time they walked away. They turned a corner on the road and the lake dropped out of sight. The long road curved ahead of them as they set back out for the house by the graves.

Cath gave a last scream, towards him, towards everyone and everything that had made such an absolute fool out of her, had made her seem so stupid and small and weak and insignificant.

—FUCKERS.

Lucy

Why'd they gone, Cath and Steph? Why'd they shouted? It had started before she'd realised, and it was over long before she'd had time to invest herself in the argument. All she knew was that one minute Cath was screaming, and next she was gone, Steph with her. DanDan sat back down in the water with Lucy. He called over to JJ, who stood chest high in the water.

—What's with her?

JJ shrugged his shoulders. He was unusually withdrawn.

—You'll have to ask her yourself.

DanDan seemed unfazed by the whole encounter. He laughed it off with a wave of his hand.

—She's off her head.

JJ swam slowly ashore, rubbed himself down with his bunched T-shirt, then dressed quickly. He collapsed onto the sand, and started to roll a spliff.

—We'll stay here a while. Give them some time.

Lucy and DanDan stayed in the water. DanDan wouldn't kiss her. She touched his shoulder, but he sat back, and let his hands float palms-up in the water.

How much time passed, she didn't know. The pill played all sorts of games with her. One moment she was dancing on the sand by herself, to an imaginary tune, or was she parping one with her lips, The Beatles maybe, 'All You Need is Love', *Perp perp perp perp peeeerp*, and JJ was standing by himself at the end of the pier looking out over the water, and DanDan had his arm around her waist, his fingers sandy and coarse on her hips. Next thing she was doing handstands, her wet hair brushing along the sand. JJ watched the black water and dashed his shadow in it with his hand. She felt ill, then she was wrapped up in a jumper, sitting on the beach beside JJ.

They could have been there for twenty minutes or four hours, she didn't know. They lay back on the sand. JJ offered a new spliff to DanDan, who murmured:

—On top of pills?

JJ said it was fine, so Lucy smoked the best part of the joint and let it float into her.

She felt her legs go mushy. She didn't know where she was. She felt mute, dumb. She needed something to feel for the strength, to find the blood in her legs. She rolled up into a sitting position. Down on the pier she'd still some wine left. She struggled to her feet and stumbled down the pier to her bag, dragging out a bottle of white wine.

She took a large gulp. The sharpness of it kicked her, burned the back of her throat, and though she was still muggy, it had done a small job. She took another gulp before bringing it back to the lads. She lay back on the crunchy, dirty sand drying herself, and feeling the sharpness of the wine mix with the drowsiness of the spliff and the thump of the pill and then the world started to turn too quickly. She screwed her eyes shut and tried to shout, to be heard once, loud and clear.

—I need to go. We need to go home.

—Yeah?

—Yeah. Getting cold.

—Fair enough.

Anything was better than sitting watching the sky spin and spin and spin overhead, so they dressed and left.

The stars were swaying as her and DanDan started on the long road back. JJ walked by himself about fifty yards ahead. The wind rustled gently through the trees, and she felt the mist they were in moving, either lifting or just blowing somewhere else, she didn't know. Her hair and head were wet and her underwear was soggy under her clothes. There was too much going on, too much that she could feel and see. She squeezed DanDan's hand, using it as an anchor.

The ground was uneven, circling under her, so she watched her feet in the dark, as if they didn't belong to her, had never belonged to her. The right foot swung up and into her vision, followed by the left, and she judged the distances by the dark pebbles they passed on the road, or she tried to count the cracks in the old cement.

DanDan's hand went limp in hers. He let it fall down as if the only natural way for it to be was poker-straight by his side. She let him go and he let himself be let go. He wandered to the other side of the road, and trailed his fingers against the rock face.

Lucy's head was spinning, or the ground was spinning, she didn't know. She needed to speak, though she'd risk sickness and collapse by doing so, but the longer things went unsaid the farther away DanDan was drifting. She opened her mouth and tried to speak through a closed throat.

—You okay, DanDan?

—Grand, doing well.

She went on walking. Every fourth or fifth step one of her legs deviated from the course, went out to the right slightly, and her body curved with it and she stumbled. Not enough to let DanDan notice, she hoped. She stopped. DanDan puttered along a few more steps before he stopped and looked back.

—What's up?

—Nothing.

—What are you doing?

—Feel sick.

DanDan huffed. Farther down, she saw the small, skinny figure of JJ turn and look back. DanDan waved him away, shouting.

—Go on ahead.

JJ put his head down and walked on. DanDan came and rubbed the side of her leg with his hand, though he didn't take her hand or put his arms around her. He stood a foot taller than her trying to look down into her eyes, even though hers were focused on the wet stains of lake water on his T-shirt. He rubbed her leg.

—Alright? Come on, it's cold here.

She needed to get sick. How the fuck had she poisoned herself so badly? Things were mixing up inside her. Things which had seemed like such a great idea at the start, wines and beers and shots and then pills, spliffs, more drink, and fug and lake water. Everything sloshing and coursing through her. She could feel the beer in her belly, and the tequila around in her liver, and the wine sting in the back of her throat, begging her to vomit, and the weed in her head and her eyes, clouding everything, the pill doing laps of her body, making her want to move and dance, but then it travelled to her stomach and met the tequila and the beer and went violent, and then in her head the love of it came musty with the spliff, and she felt sick.

—I'm fine. It's just a wave. Let's sit down.

She wandered over to the rock face and sat down against it. The sick feeling simmered down and she felt clearer. DanDan sat with her and they were as they'd been the night before. He tapped her knee.

—Okay?

She leaned in and tried to kiss him. He dodged away and shook his head. She nuzzled on his neck.

—Why not?

—You're too pissed.

—Fuck off. Was a bit woozy there. But that's when it's nice. Come on.

She clutched the back of his neck and dragged her head towards him. He resisted initially but she used enough strength to convince him she had her wits about her, she was no wilting flower. He dropped his head to her and she kissed him. She felt secure again, warm on his lips and his tongue and neck. His hand was on her face and look at her now, the love in her, she loved him she loved him and she scrunched in closer to him. His lips tasted of lake water, of cold steel. She pushed her tongue in his mouth and felt around his shirt collar with her fingers till his hands drifted down and played with her collarbone. She bit his lip so he grunted and she leaned back towards the ground so he'd to lean over her. They were almost horizontal, only her arse and hips raised off the ground kept him from flopping onto her, so she jerked her hips around again and edged out into the road, dragging him with her. He tore his face from hers.

—Hang on now, the road.

—Fuck it, there's no cars.

—Ah now.

—Come on. Come on, let's just do it.

They edged out till their bodies were stretched over one side of the road. He started to dry hump her in thrusts and they shoved right out until they were on top of a narrow run of grass in the middle of the road, and then her jeans were down. She thought she should ask him about a condom but sure what harm, it was just the once and it hadn't exactly seemed romantic the night before, watching him roll a sickly yellow skin over himself, and fuck it he was almost inside her anyway. She angled her hips up and then he was inside her and it felt good and right and he was off, on his way again, and Lucy was not sick, no, she felt full of love, but he wasn't watching her, that was the only thing; his face was buried in her neck as he thrust away, his hand wriggling awkwardly under her bra cup, the bra he'd not unfastened even, and she thought about saying his name as he went into her but it seemed weird so she just made little noises, and they went on and on and on and it was awkward because he couldn't get the rhythm right and they banged their teeth together and she breathed on him at one stage, breathed right up his nose so he coughed and then he came.

They gasped against each other. Lucy wanted to hold onto him, never let him go, but DanDan stood up and started putting himself back in his trousers. She let herself lie back and just enjoy that one moment, the warmth of him still on her and the sharp sting of cold air in her lungs as they opened for her rapid breaths. She felt again what it was to be a woman and grown up and to be a part of the grown-up world.

DanDan started shuffling near her, so she stood back up and started to pull her jeans on. She wanted to hug him but once her jeans were done up and she'd her bra fixed neatly, he started to skip and look around. He wanted to go.

—Will we go?

—Sure.

DanDan started to walk ahead. He walked quickly, Lucy trying to keep up with him.

—Why are we rushing?

—We're not rushing. It's cold.

—Would you hang on?

—We've to get back.

—Why?

—We just do.

—I can't keep up. Hang on! . . . Dan!

He stopped, and looked back at her. There was a distance between them she couldn't get to. He'd been with her only two minutes before; there were parts of himself still rubbed up into her, his skin and his clothes and everything had been on her, and now there was this electric energy that existed between them that she couldn't reach across, and in the silence she could see he was breathing heavy and she wondered why. Then there was a rustle and a loud cracking sound.

—SHIT!

DanDan shoved her away from the mossy cliff face as a large rock crashed by. A stone, a fucking boulder the size of a volleyball, tumbled down the rock face. It rolled heavily into the road, making a glassy marble sound. It came to rest in the middle of the road, right where they'd just been standing. More pebbles came skittling down after it, and then another rock, about the size of a garden gnome, tumbled down in awkward circles and clumped in the grass below the rock face. Lucy's heart was fucked as she felt DanDan's arm against her stomach.

—We're okay, we're fine. Just stay back.

—What the fuck, Dan?

He walked over and inspected the rock, trying to get his breathing under control.

—Loose rocks.

—Jesus, it scared the shit out of me. What made them come loose?

—Dunno.

—We were just there.

—Yeah.

—Fucking lucky.

DanDan looked up the road and down the road and back to the rock.

—Here though, it's dangerous like that in the middle of the road.

He lifted the big rock up. It was slippy under his hands and she could see it was heavy. He hoisted it up, and shuffled with it over to the other side of the road, swung it back and heaved it out of sight down to the trees below. Lucy could hear it punching into the first bit of soft soil then slapping down farther until its sound disappeared in the trees. DanDan wiped his hands.

—Just to be safe.

He picked up the smaller rock from the bottom of the rock face and chucked it to the side of the road. Then he came and put his arm around her. Lucy felt clear in her head. The shock had brought the world into focus, and with his arm over her shoulders she felt secure and safe. She turned into him, and nodded her head up against his chin, and he leaned down and kissed her, this time soft and tender, not harsh and quick like before, and she was happy.

He took her hand and they started to walk back. What had seemed like such a long road before them now seemed much shorter, but Lucy felt the cold now, she felt the mist and the time of night, and she went into her bag and took out the bottle of wine. There was maybe a third left. She took a swig and gave it to DanDan. He drank the wine with a renewed fierceness, and Lucy took it off him.

—Oi, calm down.

—Sorry. I just . . . I'm a bit agitated.

—Why?

—Think Cath is angry with me.

Cath had been acting weird, in fairness. There'd been a lot of shouting earlier. Maybe Cath had liked DanDan and that's what this was about, but Cath had told her time and again, repeated it over and over, she didn't like DanDan. Nothing there, nothing there. So why was it so bad that Lucy had gone for it?

She drank the end of the wine and threw the bottle at the last of the rock face they were passing. It smashed into dust against the hard rock. Good. If you were going to destroy something, better do it properly, leave no shard or splinter left that could do damage. The glass dust seemed to float away. DanDan tutted at her act, but she hugged herself into him as they walked.

—It'll be grand with Cath.

—Why should she be fucking angry at me?

—That's between yourselves. I'm staying out of it.

—Yeah.

—Come on, we're almost there.

They could see the steeple of the church through the trees. They were almost back. Lucy felt DanDan quicken his pace and arch his back, his hand strong in hers.

Malachy

Hours and hours he stayed in his chair by the door, waiting for them to return. Eventually, two of the girls arrived back. The blonde girl and the brunette, Catherine, their hair wet. They must have gone swimming in the lake. They looked cold and walked hurriedly, without joy. They sat briefly outside the house and shared a cigarette. Catherine put her head in her hands, and started to cry. Something must have happened down by the shore. The blonde girl put her arm around her, comforting her. After a while, they got up and went back inside. The lights went on downstairs in the house again.

A while after that, the skinny fella came ambling back and threw something in the stream. That just meant the tall one and the pudgy one were still out, and he wondered where they were, or what had happened to the group of them that they had split.

And then he saw them, lying down on the curved road leading to the Lodge. Two shapes rubbing in against each other. He supposed they thought no one could see them, being hidden from view of the Lodge by the undergrowth, but Malachy could see them, lit from farther down by one of the street lights. The tall lad moved on top of the pudgy one, her jeans and drawers twisted down around one ankle, his bunched down around his knees. They jerked into each other in the middle of the road.

Their pace quickened, the lad on top of the girl, and they banged into each other awkwardly, their skin rubbing and grazing against each other, the two of them eroding each other away, destroying each other, a tangle of clothes and mismatched breaths as they quickened, and he remembered her again, pressed up against him in the water, him feeling her so warm, so near, so close and her saying not now, not yet, not yet, we'll wait, we'll wait.

He wanted them gone, he wanted them gone now, the shit they'd brought up. He squeezed his eyes tight and pushed in around them as hard as he could with the backs of his wrists, till his eyeballs felt the pressure and started to ache and he tried to crush his own face in on itself.

Steph

Cath was curled up on the couch with a glass of wine. She'd told Steph what had happened as they walked home from the lake, everything about breaking it off with Paddy, then DanDan lying and fucking her over. Steph couldn't believe it. The shit she'd had to put up with. She'd had half a mind to walk back out to the shore and deck DanDan herself, but Cath had smiled and told her not to, so she just got them some wine and they talked it out in the living room.

She was still feeling a bit spacey with the pill, though the last of it seemed to be leaving her. The room was bright and yellow, the dimensions skewed, and she tried to keep her head straight as she tended to Cath. She sat opposite her as she sniffed and sniffled.

—It's stupid.

—It's not stupid.

—He's just a fucking prick.

Cath drank deep from her wine then blew into the glass, causing the liquid to ripple and stream up the sides. Steph kept silent as she played with the glass. Eventually she put it down on the tiled floor and crossed her arms.

—What do you think, Steph?

—What do you mean, what do I think?

—About DanDan.

—I dunno.

Cath's eyes were red, her hands around her knees as she waited for Steph to give her answers.

—Just tell me what you think, Steph.

—I can't tell you.

248

—Please.

Why was Cath looking to her for answers? She was probably the worst person in the world to give them. Steph pitied Cath, who was suffering, completely at the mercy of DanDan, but she dreaded the day she'd ever be like that. What kind of a person needed others so badly they'd leave themselves open to that kind of hurt? Steph could barely comprehend it. She didn't think she could ever care that much about someone to be hurt by them. Maybe Ferg was right, then. Maybe she didn't give a fuck.

—Fuck DanDan. I've not seen it till now but he's a dick.

—Yeah?

—How fucking dare he, like.

—It's out of line, yeah?

—Course.

—So I'm not being mental.

She couldn't help herself; the moon-eyes of Cath got to her. She could try to help her at least. She kneeled down by Cath and hugged her. She held her in her arms and squeezed until Cath squeaked. They separated. Cath looked in her eyes and Steph told her.

—You're way, way fucking better than him.

—Ah stop.

—No, I fucking mean it. And you know I don't bullshit. You're way better than him. Fuck him.

—Thanks.

She stayed kneeling down, right at eye level with Cath.

—And you know what, you should tell him so.

—What?

—You need to tell him where to go.

—I don't want a fight, I just think he's being a prick.

—There's a time for walking away, and there's a time for fighting. It's fighting time now. So when he comes back, don't you break. Don't cry and make up. Don't brush over it like it's nothing. I know you're not into fights, Cath, but you have to give him a bollocking. Tell him to shove it up his arse.

—I can't do that.

—Look at you. Look at what he's done to you.

—Drama.

—You need drama. Sometimes you just need to tell someone to go fuck themselves. For your own good as much as theirs. And no one here will disagree with you.

—Steph, I don't think . . .

Cath was beginning to crawl back into herself, losing her nerve, so Steph grabbed her elbow, felt it bony and awkward in her palm. She knew that Cath was softening, her anger fading, so she clenched her elbow hard, dug her fingers in.

—Cath, listen, right. You're a nice person, but people walk all fucking over you. And I can tell you, once you let people take from you they'll keep doing it and doing it until they take everything, and then they'll throw you away . . . Don't look at me like that, okay? Just listen to me, listen to me.

She'd no idea why she was saying what she was saying but she knew that it was true.

—We're completely fucking different, me and you, okay? I'm nothing like you. I use people all the fucking time. I use them for what they can give me and then I throw them away and I don't think about them any more.

Cath watched her cautiously.

—You don't.

—I do. I do it all the time. Do you know what I did yesterday? I fucked Merc. I fucked him right up against the side of the house. And this morning he took off. Everyone was making fun of him and I didn't say a word. I could have gotten him to stay. I could've gotten all of you to give him a break but I didn't. I was embarrassed because I'd fucked him and he'd run away. I wasn't worried about what was going on in his head. I was worried about me looking bad. Now he's gone and fuck knows what he's doing. I use people when I need them, but when it comes to them, I don't care. I don't care one little bit if they're in pain or any of the rest of it. I just let them do whatever they're doing and I don't give a shit.

She'd never really known she'd thought that way about things. Coming out of her were solid thoughts that seemed to have been formed and smoothed and polished over time. They weren't just ramblings, and she wondered how the hell they had existed in her before they came out, if what was happening now was a spontaneous act of putting everything together, or if it was just some trick of her unconscious to have had all these thoughts and just hidden them from her.

—What are you talking about?

—Fucking listen to me, right. What do you think I've been doing when I've been silent around you, or you ask me why I'm watching you? I'm judging you, Cath. I'm doing it the whole fucking time, but I don't really care much about helping you with what's bothering you. To be honest, we're never gonna be great friends. You know a lot of things about me, all about my problems and what bothers me, but I know fuck all about you, only what I see in front of me, because I've just never cared enough to ask. But I can tell you this from having watched you.

—Steph.

—You can take this from me, because you know that what I'm telling you is not with an agenda or with a view to do anything in the group because I don't give a shit about the group. JJ is a good fella. He's a thick but he'll stand by you. I'm not sure about Lucy. Merc's a prick. But watch for DanDan, he's a snake.

—No one is fully one or the other.

—They are as far as you're concerned. Listen, now. Listen to me. Stand up for your fucking self. You can't let people fuck you over and get away with it, Cath. You can't ignore this. You draw a fucking line under this.

—Steph, are you okay?

—I'm fucking fine. You need to deal with this, okay. Do you understand what I'm saying to you?

—I think so.

She slapped the wine glass out of Cath's hand. It shattered on the floor, the wine spilling away.

—Look at me. Not you fucking think so. I'm fucking asking do you understand what the fuck I'm saying to you. Do you understand?

Cath looked at her for a few seconds in silence, then she nodded firmly.

—Yes.

Steph knew she'd got the message. She let go of Cath's elbow, and stood up.

—Good. Then I'm going to bed. I'm high as a fucking kite and I'm going to bed. Thanks for everything, okay. Good night. Night.

She stepped away from her. She steeled her voice against Cath just as she left, so she'd know that despite all this, all she was saying to her, she was still herself.

—I'm taking the good room again.

Steph took the steep stairs two at a time and felt Cath watching her the whole way. She went into the dark room and slammed the door shut and went under the covers, her dirty shoes on, her wet clothes on, her make-up washed away, everything washed away. She knew what she'd said about herself was true. How many people had she fucked over in all her life? Plenty, no doubt. She could forget about all of them except one. Fergus was somewhere in Dublin not sleeping. She'd called him and told him she loved him when she didn't. She'd done that. What the fuck kind of a person did that to people?

JJ

He'd left DanDan and Lucy behind him and continued on to the house. The whole way home his heart was up and down and his thoughts were ecstatic and happy and terrified and he'd good and bad memories flooding him. He didn't know where the fuck he was. He'd the shock of earlier, his swim, and the sadness from his walk into Carrig, but he also had Cath clinging to him in the water, holding onto him and his hands on her. He'd a lethal past behind but a way forward. By the time he reached the Lodge, his mind had settled and a calm had come over him. He stopped by the gate, wondering what he'd say to Cath when he went in. As he waited outside, he heard the river, the whisper of it, off towards the end of the garden. He stepped away from the gate, and followed the sound of it into the grass. He walked out until he came to a ditch on the border of the field. He got to the edge of the ditch and found the river.

It was barely more than two feet wide, though it flowed quickly and forcefully over rounded rocks down to the lake. How had that made such a noise? He went down and scooped up some of the water in his hands. It spilled out until only a small pool remained in his palms.

He drank. The water was cool and fresh. He licked the last of his palm clear, then he felt in the back of his jeans and took out the little bag of pills he'd been carrying around all night. He'd scared the shit out of himself earlier with his little swim out into the lake. He'd been so close to continuing on, out farther and farther into the lake until he couldn't swim any more, just on a fucking whim.

But Cath had called him back. She'd hugged him in the water and they'd floated together, and he'd been glad he was alive, glad he'd come back. He never wanted to swim out like that again. He emptied the pills into his hand and tossed them into the river. That was step one.

Step two . . . He walked to the front door and let himself in.

He waited a moment or two in the hallway, took a breath and flattened his hair. When he stepped into the living room, he found Cath up and standing by the table. She had one foot behind the other in a boxer's stance. She looked like she was about to throw a dig. When she saw it was him she relaxed.

—Just you?

—Just me.

—Where's DanDan?

She was looking well, Cath was looking well.

—Stopped with Lucy a while back, they're on their way. You okay?

—I'm fine.

He looked in her eyes but they were so full of anger he looked away. She spun around and went to the record collection. She flipped through it, her back to him, the old vinyl sleeves slapping against each other.

JJ took a step towards her. Her mind was on DanDan. Don't be on DanDan. Be on him. Be on JJ.

It wasn't the best time for it – it was definitely not the best time for it – but he should get in there before DanDan got back. Who knew, maybe DanDan and Cath would have a roaring argument before falling into each other's arms. There'd be no more chance with her after that. If there was ever a time, it was now. Cath shoved a pile of records to one side.

—Fucking showbands.

—Ha.

He knew he should say something. Get on his fucking knees and beg. Go over and touch her cheek, and put his arms around her. Get on with it. He should say it now before she was too angry to carry on. He took a step forward and there were words on his lips.

254

—Here, there's something I wanted to . . .

But she was way ahead of him now, completely on her own train.

—JJ.

—Yeah?

—When DanDan comes . . .

—Yeah?

—I'm going to have a fight with him.

—Oh right . . . Okay.

Fuck. Fuck sake. Fuuuck. Fuuckkkk. Fuck. Fuck sake. Fuck. He tried to control his face. He swallowed and nodded his head vigorously.

—Okay . . . Do you want support, or . . .

—No. Thanks. I'd like you to stay out of it. I have to do it myself. But just warning you anyway.

He took a step away. Keep calm. Fuck. Keep cool. Nothing was lost. Just delayed.

—Okay. I'll keep out.

—Thanks.

BANG.

Fucking timing. He turned and DanDan was striding into the room, Lucy skittering in behind him. He was holding her hand so hard it looked like he was breaking it. He'd obviously been revving himself up, because the first thing he did was start shouting.

DanDan

It was only when he passed the church that he felt it rising in him, that real cool sense of him being the one in the right. He had the high ground, and he let that feeling build up. Not just anger. Righteousness. He picked up the pace, trying to get Lucy to keep up. He felt he had her support, and as they approached the house he said to her:

—I don't fucking know why she was acting like that.

Lucy, slightly breathless behind him, made cooing noises.

—Don't mind her, she was probably just drunk.

—But why was she doing that? Fucking giving me a bollocking when I've done nothing.

He could feel the anger coming up in his chest as they got to the gate of the house. He went in ahead of Lucy, and she kept a hold of his hand, and he went down the steps, the rocks wet and slippy, and he wondered if he fell and knocked his head and killed himself would Cath live the rest of her life regretting what she'd said to him. He hoped he would fall, just to spite her. He stormed down the steps to the front door. He pushed the handle in and took a step inside. He was never so fucking sure in his life that he was right and that someone else was really, really fucking wrong. Two steps forward and he was out of the hallway and into the big living room.

JJ was standing by the table, Cath farther down flicking through some records. He announced himself, dragging Lucy behind him, in a sharp fucking tone.

—The fuck was that?

Cath turned to him and Christ almighty, she was made up for a fight as well. There was a heft in her shoulders. He'd never seen her look so angry. It took him aback briefly, but he composed himself. Be strong, be fucking strong, because he was right. Cath opened her mouth to speak but he knew he shouldn't give her the advantage of an open attack so he shouted.

—What the fuck is that? We're all out having a good time and then you just go on shouting at me? What the fuck is wrong with you?

He spluttered a bit. He knew he was shouting at her and she went to say so but he cut her off quick. He was doing well.

—And I know I'm shouting at you. Don't look at me like that. I'm only shouting because you were shouting, but can you fucking explain yourself, please? We're all having a good time and you burst a fucking gasket.

He left it hanging there. It was ballsy, going straight in demanding an explanation, but he felt he had the right. What had he done? He assumed it had something to do with him and her but she'd no rights over him, and he'd never made her any promises, and save for a little intimacy the previous night he'd not done anything wrong.

Cath was silent. JJ said nothing, he just went and sat down, looking at Cath as if asking her if she was alright, so DanDan went on.

—Oh, silent treatment, is it? Fucking mature. Just fucking apologise, would you?

He felt then that he'd found his niche, he'd found a way to win but not be a bully. He softened his tone.

—Right, so I'm sorry I'm shouting, right, I shouldn't shout.

He cooled his voice and gave a swishy motion with his arms.

—Okay, I'm calm now, okay. So just apologise, yeah. Just say sorry, okay, and we'll forget about it.

Cath let him finish. She kept the distance between them, standing on the other side of the couch, beside the fireplace they'd stuffed with firelighters, rolled newspaper and cardboard beer cartons. Then she unfolded her arms and came from around the couch and spoke in a slow, scornful tone.

—Are you stupid?

—What?

—Are you. Fucking. Thick?

DanDan took a step back, but no, that wasn't the way to go, so he took a step forward and lowered his voice as well.

—Is that all you have to say, Cath? Call me stupid?

—You're a fucking thick, DanDan, so yeah. Let me tell you.

—Go on. Come on. If you're going to. Come on. Come on.

He took another step forward. Cath kept her stance steady.

—Alright, then. You're fucking thick, DanDan. Right. You are. So let me tell you. I liked you, right? I did. I fucking liked you.

Ha! So she had. He had her now. None of that was his fault.

—Sorry, Cath, I can't help that.

—No, you can't. And that's my problem. I told myself I didn't but I did, okay. That's not your fault.

—Yeah.

—But . . .

She paused. He could see it, she'd been practising this one, she'd been thinking on it a while.

—But you knew I did. We were out here last night and you said something to me.

—What thing?

—Don't play stupid, DanDan.

—Thought I was the stupid one, according to you.

—You said you were interested in me and that if I stopped seeing Paddy we could do something.

DanDan felt Lucy's hand leave his. He had forgotten it was there, squeezed tight in his fist. He didn't look around but he felt Lucy take a step back. He needed to address that before Lucy got the wrong idea.

—No, I didn't.

—Yes, you did.

—No, I didn't. I said nothing fucking like it. I thought we were talking fucking generally. I came here because I was having a hard time, yeah. I had a woman fucking die on me. And then I start to come around. I said that I was thinking of getting back out there and you said did I have anyone in mind and I said No. I actually

258

said fucking no, but if I did I was a one-woman kind of guy and that anyone I was with would have to be the same, a one-guy woman, I mean.

Cath looked at him pityingly.

—No, you didn't.

—Eh, yeah I did.

And here was his victory, here it was in front of him. So that's what was in her head. She'd thought it was about them when he'd made no promises. There'd been a hint of something there but DanDan had been sure when he said it, he'd made a very direct attempt to say it wasn't her. He could settle the whole thing now. Lucy was no longer attached to him. He spread his arms out wide, a gesture of bridging the gap, renewed friendship, acceptance.

—Now Cath, I'm sorry if I said that, right, and you thought it was meant to be about you. But it wasn't. It wasn't. But I am sorry. I'm sorry if you thought I was talking about you. I was talking generally. So this whole thing is a misunderstanding, okay. I'm sorry you got hurt, and if the me-and-Lucy thing – I'm sorry if you thought that was me being callous, but you know now that I didn't realise you thought I was talking about you. Okay. So can we hug and forget about it?

He put his arms out. That was a fucking masterclass. He felt the anger leaving him. Poor Cath, thinking that. It wasn't his fault, and it wasn't hers, so he didn't even want to win now.

—I just want my friend back, okay. We're great fucking friends, Cath. So can we just hug and forget about it?

But Cath stayed still. He expected her to cry. She usually cried at moments like this. Her jaw was clenched.

—No. You know what you did.

—Know what? Seriously, Cath, I didn't know you thought I was talking about you. I didn't. Swear. Okay.

He looked to JJ but JJ picked his nails, ignoring him.

—No, DanDan. You know what you did. I know what you meant, and so do you, alright.

—I really didn't.

259

—No. That's fine. See, I've seen it. That's enough for me. And if you want to delude yourself—

—Delude myself?

—Yeah, delude yourself. That's fine. But we both know what you meant. So I'm not apologising. I think you should apologise.

—Hang fucking on.

—But if you choose not to, that's fine as well. We've a moment here now, when we can both face uncomfortable truths about ourselves. We can recognise them, and learn from them and move on. Or we can pretend they don't exist.

Silence in the room. He felt blood throbbing in his ears, his face was getting hot. It was hot in the room. Why was it so fucking hot? He was getting so fucking angry he wanted to just lash out and fucking kill something. She was fucking wrong. JJ coughed, and DanDan glared at him. Lucy behind him spoke up.

—Cath. I'm sorry, Cath. I didn't know.

—I know you didn't, Lucy. That's okay.

—I really didn't know you liked him.

—It's fine, Lucy, it's not your fault.

—Okay. But . . .

—Yeah?

—I think if DanDan says he didn't say he liked you then maybe you misunderstood.

Lucy was on his side then. He had a fucking supporter, if not JJ then Lucy. But Cath wouldn't stop.

—Lucy, he knows. Don't you, DanDan? You know. I'm fine with you being with him, Lucy. Just be careful.

—Cath, DanDan says he's sorry, okay, so why don't you just apologise as well and we can forget about it and have a drink and talk in the morning.

Cath shook her head, and there was a snarl in her lip though she tried to quieten it.

—Lucy, I don't think you should have any more to drink.

He looked back at Lucy. She'd had her hand resting on the bannister going up the stairs but when he turned she dropped her hand and stepped forward to Cath. She was level with DanDan now. The two of them side by side. A united front.

—What's that mean?

—Honestly, Luce, I shouldn't say it now, but we're all being honest. You should think about laying off the booze.

Lucy breathed heavy beside him a moment, stunned, then she almost shrieked.

—Fuck you, Cath, we're all drinking. We're here on a fucking drinking weekend for fuck sake.

—I'm not saying it to hurt you, Lucy. But I've been thinking about saying it for a while.

—Oh fuck you, Cath. We're all trying to be nice here, we're all trying to be kind and understand each other and you start being a right fucking bitch about it.

—Lucy, I'm not saying it to hurt you.

And though Cath maybe even had a point, now was hardly the time to say it. Lucy was on his side so he should defend her.

—Don't mind her, Lucy. She's just being straight fucking spiteful. No need for that, Cath. We're all drinking.

Lucy nodded in agreement with him.

—We're all drinking, Cath.

Cath seemed like they hadn't changed her opinion on it. She looked at JJ.

—JJ? By the way, we haven't spoken about this before, Lucy. I can tell you that now. Me and JJ haven't said a word about it to each other before, but JJ, does Lucy drink too much?

JJ looked up at Lucy beside DanDan and though his face was sympathetic he looked at her straight and spoke.

—Maybe you should lay off for a while, Luce. I say that as a friend.

—Well, fuck you, JJ. Fucking pillhead. How can you talk? Stoned half the fucking time and drunk the other half?

—It's not about me, Luce, but yeah, I'm actually going to be cutting down myself.

—Well, bully for you, JJ, prick.

Cath took a final shot.

261

—We don't mean to upset you, Lucy, but yeah. Think about it.

Lucy pushed past DanDan and ran to the table. There was fury in her but she couldn't find much on the table except the cup JJ was using for an ashtray, a fine small porcelain thing, white with little green flowers on it.

—Fuck you, Cath!

She took it up and pelted it at Cath. Cath ducked, though Lucy's throw was way off. The cup smashed on the wall behind her. Cigarette ash puffed out into the air, leaving a grey stain on the wall.

—FUCK you. Fuck you. I'm going to bed. Fuck you.

—Lucy.

Cath stepped forward but Lucy barged by DanDan and went stomping up the stairs. She slipped on the high steps and banged her knee. She whimpered and gulped for air, and it looked for a second like she might just collapse down and sleep on the stairs, but then she started stomping up again. There was quiet except for her footsteps as she disappeared out of sight. They listened to her push in the door to their room, and slam it after her. It was quiet again.

DanDan turned to Cath.

—That was fucking harsh, Cath. Not on.

Cath shrugged her shoulders.

—I'll talk to her, DanDan. I didn't want to do it, but she has a problem and you know she does and you shouldn't tell her otherwise.

—You're being a complete fucking bitch, Cath.

—Whatever about it. We'll sort it out. But for you and me now, you do know what you did. You know.

—STOP FUCKING SAYING YOU KNOW.

—You should go in the morning. And when you're going maybe just have a think about it.

—I've a clear conscience.

—You shouldn't. You can be a great fella, DanDan. Great fun and all that. But think about what happened. You do know.

What fucking right had she? What right at all? Her standing there so calm and self-righteous in front of him made it all the worse. She was wrong, she was so, so wrong, and it was burning hot in the room but he wanted a drink as well.

He went into the dark kitchen and found the vodka. He took a swig from the bottle. He knew Cath was still standing in the living room, her arms folded and feeling so smug with herself. How had he never seen that nasty side of her? All the while he'd thought everything she'd ever done was sweet and considerate, but when she'd been helping him, calling round to him when he was upset and sending all those texts, it was just because she liked him. And now, when the possibility of him liking her back was gone, she was turning on him.

The vodka stung his throat. She couldn't be happy for him, not if he was happy without her, and he felt the tug of his former heartbreak coming back into him; he felt the darkness coming, the shame of it.

He wondered had he said something to Cath, had he really honestly meant it about her. He tried to swim back in his memory to the night before, them both outside, he was in his bare feet. Or was he? But fuck that, fuck, no. He remembered what he remembered. He hadn't said anything that made it about her. If there was a fault, or an error, it was hers. He'd said nothing wrong.

He slugged the vodka again and it retched up in his throat and his eyes burned and watered. He walked into the living room, JJ leaning back in his chair and Cath there waiting for him. What use was any of it? He shouted at her.

—You're full of shit.

She didn't move. He marched to the fireplace and grabbed his guitar up from where it lay on the floor. His stupid fucking guitar that hurt his fingers and never worked the way he wanted.

He took the guitar up in one hand, swung it over his head and brought it down on the ground. It made a twangy clunk. Cath jumped. JJ creaked his chair back down on all four legs, and shouted at him.

—Dan!

The first blow on the tiles hadn't broken it. It just bounced it up. Again, fucking again.

—Dan!

—Fuck off, JJ.

He took the neck of the guitar in both hands, raised it right up over his head and smashed it down. He felt the structure of it rupture as splinters flew in all directions. Christ, it broke well. The face of the guitar dangled above the ground, still attached to the neck by the strings. JJ tried to calm him down.

—DanDan.

—What?

He glared at JJ. Cath shrugged her shoulders.

—Let him, if he thinks it'll work.

—Fuck you.

He stuffed the remains of the guitar into the fireplace. It kept falling out, heaped on top of the rubbish already in there, so he put his foot up on it and smushed it in until it stayed, then he went and gathered up the pieces of wood left on the tiles. He threw those into the fireplace as well, along with a handful of firelighters from the mantelpiece. He breathed heavy as he turned to Cath and she sighed.

—You finished?

Oh, the last fucking straw. DanDan took his lighter out, then he got one of the rolls of paper out from under the fire and had it lit before Cath could step forward, hissing at him.

—Are you fucking stupid?

—Fuck off.

He threw it in on top of the guitar. It lay there a while, and Cath stopped mid-tracks, while JJ rose from his chair and watched it. It did nothing. The roll of newspaper just lay there burning quietly, not stunning anyone, and DanDan was disappointed, until the paper shifted. The roll fell to one side and touched a bit of cardboard at the back. Then whoosh, it started to go up.

Cath shouted at him.

—For fuck sake, DanDan, put it out. Put it out.

—Fuck off, it's fine.

DanDan watched as the bits of the guitar were swallowed up in flames. The fire flickered large and bright, spitting a little up out of the grate.

—It's fine.

Something else took. It wasn't just the stuff DanDan had thrown in. There was other fuel on it somewhere. Then he saw the little puddles lying about the floor, wet stains soaking the carpet and the cloth covering the mantelpiece.

Flames exploded out from the fireplace.

—FUCK.

Cath screamed. The heat of it forced DanDan back. The fire blazed up, dancing from spot to spot across the mantel. The whole front of the fireplace seemed to go up. It burned bright and hot. There were snaps and bursts as sparks shot out onto the old woollen carpet on the floor. Black stains were burning into the wall over the fireplace.

—Fucking Merc!

—What?

—He threw fucking sambuca everywhere. Put it out!

—Shit, shit, shit.

DanDan stood back as JJ ran into the kitchen.

—Where's the fire extinguisher?

—What?

—Fucking fire extinguisher.

Cath ran after JJ and he could hear them.

—There's fucking none.

—What?

—I don't know. I don't know!

JJ ran back in and DanDan stood there dumb, and he felt the first sting of smoke in his nostrils. The cloth on the mantelpiece was up in flames, and the fire started to climb up the back wall. JJ shouted.

—Right. Out.

—What?

—OUT.

Cath ran in.

—No! We've to put it out.

—Get out!

JJ ran upstairs and DanDan heard him shouting in Steph's room, waking her.

—Get up!

—What?

—Get up, get up, get out.

Steph stamped down the stairs. Halfway down she saw the fire.

—The fuck? Shit! Shit!

—Get out!

She ran down to the end of the stairs, and grabbed Cath's hand.

—Come on. Come on.

—No.

—Come on.

JJ came down the stairs after them, dragging Lucy with him. As JJ struggled with her out the door he shouted at DanDan.

—Out!

He ran after them.

Cath

She struggled as JJ held her back. He didn't understand, he couldn't understand. It wasn't her fucking house, it was her mam's and she couldn't let it go. She couldn't let it burn.

—Let me go. It's fine, right. It's fine. I'll deal with it.

—No, Cath, no. Just stay out for the moment. Who has a phone?

—What?

—Who has a phone? Call the fire brigade.

—Just let me go in. No!

JJ dragged her up the steps and out to the little gate on the latch. He pushed her into Steph, shouting at her to hold her. She felt Steph's arms wrap around her and hold her tight.

JJ ran back into the house. He came back out with a phone, tossed it to Steph then went back inside. Steph tried to hold on to her and dial the phone at the same time. DanDan stood still holding Lucy, who was shivering. Through the windows, Cath saw JJ grab a blanket and run towards the back wall. He beat at it with the blanket, then it caught as well, and he threw it to the ground. The fire threw light out the windows, illuminating the garden, and the forest around them seemed to howl and invite the flames.

She struggled free of Steph's arms.

—Cath!

She ran to the door of the house and looked in. The room was filling with smoke. Fire had engulfed the back wall. There were flames rushing up the curtains of the side windows and through the woolly dog blanket that JJ had kicked to one side. JJ coughed. He was running out of objects to beat the fire with. In

267

desperation, he picked up one of the wooden chairs by the table and he threw it at the wall. It smashed against the plaster. A leg broke off and the whole thing clattered down to the floor.

—JJ, leave it, leave it!

It was beyond their control now. They'd started it but now they could do nothing. The room was getting warm, smoke was billowing off the curtains. Cath couldn't believe what was happening. JJ looked around at her. His eyes were wild, scared. The fire climbed the walls behind him as if a gate of fire was opening up for him. His hands were empty, he started to cough and the fire roared.

Malachy

He saw something golden down the way. It was flickering in the dark. He watched it lazily as it seemed to dance in front of his eyes, until he heard a scream.

Malachy stood, his eyes fully open, and looked down. They were running from the house, pouring out the front door. The pudgy girl was screaming, the tall one was shouting. The skinny lad pushed Catherine outside then ran back in. Then Malachy knew what it was coming from the window. In the misty night he'd not recognised it at first. They'd set fire to the goddamn house.

Shouts came rushing through the mist towards his home. He went into the wardrobe and found the big extinguisher, the one he'd had for the barns before. It was large and heavy, about the size of his torso, but he heaved it up. He was strong still. He took it with him in one hand towards the door, and from there, he took big long steps down towards the house.

When he got to the start of their drive, he noticed two were gone. The tall lad was holding the pudgy one in his arms, and the blonde girl was shouting into the house. He walked right on by, through the centre of their group without acknowledging them, and then he was inside. Catherine was in the doorway, in his way, so he pushed past her, the extinguisher still in one hand.

The back wall around the fireplace was ablaze, with a fierce heat that got worse as he made his way in. Smoke was filling the room. The skinny fella was trying to beat at the wall with a towel but kept getting repelled by the heat. The room was covered in half-empty, spilled-over bottles of booze and fag ends and candles.

The curtains were on fire, the carpet in front of the fireplace was ablaze.

He went over, shouting at the skinny fella.

—Out of the way.

The fella didn't seem to hear him first, so Malachy put his hand out, and knocked him aside. The lad fell away behind him as light as a scarecrow. He shouted at him.

—Out! Out! I'll deal with it.

He aimed the nozzle at the burning curtains, the heat hardest on his outstretched hands. Foam burst out of the extinguisher, sputtering. It hadn't ever been used, and was most likely expired. He clamped down on the handle. The extinguisher gave an almighty whoosh and picked up force and speed. He turned one last time to the skinny boy and shouted:

—OUT! And close the door.

The young lad ran to Catherine and dragged her out. Malachy heard the door close behind him. He directed the jet of foam at the curtains. The rest of the place roared as he managed to get the curtains out. The sweat soaked his face and his breathing was laboured as the fire on the walls and the carpet continued to rage. He forced himself into a wall of heat as he stood in front of the fireplace and took aim at the source of the fire in the grate. He stopped a moment, to calm himself, to do it right and with a clear head.

It was then he felt the smoke scoring his lungs, and his heart beating fast under his chest. Everything was crowding in on him, trying to fold him in.

The room around him seemed to vibrate, seemed to groan in complaint as the rushing flames hurt his eyes. There was a wet roaring in his ears, the sound of the room drowning in itself, being destroyed. His nose filled with the breathy, sour smell of the extinguisher and the acrid stink of burning plastic and fabric.

Though the fire grew around him and he felt the air growing thin, he remained standing, the extinguisher ready in his hand, but not moving. The fire seemed to have contented itself with just eating the back wall, though with every second Malachy knew he was inhaling more smoke and he was already feeling light-headed. Standing there, a thought took a hold in him. Why should he put it out? He tried to think quickly, but try as he could, it seemed he had no good answer to give himself. There was a bottle of vodka nestled in an arm of the couch beside him. Malachy picked it up as the flames ate into the walls. The extinguisher was a dull weight in his right hand, but in his left he held a bottle of clear, powerful liquid that could fix everything, make everything come right. He lifted the bottle in his arm, and it seemed right, everything in this room should go, get rid of all of it.

He hurled the bottle into the corner where the back wall met the side one. The bottle smashed and a blast of warmth seared Malachy's cheeks. The fire roared and flames spread out over both walls fiercer than before, spraying over everything.

Malachy tripped as he retreated and fell to his knees. He slowly struggled to his feet and tramped for the front door, coughing. He pumped the handle of the heavy extinguisher as he left, the nozzle trailing aimlessly on the ground, and it let off a few mild, throaty bursts. As he reached the front door, he took one look back. The whole room was going up. It'd spread far beyond the fireplace and was consuming the shelves. Black, black smoke was filling the upper areas of the room, and Malachy coughed and coughed. He opened the door, and stumbled out, dragging the extinguisher with him.

The air was sharp and cruel and he dropped the extinguisher a fair distance from the house. Back by the gate, the group of them were clustered around holding themselves and each other. The skinny lad was sat down coughing. Catherine looked frantically to each person, before she shoved off and made to go towards the house. Malachy grabbed her arm as she passed, and said in a hoarse voice:

—Don't. It's gone.

—No. We can stop it.

—It's over.

She struggled with him a few moments before she pushed him off and walked into the long grass, her hands on top of her head.

He sat on the stone steps up to the road, coughing. The wet stones soaked his trousers as he watched the Lodge burn.

Over in the grass, illuminated by the glow of the fire, Catherine looked out into the sky. She'd not have to deal with it, any more of it. Both her grandmother and her mother had suffered in that house. What good would have come from saving it? Why bother, when all that would happen in it would be more heartbreak. More violence and carnage and sadness, and more for him to look down on for the coming years. Billy had lived here, and Mona, and the Nevilles, and many other families. It had always been rotten underneath. There was only pain waiting in that house for her, for anyone that went into it, and now with it burning, that'd be the last pain it inflicted. Once it was gone, it'd be gone, and it'd give no more grief.

After a few moments, Catherine turned around and sat down, stunned, beside Malachy. There was a silence among the rest of the group as they walked about each other, dazed. Malachy watched the house burn. The fire brigade wouldn't come in time. Each second that passed was one bit more of the house getting scorched, one square foot more of wall getting eaten. There'd be no painting over this one. He watched the house and waited to get his breath back.

The mist gathered round all of them, cloaked them, hid them from each other, but Malachy could see just enough. Catherine sat beside Malachy, blinking, as the heat from the house warmed their faces. Next thing, the young one, the pudgy one, blurted out back by the gate:

—Oh my God.

She clamped her hand over her mouth and gagged. She stumbled across the road to the church and vomited over the steps, splattering the stone, crying and moaning as she did. The blonde one ran across to her and held her hair back. The other two lads leaned on the gate, looking like they were in shock.

The downstairs windows of the Lodge glowed yellow, and black smoke tumbled upwards out of the open ones. Some cars had started to pull into the car park, locals from the houses around the hills, though there was nothing any of them could do to help. The girl continued to vomit up on the steps of the church, and the skinny fella coughed and coughed. Finally, Malachy stood and spoke down to Catherine.

—You'll be okay without me now. They'll look after you.

She nodded slowly. Her brown hair was frizzy and messed about. She ran her fingers through it as she stared at the house. Malachy waited a moment for a response. When one didn't come, he walked away.

He walked up the road and away from them without looking back once, and as he left he heard their cries and their tears. He heard them console each other. He didn't turn, he just started walking, not back towards his house, but away towards the Doon Shore. He heard Catherine shout after him.

—Malachy!

But no, he was walking away. He continued on, until he heard her footsteps coming from behind. He stopped and turned. Catherine was standing in front of him, breathing heavily. She was so fucking young. Only a baby.

—Where are you going?

—There's nothing more to be done.

—But, you can't leave us.

—I can. You'll be fine.

Catherine looked around him, down the dark road Malachy was walking.

—Where are you going?

—It's done. It's fucking done. It's over.

—What?

She looked confused, but how the hell was he supposed to tell her?

—It's done.

With that he turned and walked away again. She shouted after him, pleading, but he ignored her. He heard her turn and start to walk back her own way. He set off on the dark road to the Doon Shore.

He kept a steady, plodding pace on the way down the road. At one point there'd been a rock fall; a bunch of loose gravel and some larger rocks were scattered in the road. He stepped over them. All along the way he recognised the rock walls he'd built and repaired, paving his way, leading him to where he was going, down and down the sloping road until he was out by the lake in the mist and it was black again. Away in the distance, across the lake, he could see flashing lights and the glow of the Lodge burning. The lake was quiet, though, shushing once again, gently, gently, the black water smooth until it rippled by the pier.

He took off his jacket and threw it down, then walked to the end of the car park and lifted a large, flat rock off one of the walls. He carried it to the pier, crushing his way through the sand, past discarded beer cans and wine bottles. He reached the end of the pier, the rock in his arms. He closed his eyes and shuffled forward so he was balancing on the edge of the concrete, his boots half on, half off.

It was fucking useless. All of it. Fucking done. Over. He listened to the water and felt the air cold on his face.

What was there left for him? What fucking point would there be, what gain? Some days he'd just get on with it. He knew that. He'd drag rocks up out of the soil and put them in walls and that'd be his day. He'd deal with it.

But then there'd be the other days. The days when he'd lie in bed too tired to dress or wash or feel any joy or work in the fields. He'd moan and curse himself and he'd feel Elaine saying goodbye every night in his head, every night she'd say goodbye, goodbye goodbye and he'd watch her leave, knowing he could never turn it back, even in his dreams. Goodbye goodbye goodbye, Malachy, I'll see you.

What would come of it, what the fuck would come of it, what little was left? Nothing new in store for him except pain and brokenness and dying and indignity. Pains in his hands and pains in his knees and his back and his feet, and alone, always alone, sitting in front of the fire, looking into it and hearing Elaine, her voice in his ear as he creaked slowly to death.

The rock was heavy in his hands, the weight of it dragging his arms down, straining his shoulders and bending his back towards the water. He lifted it and held it tight to his chest, hugged it close. He knew what to do. Just hold on until you're too far gone to save yourself. The water below was so horribly, horribly fucking cold. One last time. He held the rock strong. One last fucking pain to take and it'd be done.

Day 3

Merc

The sun rose slowly over his parents' front garden. He felt sick standing alone in the morning air. With no one to talk to, all he could do was think on how he'd left and what had happened once he'd gone. A fucking fire for one.

Apart from the fire what bothered him most was why he'd left in the first place. He'd been so sure when he left that he was in the right, but when he got home his house was dark, his parents away, and he'd had to sit in and think it over. He'd stayed up all night unable to sleep.

After he heard from Cath, who rang him at six in the morning, screaming at him for the fire, he'd walked out his front door and stood looking at the houses opposite him in the estate. Everything was quiet and still. One small thought entered his mind. He held onto it for a brief moment, like a small butterfly in his hand. It was his fault.

He let the thought go. If it came back again, he'd listen to it. If not, then it probably wasn't all that important.

Merc shut his eyes and let his thoughts slip to daydreams.

DanDan

Lucy was lying on his arm and he watched the sun rise through the window. What a lovely, lovely morning. Despite all with the house fire and Cath, it was a beautiful morning and he was no longer heartbroken.

They'd stayed the night on a neighbour's living room floor. All night people came in and out, checking on Lucy and whispering to Cath, while others gathered in the kitchen. The fire brigade had come and soaked the house up and down, then gone in with their bars and torn out the walls and anything that might still be a danger. They had to wait until morning, they said, to see what the extent of the damage was.

They were all ready to turn in, to switch off and try and get a few hours of sleep, when Cath started asking about Malachy, about where he'd gone. Word went out he was missing. She was the last one who'd seen him. They'd started a search for him while Cath was up in the kitchen, talking to her mam on the phone, telling her she was okay, and listening to her mam say she was on her way out, she was driving out now. DanDan tried to catch Cath's eye, to say sorry, but any time he did she turned away. Not out of spite or anger. She just looked at him like he was irrelevant, like he didn't bear dwelling on any more. Once it was quiet, Cath had phoned Merc and given him a bollocking.

In a few hours, they'd go back out to the house. Cath would stay on, and her mam would come out and meet her, but the rest of them would go home. DanDan would offer to help, he supposed. Offer to stay. After all she'd said to him, though, before the fire, he wasn't sure if he could forgive her. A lot of it was hazy in his mind, what exactly had been said, but he was more than sure she'd called him out, that she'd said everything was his fault, that he didn't know what he was doing. All of it was out of line. He knew his reaction was over the top, but he'd put nothing on the fire that wouldn't have gone on it anyway. Anyone who lit it would've had the same result. It was Merc's fault.

With all the talk of death and blame about, he couldn't help but think of Jess. But when he thought about her, he didn't want to close his eyes shut and never let them open again. He just imagined her smiling at him, and it made him feel warm. He laughed, just a little, when he thought of it, the absurdity of being dumped in an arcade. Crying behind the air hockey tables.

He was coming through the whole thing. He was over the hump. And he'd done it himself, he'd gotten himself over it, that was what was important. He could rely on himself now. He knew if he could survive this he could survive anything, and with Lucy sleeping on him he felt warm and energetic, ready for the next part. Whether the rest of the group would be involved in that, he didn't know. He was having a good time with Lucy, but he doubted if he'd continue it on back home. She was actually a pisshead at the end of all things and he didn't want to corner himself in just now that'd he'd gotten himself free. He didn't suppose it'd ever be the same with Cath again. There were some things that you just didn't let go. He'd seen the true side of her that weekend.

He couldn't wait to get back to Dublin, to start over, to begin running again, playing guitar and going out and enjoying himself, embracing everything that'd felt dull and sad in him before. He felt so, so excited about what lay ahead of him.

Lucy

She felt a little jump in her. She'd done what she'd hoped with the weekend. That last part of her was gone and she was a new woman.

Cath had gone on ahead to the house. Lucy had woken later and walked with DanDan down to the Lodge. Her head was still sore but she'd mostly emptied herself out the night before, so she wasn't feeling as ropey as she might have. She remembered all of them fighting during the night. They'd fought at the lake and at the house before it'd gone on fire. She didn't care that much to try and remember all of it. She just knew that she'd been with DanDan again and Cath was jealous. She'd said all kinds of mean things to DanDan and to Lucy. Telling DanDan he was a dick, and getting on her back about drink and all kinds of things. Showed you how messed up Cath had been when she'd told her to lay off the booze. Ridiculous. She was fine.

They saw the blackened Lodge away in the distance. Some of the roof had collapsed and there were piles of charred debris left outside in the garden. It was none of her concern, really. They were going to head back whenever Cath's mam came out to take charge. They'd all called their parents and told them what had happened. Lucy's parents had tried to say they were coming to get her, but she convinced them to let her go back on the train with DanDan.

Just the two of them. Something brilliant was starting.

Steph

She waited outside the burnt house to take DanDan and Lucy to the train. Afterwards she was going to drive straight to Wexford, spend some time at home with her parents. She sent a quick text to Fergus just to say sorry, and that he'd never hear from her again. He hadn't replied.

Cath was sitting by herself out in the garden. The door to the house was closed off with yellow tape and there were trails of debris all around the front, charred beams and floppy sections of wallpaper and plaster torn from the walls. It was a beautiful day, though. The mist had cleared and there was not a cloud in the bright blue sky. Steph walked over and sat down in the grass next to Cath.

—How's it going?

—Fine, yeah.

—What're you thinking?

—I was talking to some of the neighbours. They were saying, it looks like Malachy walked into the lake.

—You serious?

—Yeah. After he left us. They found his coat down by the Doon Shore. Out where we were. They think he walked in.

—Jesus, Cath.

—No, I know.

—I'm sorry.

—It's fine. I mean, it's sad, but I only ever met him the two or three times, just the same as you, and only even barely then.

—Fuck, though.

—Yeah, I know. And here, see there, up the way, the house?

Cath pointed a finger to a house up on the hill, its large windows facing out towards them.

—Yeah.

—That's Malachy's house.

—Oh right.

—I thought initially that it was just empty, vacated. But no, he was there the whole time. And he could see us.

—Shit, really?

—Well, we can see him, can't we? We can see his door and his garden and even inside his windows, see. So he could probably see us. He could see everything we did.

—Jesus.

She dropped silent beside Cath and the two of them looked on up to the house. Sure enough, they were so close they could see right in, into what looked like his kitchen. An empty chair was placed by the screen door, facing them.

—Why do you think he . . .

—No idea.

—You don't think it was anything to do with us?

—Don't know. Maybe. Probably not. I don't think we're that important. Maybe he was just fucked up. Had his own stuff going on.

—Jesus.

—Sad.

—Yeah.

They were quiet for a moment. There wasn't a huge amount they could do or feel about it that would help. Steph switched subjects.

—So, what now then?

Cath sighed, but kept her face to the sun.

—Wait to see what the damage is. The insurance people are coming out tomorrow, and the fire lads will have an assessment on it.

—Fucking hell.

—My mam's going to be here in a bit.

—I can stay with you.

—No. Thanks. I want everyone gone. You need to drive them.

—Everyone?

—Yeah, everyone.

—You sure?

—Yeah, thanks, Steph. Get the others to the train. I'll be grand here.

—Okay. You know JJ thinks he's staying, though.

—I'll speak to him.

—He seemed like the good one out of all of this. He's done right by us.

—I know. He has. It's shit, I know. But I need a clean break. I'm done with this.

—Even when you get back?

—Yeah.

—Jesus, Cath. I know it's bad. But just . . .

—Look at us. Look at the house. JJ doesn't deserve it, but I just need to look after myself, you know?

—Yeah, I know. I'm sorry. He'll understand.

—Will he?

—Course he will. We give him grief all the time, but actually when it comes down to it . . .

—Yeah. He's solid.

—And DanDan?

—That's gone.

—Sorry.

—Steph, it's grand. Better to learn it now.

—Fucking hell.

—The weekend.

—Yeah.

—I wouldn't say disaster now, Cath, but eventful.

—Ha. One way of putting it.

Steph took her eyes down, her head down, from the sun, and she turned to Cath.

—Listen, Cath. What I said yesterday. I didn't mean it, you know.

—Yeah, you did.

285

—Pills, y'know.

—It's okay, Steph. Really. You were actually honest. In a good way. We can be friendly like, when we get back, but we're never gonna be best buds.

—I feel shit about that.

She actually did. Steph did feel shit, though the more she looked at Cath the more she knew she could handle it.

—You're fine, Steph. Listen, just for yourself, you know. You can be really good. You just have to actually try.

—Yeah.

—Lucy told me what you were saying about being cold.

—The fucking . . .

—You shouldn't tell her things, she can barely help herself. And then I remembered what you said to me about a year ago, when you were asking how to be friendlier.

—Fat lot of good that did.

—You know, that was when I got on best with you, Steph. You were really nice then. And you actually seemed happier.

—It didn't work, all that nice stuff.

—It did. You just got lazy. You're not cold, Steph. You just need to give more of a shit. I know it doesn't come natural to you, but just try harder. If you can't feel close to people then just do the things people do who are close to each other, listen and be kind and all that.

—Yeah, maybe.

—Just try it.

—Okay.

—Come here.

They hugged close. Cath was never exactly Steph's kind of person. Too earnest, but she felt close to her all the same. She allowed herself hold on in the hug until Cath broke it.

—Okay.

—Okay.

She stood up out of the grass and took her keys out of her back pocket. DanDan was shuffling around by the car. Lucy was tagging along behind him, trying to make conversation. She nodded towards them.

286

—Best get these to the station then.

—Right.

They walked to the car. Cath went over and hugged Lucy loosely. Steph could make out an apology from Cath, she heard the word drinking, so she moved closer to hear them.

Cath rubbed the side of Lucy's arm.

—I'm sorry, Luce.

—It's okay.

—But do think about it, maybe going easy for a while.

Lucy stiffened under her arms, and broke away.

—Yeah. Whatever.

Lucy turned back to the car. Cath and DanDan stood square opposite each other. He spoke in a sulky, quiet voice.

—Sorry about the fire. I didn't mean it.

—Forget about it, DanDan, it's over. Just forget about the whole thing. I'll see you around.

—Around, Cath?

—Yeah, around.

Then Cath left them. Lucy and DanDan got into the back seat of the car and closed the door. Steph got into the driver seat and watched through the window as Cath made her way down to JJ, who was gingerly stacking stray bits of debris around the house.

They'd be home in a few hours. She thought about calling out to Fergus, maybe. Apologise in person. But no, that'd just make things worse. She supposed Cath was right, she could try harder in the future. She'd work on it, maybe. Give it another try. A small one anyway, though she hardly saw the point in it.

JJ

He tried to make things as neat as he could, shovelling all the little bits of plaster and ash and broken bottles into a big pile. He'd told Cath he'd stay on to help clean for a day or two. She'd been brilliant the whole weekend, whatever had fallen apart, and he wanted to help her out.

He'd expected the mother of all come-downs from the pills, considering he'd been on the razz for two days, but aside from a slight uneasiness, it was nowhere to be found. He'd said goodbye to Steph and the others, but when he looked up to their car, he noticed they hadn't moved.

They were sitting in the car in a moody silence. Cath was making her way down to him. She kicked at the gravel as he walked to meet her halfway.

—What's up?

—Hey.

—Are they going?

—They're waiting, JJ.

—For what?

—For you.

—What? I thought I was going to stay on?

—No, I need to be alone with this for a while.

Shit. Shit, she was bailing. He knew it was the wrong time now, it was almost certainly the wrong time, but he couldn't go without saying it. He just couldn't. And if she was sending him away, then he might as well do it now. He tried to make his voice hard and confident.

—What if I wanted to stay?

—What?

—What if, you know . . .

He made a faint gesture. He tried to link her and him with his arm, a you-and-me wave, but it felt small and useless between them. Cath seemed genuinely surprised by it. A small breath escaped from her.

—Oh . . .

He knew then he'd failed. Her eyes right on him. He looked in her eyes and he wished so much there was love in them, but he knew there wasn't. No flicker there for him, no softness. It ripped a hole in him that he'd never felt before. He felt small and stupid and completely fucking foolish. How had he ever thought that there would be something there? She made a small conciliatory wave at him.

—JJ . . .

—No. It's fine.

—I didn't really think . . . I'm sorry, JJ, I can't. I don't think about you, you know . . .

—Yeah. DanDan, the fire.

—No, it's nothing to do with DanDan. I was wrong about that. But it doesn't – it doesn't mean that, for us. I'm sorry. I'm really sorry.

—It's fine. I was only, you know . . .

Cath came to him, and he realised he was smaller than her. He was fucking smaller than her. He probably weighed less, for fuck sake, and how could that work? She came right in front of him and he twisted to go away.

—I'm gonna head then.

—No.

She grabbed his arm. She clamped her fingers around his wrist and held him and he turned back to her. She held his arm so tight and looked at him.

—What do you want? What did you think would come from it?

—I dunno. I just started liking you is all. I don't, it's stupid. I'll get over it.

—I'm sorry if I did anything to make you think . . .

—It's fine. You didn't. I dunno, it was stupid. I just started to get a bit hopeful. Not through any reason of yours, you didn't do anything to make me think that.

—I'm sorry.

—Don't say sorry. Don't start to pity me.

She left her hand down by her side and nodded.

—I won't.

—I'm actually grand.

He walked a few steps away and took out a cigarette. His hand was shaking. Cath followed him.

—JJ, I'm not going to see the group for a while.

—Even me?

—Even you, yes. I'm sorry.

—I shouldn't have said anything.

—No, JJ, it's not that. You were right to, and it was brave. But it's nothing to do with that. You've been fucking brilliant. And I'm sorry. I'm so sorry, but you kind of helped me with this. What you said to me last night, when we were swimming, it made sense. I need the others to go. I need to look at what I'm doing. And to do that I have to not see you. Even though you've done nothing wrong, even though you've been really kind and good to me, and you don't deserve it, you deserve the opposite, but I can't give that to you. I'm being selfish.

She gritted her jaw as she looked at him. He was barely able to look at her. Why was she doing this? It wasn't fair. After what they'd done, and been through, and all that shite, all that had happened the night before, and what he'd just done, the pills gone and his weed gone . . . But he made himself look at her, and he knew she needed it.

—Okay.

—I'm sorry.

—It's fine.

—I'll see you.

—Yeah, see you.

It wasn't fair. It wasn't fair at all, but maybe she deserved it. He didn't but she did.

He just couldn't look at her.

He walked away, back towards the car. It wasn't fair. He was alone. What wrong had he done? No wrong, so why was he getting thrown away? His head was clear but in the clarity of it there was sadness and the regret for everything he'd done and said and what had been done and said to him, and he felt like crying, but he told himself he wouldn't. It bucked in him. He'd fucked away his pills and decided to go straight and clean then this happened.

All he wanted was to run back and grab Cath and hold her, but that was gone, that was never going to happen, and it had never been going to happen, though he'd been stupid enough to think it might. And now he was being thrown away with the rest of them. He got into the car and shut the door in on himself and kept his eyes on his feet. He'd not go back to what had been before, he knew that much. He was going to be strong and do something good, but all he had for the moment was sheer fucking pain right there in his chest, stabbing him in waves over and over again as they pulled away and he didn't look back.

Cath

Steph did a little two-beep at her as she pulled away from the house, the car scrabbling over the gravel of the church car park. Cath waved goodbye from the long grass. Her mam texted her, said she'd be there in twenty minutes. She looked up to Malachy's house.

It was in full view. Looking at it earlier, she'd realised he must have been watching them. All weekend they'd been cruel and drunk and stupid with each other, Cath included, and he'd sat up there, watching them fight like dogs. She'd run after him the night before, followed him away from the burning house to thank him, but when he turned to face her she could see something was wrong with him.

His eyes were wild, though every other part of him looked tired. She'd just supposed it was from inhaling smoke, fighting the fire as best he could. As he faced her on the road, she'd felt ashamed of herself, for all that they'd made him go through and for how tired he seemed. It never occurred to her what he'd had in mind. But looking back now, there was something so final about the way he'd turned away from her, only she'd been too caught up, too preoccupied with the house, to notice.

Malachy was gone, her friends were gone, and her mam yet to arrive. She knew she'd done wrong by JJ. But he was a strong fella and he was the one who'd said it to her, as they'd drifted in the lake, to cut them loose. As for the rest, she was probably better off without them. She still had others back home, people she cared about and who cared about her. She'd spend more time with them. She knew people who were kind and lovely. People who did more than kick up a fuss and dance on tables in the nip.

She could hear the river off in the distance running down the hill. She'd be gone soon and it'd keep going, keep flowing all the way down to the lake, mixing in with the rest of the water. It'd move silently under the chains on the Rockadoon Shore and lap up on the sand, and with everyone gone it would be quiet and still on the shore side. She listened to the river and felt something new in her, something hard and determined that had never been there before.

Acknowledgements

Huge, HUGE thanks to Mark Richards, who came after this book, bought it, edited it, and put it out into the world. Everything came from him. Holy Fuck. Thank you.

To Becky Walsh who found the first bit of this work, and whose intuitive, sneaky edits made everything better. Thank you to everyone at John Murray who helped bring this book into being.

To Lucy Luck for being such a sure presence. Sometimes I imagine I'm lost in the wilderness, totally unsure of what to do, then this huge, hulking tank comes smashing through the trees to back me up and everything's cool. Thanks, tank. Thanks to everyone at Aitken Alexander who's been pulled into the orbit of my messiness, and had to suffer it.

To Meg Stapleton, a fucking hurricane and one of the best people I know, for coming into my life when it was changing and helping me change.

To Federica Sciori, Wonder Woman, for dealing with me, for keeping my head in a good place, for dancing.

Thank you to the many lecturers, admins, supervisors and students from Manchester, Oxford and UEA. Go Unrulies. Thanks to everyone who read different pieces of varying quality, and to Dan McVey and Ayòbámi Adébáyọ̀ for the first and last full length reads. Thanks especially to Geoff Ryman, who guided the ship early on, and to Giles Foden who got me to stick with it.

Thank you to all my friends and family for their kindness, humour and support.

To my brothers Domhnall, Fergus and Brian, who helped form my sense of humour, and continue to make everything such corking good fun.

I owe everything to Mary Weldon and Brendan Gleeson, who made me. They pushed my head into books and held it there until I didn't want to take it away. They loved, encouraged and supported me all the way. Thank you so much.

From Byron, Austen and Darwin

to some of the most acclaimed and original contemporary writing, John Murray takes pride in bringing you powerful, prizewinning, absorbing and provocative books that will entertain you today and become the classics of tomorrow.

We put a lot of time and passion into what we publish and how we publish it, and we'd like to hear what you think.

Be part of John Murray – share your views with us at:

www.johnmurray.co.uk

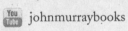 johnmurraybooks

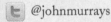 @johnmurrays

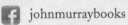 johnmurraybooks